An Astrological Guide
for Broken Hearts

ATRIA
PAPERBACK

An Imprint of Simon & Schuster, Inc.
1230 Avenue of the Americas
New York, NY 10020

Originally published in Italy in 2015 by Nord (Gruppo GeMS) as *Guida astrologica per cuori infranti*

License agreement made through Laura Ceccacci Agency

First Atria Paperback edition November 2021

ATRIA PAPERBACK and colophon are trademarks of Simon & Schuster, Inc.

For information about special discounts for bulk purchases, please contact Simon & Schuster Special Sales at 1-866-506-1949 or business@simonandschuster.com.

The Simon & Schuster Speakers Bureau can bring authors to your live event. For more information or to book an event, contact the Simon & Schuster Speakers Bureau at 1-866-248-3049 or visit our website at www.simonspeakers.com.

Interior design by Dana Sloan

Cover art and title font © Netflix 2021. Used with permission.

Manufactured in the United States of America

1 3 5 7 9 10 8 6 4 2

Library of Congress Cataloging-in-Publication Data

Names: Zucca, Silvia, author translator.
Title: An astrological guide for broken hearts : a novel / Silvia Zucca.
Other titles: Guida astrologica per cuori infranti. English
Description: First Atria paperback edition. | New York : Atria Unbound, 2018.
Identifiers: LCCN 2018002377 (print) | LCCN 2018034396 (ebook) | ISBN 9781668004128 (trade pbk.) | ISBN 9781501116957 (ebk.)
Subjects: LCSH: Single women—Fiction. | Man-woman relationships—Fiction. | Astrology—Fiction. | GSAFD: Love stories
Classification: LCC PQ4926.U75 G8513 2018 (print) | LCC PQ4926.U75 (ebook) | DDC 853/.92—dc23
LC record available at https://lccn.loc.gov/2018002377
LC ebook record available at https://lccn.loc.gov/2018034396

ISBN 978-1-6680-0412-8
ISBN 978-1-5011-1695-7 (ebook)

An Astrological Guide for Broken Hearts

A Novel

SILVIA ZUCCA

ATRIA PAPERBACK

NEW YORK • LONDON • TORONTO • SYDNEY • NEW DELHI

To my father,
on his special birthday.
And to my mother,
who taught me to read.

Thank you to Simon & The Stars for the astrological advice
Facebook.com/simonandthestars

An Astrological Guide
for Broken Hearts

PROLOGUE:

The Heavens Can Wait

Some days, you just feel it in your bones. You wake up, and you're sure that nothing is going to go your way: it would be better to turn around, pull the covers over your head, and go back to sleep.

In a movie, this would be a voice-over explaining why I would much rather grab the box from under my bed labeled "Survival Kit" than go to work.

In my survival kit, along with a photo of Hugh Jackman's abs, gummy worms, and a bag of kernels primed for popping, there are films—strictly on VHS—that would not normally appear in the library of the 1" film aficionado I make myself out to be . . . As if to spite the ABCs of cinema (that does not stand for the American Broadcasting Company, but for Allen, Burton, and Coppola), whose posters are proudly displayed on the IKEA bookcase in my living room, under my bed I hide pop culture hits like *Notting Hill*, *Dirty Dancing*, *Pretty Woman*, and *Ghost*.

It's true. When everything goes wrong, I overdose on sugar in cel-luloid form. But why these films in particular, and romantic comedies of the '80s and '90s in general? Because I am an eternal child, and those films are my version of Proust's madeleine. From their very first scenes,

1

they take me back to the safe, protected world of my childhood. They make me believe that there is an order to my life; that even when everything seems to be going wrong, there is a happy ending right around the corner—at 120 minutes, just in time for the closing credits.

Today is one of those days. I know it as soon as I open my eyes to the whining of the alarm. I'm tempted. *Very* tempted. But, of course, survival kit days do have a tendency to occur on Mondays, when you have a meeting on par with a United Nations summit.

And yes, last night I had an inkling that an intravenous dose of *Eternal Sunshine of the Spotless Mind* was not a good idea. Especially from the moment I decided to wash down both the film and my sorrows with a bottle of champagne. To be precise, the bottle of Louis Roederer champagne that was supposed to be drunk on a first anniversary that never happened.

In life, there are some moments when you deliberately set out to mess yourself up.

So, as I push aside the covers, I can't help but regret the big night that ended in grand style with me hugging the toilet and squeezing out stupid tears in between retches.

On my pilgrimage to the kitchen, I hope that a double dose of caffeine will work the magic of our Lady of Lourdes and rouse me from my catatonic state. Still on autopilot, I turn on the radio to listen to the news, and take great delight in the fact that there is someone who is worse off than I am.

Finally, I gather the courage to inch toward the bathroom. *Oh my god.* Looking back at me in the mirror is a female version of the picture of Dorian Gray—in pajamas. The dark circles under my eyes make me look like a panda in a wig.

Carlo, I hate you, I think as I try to gather together what's left of myself and the orgy of junk food scattered around the house.

Carlo is my very-ex-boyfriend. Five years together. Seven months, twelve days, and four hours (give or take a minute) of cohabitation that ended almost two years ago. Of course, in two years, a life should be completely rebuilt, and I've done that. Or at least I've tried to, given the sequence of wrong men I've fallen for after him—the last of them, Giorgio, left me the legacy of that damn champagne. The problem is that while the others came and went, Carlo has always remained, even though we're not together anymore. I always thought that in the end our bond went beyond the normal definition of love, that it was something more complex, something that transcended physical attraction. Like in *When Harry Met Sally*.

But now, Carlo is getting married.

In seven months.

And I had to find out from Facebook. And not even from him, but from that idiot Cristina who announced it for the whole world to read: "I'm pregnant and Carlo and I are getting married in September, on my birthday!"

Fantastic. Congratulations. Best wishes. And a nice fuck-you the size of Milan Cathedral, OK? And to think that, at first, I thought she was my friend.

It's not that I wish I were in Cristina's place. But between Carlo and me, I should have been the one to get married first. They always say "ladies first," right?

And here we come to my other pressing problem: age. I'm already way past thirty. I'm no spring chicken, as they say. I so badly want to meet someone, to really fall in love (and he with me, preferably) and start a family. But instead, I'm so unlucky in love that I seem to be competing for the Nobel Prize for Spinsterhood.

I am on the toilet with my head resting on my knees when the sound of the radio filters through:

"Unions have confirmed the general public transport strike planned for today. Remember that strike action is scheduled from 8:45 this morning until 3:00 p.m. and then from 6:00 p.m. until the end of service . . ."

"Oh shit!"

The news hits my system like a shot of adrenaline. The meeting starts at 9:30 and my car will be at the mechanic until Wednesday.

Alice, wake up! It's already 8:04, assuming that the clock in the bathroom is correct. And since it takes about ten minutes to get from here to the tram stop, I barely have twenty minutes to transform myself from *Carrie* to a low-budget version of Alice Bassi.

So long, shower. So long, hair straightener. And so long, nail polish. Actually, no, I'll throw that in my bag; I may have time for a quick retouch once I get to the office. Clocking a time that would make Carl Lewis weep, in ten minutes flat I'm out of the house and cursing the chronic disorganization syndrome that made me give up before even trying to look for an umbrella.

I run to the tram stop through the torrential downpour.

It's 8:16 and someone comments that we won't make the last train. In my head, I start doing calculations again. It's a fifteen-minute walk from here to the train that I need to take, and I'm already crossing the road at a steady pace, trying not to give a damn about the rain that is drenching my hair and my jacket.

"What a shitty day . . . What a shitty day . . ." I growl like a mantra through clenched teeth.

As my brightly striped stockings become drenched up to my knees, I miss my survival kit, especially *Ghost*. Because at least Patrick Swayze is a ghost, and you can be sure there's no possibility that after the end of the movie he might change his mind, leave Demi Moore, and get another woman pregnant.

"I'm sorry, the last one just went by," says the little man closing the gate to the commuter train.

It's not possible. This is a nightmare.

I cling to my last hope: the phone numbers for taxis saved in my smartphone. And after another quarter of an hour under water, my saving angel arrives: Wapiti 28–47.

The guy, with a gaunt face and a tan like Crocodile Dundee's, stares at me for a moment and then shows me the newspaper resting on the backseat. "Couldn't you sit on that, ma'am? Otherwise you're going to soak my whole seat ... "

Of course. Perfect. I hate when people call me ma'am. And now I have to wrap my ass in newspaper, as if I were a sea bass being taken home from the market.

"You look like you need to get your energy back, if you don't mind me saying so," he says, starting up again. "You know, the wapiti is a Canadian elk. In shamanic medicine, it's considered a sacred animal, a good help for people ... At your age, you should start taking care of yourself. Have you ever tried crystal therapy?"

At my age? *At my age?* Good Lord! How old does he think I am? Sure, I have no makeup on, I still have panda eyes; and right now my hair must look worse than Johnny Depp's in *Edward Scissorhands* ... but, heck, I do not have one foot in the grave!

One foot in the ditch is what I get instead a few minutes later when Wapiti pulls into the driveway of Mi-A-Mi Network, the small TV station for which I have been sweating blood every day for the past ten years. Opening the door and putting your foot in a crater full of water all in one motion? Priceless.

"How much do I owe you?" I ask, holding back a grimace of anger and disgust.

"It's twenty-two euros and sixty-five cents. Call it twenty-two fifty."

I open my wallet and realize that I have only ten euros in cash. Shit. Now what am I going to say to Wapiti-Crocodile Dundee? "Just give me a second . . ."

When I raise my head, I spot my colleague Raffaella, wrapped in an impeccable Gucci raincoat, her umbrella and boots in a matching dusky mauve color. Not a single hair out of place. The raindrops dodge her obediently.

"Taxi? Very nice," she says with a wink. "Somebody's treating herself."

"Raffa, wait!" I call out. "Could you lend me thirteen euros? I'll pay you back at lunch, I need to go to the ATM."

"Of course, sweetie. Are you sure that will be enough?" she says, giving me a twenty. "Keep it so you can get yourself a hot tea at the machine. You look exhausted." Pointing to my behind, Raffa adds, "Alice, what have you done to your skirt?"

Lifting up my jacket a little, I understand why: I have a newspaper article printed across my butt cheeks, and it's all thanks to Wapiti-Dundee and his brilliant idea to make me sit, sopping wet, on a newspaper.

I quickly say goodbye and race down the stairs that lead to the recording studios. There are bathrooms there, but more important there are dressing rooms where they keep a few stage costumes. I hope I can find something in my size.

"Good morning."

There is a man in front of the coffee machine next to the production room. He turns around and looks me up and down. "Are you new? Are you lost?"

New, me? He's the one who must be new. Judging from his height, jeans, magnetic glance, and salt-and-pepper hair, he must be an aspiring actor from *Mal d'Amore*, the soap we shoot in the Alpha studio. Maybe they're holding auditions today. And this guy, who looks like Richard Gere but taller, has a good chance, if you ask me.

"Really it's been a while since I was new—" I tell Tall Richard Gere.

I shoot straight into the dressing room, where I find a skirt. It is a dark, pleated kilt, which would be fine if it weren't stitched with sequins.

"Nice, it looks good on you. Which show do you host?" Tall Richard Gere asks me as he finishes sipping his coffee and hits the basket with his paper cup.

"Oh, I . . . No, I don't do any broadcasts," I reply, my face softening into a smile. If he thinks I could go on camera like this, perhaps I don't look such a fright.

"Ah, yes," he says. "That's what I thought, but since you're wearing that skirt from Wardrobe . . ."

Meanwhile, I'm already waving goodbye as I start walking away. I still have another Everest to climb: the meeting is starting in less than ten minutes.

. . .

When I get to the meeting room, everyone is a little late. I have time to organize the notepaper, pens, and water pitchers, and check that the whiteboard markers are working. Then, since I'm still alone, I tell myself that I have maybe a minute to fix that nail where the polish came off. It won't take long.

I'm just doing the last touches when Carlo comes in and casts me a knowing smile. God, I wouldn't even be able to steal candy without him catching me. I pretend not to notice. The code of conduct of the true strong and independent woman calls for the flaunting of a certain level of indifference. I continue to apply polish to my other nails, concentrating on my hands, as if I were Leonardo da Vinci painting the *Mona Lisa*.

Out of the corner of my eye, I see Carlo take a seat far away from me. I blow on my nails and wiggle my freshly polished fingers to show him that I'm the important one here; the rest of the world doesn't exist.

Then I hear someone clearing their throat.

Everyone has arrived. Raffa shakes her head and walks over to Enrico to whisper something in his ear. Cristina rests her hand on Carlo's arm—he has a furrowed brow and looks almost sad. To top it off, standing in front of the whiteboard are Our Lord the President of the Network and Tall Richard Gere. The latter clears his throat again. "Well, if the *young lady* has finished doing her nails, I would say we can begin, Mr. President."

I close my eyes and think of the *Dirty Dancing* video under my bed, and that moment when Baby confidently stands up and shows everyone what she's made of. But there is no Patrick Swayze here to hold out his hand for me. In his place is that guy I thought was a handsome actor—the type who if he gets to say more than three lines already feels like he's De Niro in *Taxi Driver*—and he's no longer sporting the friendly smile that he greeted me with at the coffee machine.

"Good," says Mr. President, calling everyone to attention. "As you know, we are a small network. One big, little family with a great desire to grow. This will mean all hands on deck. It will not be easy, since we're in the midst of a crisis . . . but we must change if we're not to surrender. So, in order to give the network a makeover, Mr. Davide Nardi has come to help us. In the coming months, he will observe and evaluate the work being done in our company, and then tell us how and when to intervene. Where to change, expand . . . or *cut* . . ."

And I, with my skirt and my nails, just gave him the worst possible impression.

At the end of the meeting, I have one foot out the door, when I hear Nardi say: "Of course, your ideas for the development of the network will be most welcome. If anyone has an idea for a program, a new format, anything interesting, please let me know and we will consider it."

Maybe a program on how to search for a new job, I think. *Hired or Fired?*

"There are germs on that."

I lift my head out of my hands. I am sitting on the floor in a bathroom stall with my elbow resting on the closed toilet lid. It seemed like the best place to reflect on my future.

In front of me stands a tall guy with blond hair and a very flashy earring in his left ear.

"Sorry?"

He smiles, crouches down next to me, and shakes his head. "Honey, excuse me for saying this, but you do not look well at all."

"Let's say that it's really not my day." I sigh.

He puts his hand on mine. On his middle finger, he's wearing a ring with strange symbols. "I know," he says, nodding.

I look him in the eye, and it is as if he really does know. I have the feeling that he has all the answers. Like Cinderella's fairy godmother, except that he's a man with bleached hair, thick eyeliner, and an earring. He stares at me in turn, kindly, and then says, "You're a Libra, aren't you?"

1

Swept Away (by a Libra)

And that's how it all started. When you talk about the important moments in your life, you expect them to happen when you're at the top of your game. That is, with smooth legs and perfumed underarms. But I like to be different, so my defining moment had to happen in the stall of a company bathroom, with my hair still wet and mascara streaming down my cheeks.

"A . . . Libra?" I repeat.

"It's a zodiac sign," he explains to me.

"I know what a Libra is," I reply. But I'm genuinely stunned, because I actually am a Libra. "Anyway, I . . . sorry, I don't believe in that. Astrology is for idiots. We're not in the Middle Ages anymore."

He shrugs and holds out his right hand again. "I'm Tio."

"What kind of name is Tio?" I ask, taking his hand. "Um, Alice."

"It's a stage name. An abbreviation for Tiziano. I'm an actor. And don't worry, most people don't believe in horoscopes . . . but they all read them anyway."

As I move toward the sink, I acknowledge that he's right. After all, even I have found myself looking at my stars on occasion.

"Do you know what really pisses me off?" I tell him, trying to flash at least the semblance of a smile. "When I read in my horoscope that this is a great period, that I have at least three stars for love, business, and health, but instead I feel like a wreck. I've just been dumped and I'm in danger of losing my job. So I feel like picking up the phone and calling the guy who wrote the horoscope, hurling insults at him, and telling him that I'll see him in court. When I read a great horoscope and my life is going to hell, I feel like an outcast. I imagine that everyone else with my sign has happily boarded the good luck bus and I got the door slammed in my face."

Tio looks at me puzzled, then smiles and says, "Well, now you're on the bus, honey. Or rather, a business class flight." He winks and takes me by the arm.

We walk toward the door.

"And you know what your first stroke of luck is? I'll buy you lunch. I have to celebrate; I just got offered a part in *Mal d'Amore*."

I smile at him. "That way you can explain to me what you were doing in the ladies' room . . ."

"Um . . . actually, this is the men's room."

And as I open the door, we find ourselves face-to-face with Carlo, who gives a start when he sees me.

"A . . . Alice!" He scratches his head while his smile reduces to a grimace. "Look, I . . . I wanted to talk to you."

Of course. The last thing I need is a firsthand account of Carlo's happiness about his impending fatherhood.

I shoot a look at Tio, wishing that he would throw me a rope to get me out of the quicksand I'm sinking into.

Miraculously, Tio behaves like a perfect fairy godmother. "Excuse us, but we were just going to lunch . . . to discuss work," he says with such a professional look that I almost believe him. He's not a bad actor.

. . .

"You must be deceptively thin." Unless he's been locked in a cage with no food for three days. The speed at which Tio manages to gulp down everything on the tray must be a Guinness World Record. Meanwhile, I'm still fiddling with my overcooked macaroni.

"I have a good metabolism, and like many Gemini, I have a mercurial structure. I'm nervous and agile."

"More astrology? OK, so tell me how you guessed I was a Libra."

"Well, at the moment the sky doesn't look good for Libras. Saturn is retrograde for the whole month. The Sun went into Aries a couple of days ago. And complicated situations and stress are accumulating in the Libra constellation, both from an emotional point of view, with Venus negatively squared with Jupiter, and from a professional point of view, with the Opposition of Pluto and the Negative Transit of Uranus."

I blink because, although on the one hand I didn't understand a word of what he said, on the other hand my ears filtered all the words, coming to an immediate conclusion: I have interplanetary bad luck syndrome. "So, basically, there is nothing I can do: it's not me . . . it's not like I could do something about it. There's no escape."

"No, come on. It's just one period and the Transits will soon change . . . And actually: knowing what is happening to you on an astrological level can help you to prevent certain issues. Like if you know that it's going to rain, what do you do? You bring an umbrella."

I snort. A flawless argument.

Tio sighs. "Libras haven't had an easy time. It's due to the Transit of Saturn in their sign. It's been there for almost two years. What can you do? It's the planet associated with tough times, discipline, and the trials of life. But the good news is that now it's moved on to Scorpio, and since it's one of the slower planets, it will not come back into Libra's orbit for another thirty years."

"Alice ..."

When I lift my gaze and look over Tio's shoulder, I see Carlo. Great. "What do you want? Can't you see that I'm talking?"

"Alice, please, I know that—"

"If you know, then why are you disturbing me? Can't you see that I'm busy? Would I interrupt you if you were in a meeting?"

Tio also turns around for a second, then looks back at me and rolls his eyes.

I watch Carlo walk away.

"It's a real shame that *he's* not a Scorpio." Saturn's bad luck won't touch him for another twelve years. Too late to rely on that.

"You must have negative Mars in Midheaven; it makes a person very aggressive and not particularly diplomatic," comments Tio.

"Oh, it's just that he's my ex . . . that is my *very*-ex . . ." Actually, counting all the unfortunate relationships that came my way after him, I should say that he is my ex-ex-ex-ex-ex . . . assuming I haven't forgotten anyone. "We have a very . . . complicated relationship . . ."

"What sign is he?"

"Aquarius."

Tio distractedly checks his watch. "Aquarius is the sign of freedom and experimentation. It' s difficult to make them put down roots . . . They love risk and unpredictability."

Ah, two birds with one stone . . . Carlo evidently did take a risk and now a positive pregnancy test will force him to put down roots, whether he likes it or not. In spite of everything, I feel a little guilty for how I treated him. I glance around for him in the café, but he must have already left. Can I really blame Mars for having spoken to him like that?

"Between Aquarius and Libra there is, in fact, a certain harmony," continues Tio, "but if the understanding is not reinforced on an erotic level, Aquarius has the tendency to wander. The good news is that they can have a loyal and sincere friendship."

He's not telling me anything new, really. Living together just proved that it wasn't going to work: even though we were in love, we drove one another crazy. One example: I am completely disorganized, while he has always been practically obsessive-compulsive, trying to put everything in alphabetical order, from DVDs to the contents of the kitchen cabinets, which meant I had to remember to look for biscuits near baking soda and not where you kept the tea or sugar . . .

"See? Now you know that potentially things won't work out well with an Aquarius. Libras usually suffer with signs that don't know how to take care of them. For you, a strong Leo would be great; an alpha male, dominant, but able to pay real attention to his partner. Or an adventurous Sagittarius. Or with Scorpio . . . Let me think . . ."

"I don't want a Scorpio," I say, getting up. "I've already had enough trouble. He can deal with Saturn on his own."

2

I'm Starting from Aries

I leave Tio in Wardrobe. We exchange numbers and he promises that he'll call me soon. When we say goodbye, he plants two kisses on my cheeks and says it was the lucky Trine of Venus that brought us together.

As skeptical as I am about Tio's astrological theories, I can't help but find them fascinating. And deep down, I love this stuff. The thought that there is some kind of predestination, a Grand Plan, makes me feel less in jeopardy. A while ago, for example, I toyed with the idea of devoting myself to feng shui, but not just casually dropping a pink pillow here and a green curtain there. I made up my mind to completely reorganize the entire house.

This was right after my best friend, Paola, got married.

I haven't always lived alone. I am a very sociable person, and Paola was my third and last roommate. Just like the two before her, Sara and Marta, she fell in love and packed her bags after less than four months.

After she left, I began to think that my apartment was a catalyst for supernatural forces that stimulated marriage. Some sort of holistic dating agency: come and live with me and you'll be settled down in no time.

Now, I really love my friends, but it wouldn't be such a bad thing if the magic also worked for yours truly. And, given that the first, Sara, left me to live with her boyfriend; the second, Marta, got married; and Paola, the third, has even had a baby, it seems that the miraculous power is only increasing with time.

Hence, feng shui. I tried to reorganize the layout of the furniture to channel the energies toward me. I even changed bedrooms, occupying what had once been theirs. Nothing. I even managed to make things worse. Seeing me so fully committed, the man I was dating at the time suddenly had second thoughts about our relationship and decided to break things off.

In a fury, I put everything back the way it was, and I used the feng shui manual to wash the windows. At least I can say that it helped me to gain some clarity.

Don't get me wrong, I am truly happy for my friends, especially Paola. The fact that she found a man like Giacomo and that they are madly in love gives me some kind of comfort. In short, it makes me think that there is still a little hope left for true love in this world.

Today, I am extra happy to see her. Ever since the new baby arrived, our opportunities to see each other have dwindled. In fifteen years of friendship, Paola and I have become well versed in the analysis of each other's emotions. If universities had such a thing as a Department of Emotional Anatomical Pathology, we would be awarded an honorary doctorate and invited to teach the course.

The first spritz is dedicated entirely to childbirth, and to the monumental change for a woman when going from being an individual to a mother. Philosophy doesn't last through the second round of alcohol, where we glide through more mundane topics, such as men and sex (which neither of us has had recently for various and very different reasons), and finally the signs of the zodiac (astrology applied to sex and to the search for Mr. Right).

"According to Tio, the important thing is not a sign's propensity to love, but how compatible it is with yours. If you think about it, it's true. It's like saying that it's personality that counts," I explain, lifting my half-empty glass. "Take Carlo. He's an Aquarius. With Libras like me, there is compatibility but only to a certain point. Plus, they're fickle. And Carlo is the fickle type."

"What do you mean? I thought you were always complaining that he was so persnickety."

"Well, yes, but he's fickle in relationships. How many women did he have after me? He loses interest right away. He even lost interest in me. He's not the marrying type."

Paola clears her throat. "But Cristina is pregnant . . . And they are getting married."

I empty my glass in one long gulp. "Yes, but he's still fickle," I say resolutely. Because I cannot bring myself to believe that he was fickle only with me. That I was the one he didn't want to marry; that there was something wrong with me.

Paola doesn't rub it in and lightens our conversation with a shrug. "Well, he was a bit fickle with his semen."

We both burst into laughter.

"Hey, on a more serious note, how are you going to deal with this new problem at work?"

The new problem at work has a first and last name: Davide Nardi.

I sigh and raise my hand to call the waitress. I need a third spritz to address this question.

"I don't know. My idea is to lie low. You know those tiny animals with terrified eyes that escape predators by camouflaging themselves as a leaf or a stone? I hope that he will forget I exist."

"Why not treat this as your big break? Your problem is self-esteem!"

Paola gives me her analyst's stare. "If you don't believe in yourself first, how can you expect someone else to? Let's take the issue of men, for example: What kind of partner are you going to find if you only offer your need to be loved? You don't want a man; you want a crutch."

The problem with Paola is that she's always dead-on. "Back to Nardi, then. What do *you* think I should do?"

"Well, you shouldn't hide, that's for sure. Instead, be proactive and efficient. Show him what you're made of. You're more intelligent than most of the people working there."

Proactive and intelligent.

I can almost hear the beginning of the theme from *Working Girl*: "Let the river run / let all the dreamers wake the nation . . ." I feel like Melanie Griffith. I'm ready to fight for my job and earn myself an office with a view. And in the meantime, perhaps, wed my Harrison Ford. But who would he be . . . Nardi?

Oh. My. God.

"Excuse me for a second . . . I have to pee." I get up and head toward the bathroom.

I run cold water over my wrists and my mind cools down, too. How absurd to think of Nardi (even for a second, just one tiny second!) as a possible candidate for the role of Prince Charming. Perhaps I have Stockholm syndrome?

When I return to Paola, for a second I think I must have double vision. Then I realize that there is someone else at the table with her.

"Hi, I'm Luca."

Scan: Male, white. Age: Thirty-five to forty. Hair: Light brown. Eyes: Brown. Shoulders: Not bad . . . And most important: No ring on his left hand.

"Nice to meet you. Alice." I shoot a glance at Paola that says: *How is it that I leave you for just one second and a man approaches you?*

"Luca is a colleague from the newspaper," she explains.

"Yes. A colleague who is amazed to see a mom out on the town."

I grin and take my place between them. "Oh, I am the bad influence."

"Excellent!" This time, he is scanning me with his gaze. The result is a smile of appreciation. "Don't ever lose your social contacts. Don't do what I did. I did everything for my girlfriend: romantic outings, trips, candlelit dinners . . ."

Girlfriend? Stop. Not single! Danger. Red flag!

My eyebrow rises the extra millimeter that changes my expression from bewitching to the sympathetic look of Grandma Duck.

"And in the end . . . BANG! Anna left me because she needed her space."

"Oh . . ." Paola and I say in unison.

"I didn't know, I'm sorry," says Paola, who sneaks a glance at me.

"Now I'm recovering my friendships. Trying to enjoy life."

Poor, poor guy! Imagine how much he suffered, thinks Nurse Alice.

"But it's fine. I was actually just waiting for some people to go dancing." Luca gets up. "I hope to see you again, Alice. We can arrange it with Paola if you like." And we watch him walk away to meet three or four guys standing at the bar.

"Poor thing, I'm really sorry," says Paola. "He's a really nice guy. And a hard worker."

I nonchalantly sip at what remains of my spritz.

"And . . . do you know what sign he is?"

Paola squints thoughtfully and then flashes a smile. "Aries, I think."

3

Dog Day Libra

A woman at the wheel is a woman in control of her life. Although you wouldn't think so from looking at the dents on my jalopy. But as I always explain to those who reproach me for not getting it fixed, my car is something of a metaphor for the soul: there are some scratches that cannot be erased.

After last week's little incident, this morning the two of us are finally reunited, and I am on cloud nine as we head to work.

I'm almost there, but I think I have time for a tune. If only I could find the radio. I reach down, stretching my hand under the seat, and my car swerves across the road.

Someone behind me honks their horn.

"Oh, calm down!" I raise my hand at the motorcycle that passes me only to brake a little farther ahead at the red light. "There, you see? All that rush and now you have to stop, too," I say as I reach him.

In the meantime, I've finally found the front panel of the radio, which, as soon as I attach it, starts blasting out ABBA. It's "Dancing Queen," which is perfect, because that's exactly what I want to be.

When I turn around, the motorcyclist is looking at me.

I have the window down, so I imagine he's listening to me wailing along to ABBA. Oops . . .

But today I'm not going to let anyone burst my bubble. What did Paola say? Confidence! I have to be sure of myself and not let the little things rattle me. I look at him nonchalantly, keep singing for him, and then, as soon as the light turns green, I wink and hit the gas.

I start laughing hysterically. For the last few miles, the motorcycle and I are in a race between one red light and the next.

At the last traffic light, I hear my phone announcing the arrival of a message on WhatsApp. As I'm parking, the motorcycle finally passes me and I wave goodbye before grabbing my smartphone to see who it is.

I ignore the missed calls from Carlo, sticking my tongue out in disgust as I swipe them away.

Just above Carlo's, however, there is another message. This time I smile. It's from Tio.

Good morning, dear Libra!

The day will seem to be two-sided. You are energetic and spirited, thanks to the Trine of Venus in Positive Transit with Jupiter, but your desire to do and to prove will be tested by Saturn and Mercury. This could lead to unexpected revelations, which may slightly dampen your enthusiasm, or to unexpected workloads that will require all of your patience. Possible clashes with people who hold opposing views are also on the cards. In matters of the heart, the Square of Venus in Negative Transit with Pluto calls for caution and hints at the possibility of a powerful and stormy love.

With a smiley face, he concludes:

Tio is arriving at one for hair and makeup. He loves tuna sandwiches.

Still smiling, I lock the car. And it's only when I look over to the entrance gate that I realize that the motorcycle I had been racing is parked right beside it and that the driver is just getting off his bike.

I toy with the idea of burying myself in the café next door until he's gone, but I don't want to hide just yet. I brazenly cross the street while he removes his helmet.

Where is a *Wizard of Oz*–style tornado when you need one?

Davide Nardi finishes removing his motorcycle gloves and fixes me with a serious glare. "It's dangerous to take your eyes off the road to look for the radio."

It is also dangerous to sing and pull faces at a man who could get you fired, I think. I stammer, "Umm . . . morning."

With his disheveled helmet hair and bright red face, he looks even more like Richard Gere—in one of the steamy scenes from *American Gigolo*—and despite my recent Oscar nomination for most embarrassing performance, my circulation seems to be going haywire, like when you hit the maximum score in pinball. Hot. Cold. Cold. Hot.

"But you have a nice voice," Davide Nardi says to my back.

I blink, and when I turn around, he cracks a smile. I sigh and decide I should punch in.

I don't have much time to dissect the effect that Nardi (Nardi, the Hatchet Man; Nardi, Public Enemy Number One) had on me with his leather jacket and his unkempt bad boy look.

As soon as I set foot in the editing room, I feel like I am in the middle of a screen test that Enrico, my boss and the head of production, is doing for a movie about hunting grizzly bears. All signs point to Enrico in the role of the bear.

"What do you mean the studio is not ready yet?" Enrico shouts before unleashing a diatribe laden with profanities that would make the perfect opening for another *Exorcist* movie. "You didn't get the memo? Where the hell is Alice?"

"I'm here!" I squeak.

Before him, the head of photography and the director of several of our programs are reduced to Lilliputian dimensions by the roar of Grizzly-Enrico.

They seem relieved to see me, but I'm under no illusions: I am not the network's Mother Teresa, I'm just fresh meat.

"Where the hell were you? Do you or do you not have a work schedule?"

It's useless to remind him that it is nine o'clock and that's the time we always start on a Tuesday. "What happened?" I ask him instead. Great. Active. Proactive.

"Luciano says that the boys don't have the studios prepped because no one received memos beforehand, or that this week we would be taping two shows, since Marlin will be in Rome next week."

I blink. I'm the one who sends the memos, but they are based on the information that is sent to me. And no one told me anything about taping an additional episode today. "Enrico, you didn't send me an e-mail about this."

Enrico turns blue, and for a second I fear he is about to sprout Dracula fangs.

I reach my desk, grab the folder with all the sheets for the production of *Buongiorno, Milano*—the show we're supposed to be filming—and run straight to the studio.

Halfway down the corridor, I hear the ambulance-like Doppler effect of Enrico yelling above the production team, all of them drowned out by Marlin's voice booming from the makeup room. Marlin fidgets under the makeup artist's brush and huffs, "Two episodes and you're not ready yet! Bloody incompetence!"

Without even stopping to greet her, I run directly to the studio, where I find the director of photography dangling from a ladder as he adjusts the lighting. "Flood her with lots of light," I shout. Marlin likes to be lit like Our Lady of Lourdes, since she thinks it makes it harder to see her wrinkles.

Next, I make a mad dash to our director, Luciano, to go over the lineup, as the first guests are already being corralled into the lounge next door. "We'll do both shows calmly, without any strokes of genius, Lu."

Luciano nods and looks into my eyes. "Today of all days, Alice!" he chides me gently, looking over my shoulder.

I turn around for a second and see Mr. President at the end of the corridor, leaning against the makeup room door and flirting with Marlin. Davide Nardi is just behind him, feeding coins into the soft drink machine.

"I know, Luciano . . . I'm sorry," I stammer. "I didn't know anything about the extra episode."

"The guys are really nervous with all the talk of a network restructuring and possible cuts. Upstairs they're saying that they want new ideas, new shows, new people, and we get caught unprepared from the start!" And with that, he walks away, shaking his head.

New ideas! I shudder to think of what that might imply.

Someone from the waiting room yells, "Could we get some coffee?" and once again off I trot.

I flash my best Colgate smile as I ask the guests, "Coffee, tea . . ."

Davide Nardi turns toward me and I can't help but think of the line from *Working Girl*: "Coffee, tea, me?" I add the third word silently as I meet his glance.

He stares at me for a second and then smiles. "No coffee, thanks, but I would love a bottle of still water. The machine outside ate my money."

Action and reaction, Alice. It's pretty simple.

Instead I stand there, dazed, while the guests shower me with their orders.

After a few seconds too long, I turn like a robot toward the machine and say, "Of course." This is not the first time that the damn thing has jammed, but we have developed an almost infallible fix.

I stop a colleague who is passing by. "Sergio, I need the *shake*, please."

Sergio nods while Nardi comes over to join us. "Can I give you a hand?"

"Grab the other side of the machine," says Sergio before I can interject.

They tilt it back, and I stand motionless, staring at Nardi playing X-Man with the soft drinks machine.

"Alice!" Sergio brings me back to reality, because now it's my turn. I gave the order for the *shake*, I can't back out now.

I sigh, and under the scrutiny of the Hatchet Man, I give a wiggle, and swing my backside hard into the side of the machine.

Immediately it dispenses two bottles, which I remove and deliver to Nardi. "Here you are." I feel my neck burn with embarrassment and walk away immediately, using the coffee run as my excuse.

"Thank you for the . . . *shake* . . . Alice," I hear him say.

Oh god.

In the meantime, Enrico has reached the production room and is screaming, "Well? Not ready yet?"

Luckily, I again manage to transform myself into the bionic woman and I have the opening theme music playing within three minutes.

"Today, we are joined in the studio by Mr. Claretti, who has one of the largest record collections in the world. The old LPs, remember them? They played at thirty-three revolutions per minute.

Now, on the other hand, we have CDs that play at forty-five revolutions—"

"CUUUUT!" Enrico claps his hand on the wall with such force that the partition shakes.

In the studio, some of the guests giggle while Marlin looks around, lost, and asks, "Why have we stopped?"

"Because you're an idiot!" Enrico barks. "That's why we stopped, damn it. We're already short on time and Your Chestiness doesn't even know that CDs don't play at revolutions per minute. Now, I'm going to come in there and . . ."

I rush toward Enrico. The engineers dubbed Marlin "Your Chestiness" right after her mammoplasty last year, but Enrico is generally careful not to use that nickname, and he should be especially guarded when Mr. President, who seems to be Marlin's benefactor, is around.

"I'll handle it," I say, without broaching the subject. "But please don't get yourself in trouble."

I head to the studio where I tell Marlin that we have to start again from the introduction of Mr. Claretti, and explain in broad terms the difference between an LP and a CD.

When I leave the studio, I lean for a moment on the iron door, close my eyes, and sigh. I can't believe the day's not even halfway over yet.

When I open my eyes again, there are two people staring at me: Davide Nardi, from the door, and Carlo, from the end of the hallway. Carlo raises a finger, as if to call my attention, but I shake my head and dash back to the production room, almost colliding with Nardi in the rush.

4

A Gemini for All Seasons

I can hardly believe that we managed to record both episodes.

I want to strut over to Enrico, proud as a peacock, but when I turn around, I see him behind the glass door of the production room, arguing animatedly on his cell phone.

Instead I call out "It's a wrap!" and after a trip to the café, I stop at the *Mal d'Amore* makeup room with two large tuna sandwiches. The smile plastered across my face falters a little when I see Tio with a ton of fake tan on his face and a pair of round glasses.

"And who the hell are you supposed to be?" I ask Tio as he takes his first bite of the sandwich, trying not to ruin the greasepaint.

"I ... am Marshush ... Alvars ..." he splutters, in between mouthfuls. "Marcus Alvarez de la Rosa, cousin of Ferdinando Prandi, and an old flame of Ferdinando's current girlfriend. We had a fling when we were kids, when she was on vacation in Tenerife."

I shake my head. I can't get over how they've tanned him! He looks like a cross between George Hamilton and Eduardo Palomo. They've even put extensions in his hair.

"So, did you get my message?" asks Tio as they finish giving him curls that would be the envy of Shirley Temple.

"Yes..." I say, a little distracted.

"And?"

"And I read it... But today has been chaotic and..." I turn toward him and stare.

I rummage in my pocket for my cell phone, to reread his message from this morning.

The day had started well, and after my evening out with Paola, I was so keen to prove what I was capable of. Tio had written that I would be energetic and spirited, but that then Saturn and Mercury... The message mentions "unexpected workloads."

"How did you do it?" I ask him, staring at the screen.

"I told you, it's your horoscope. The position of the planets in your sign is clear."

"What about the powerful and stormy love?" I bat my eyes and stop in front of him, blocking his path. "Because I want it now! 'Powerful and stormy,' like it says here in black and white! Passionate, etcetera, etcetera." If it turns out he has only guessed the negative aspects of my horoscope correctly, there's a high chance I may scream.

"I don't know, be patient. I'm not a matchmaker. That's what the Transit of the planets says."

We are walking down the hallway when I see Carlo, and I give thanks for the character designer who came up with Marcus Alvarez, especially Tio's lion's mane, which easily serves as a bush that I can hide behind.

"You won't be able to avoid him forever, you know."

I snort and slip the phone into my pocket, only to jump immediately as I feel it vibrating furiously against my thigh.

Above Tio's message there is another, from a number that's not in my phone book.

Hello, this is Luca, Paola's colleague. We met last night. I was wondering if you'd like to go for a drink sometime.

I look up at Tio as incredulous as Luke Skywalker when Yoda makes objects levitate in front of him using the power of the Force. When he pats me on the shoulder, I half expect him to say: "May the Force be with you." Instead, he jumps up and down and whoops like a cheerleader.

"Don't tell me it's a MAN?!" When I nod, he starts improvising a dance in the hallway. "Am I or am I not good?"

"You are . . . phenomenal," I say unconsciously.

Fireworks are exploding in my head. Luca is cute. And in his favor, he has:

+ A thumbs-up from Paola, who describes him as brilliant and kind;
+ His message is written with impeccable grammar. These days, with all the U's and R's and dangling prepositions floating around, this is not something to be underestimated.
+ He asked for my phone number and asked me out on a date! Isn't that a sign that he has good taste?

Tio is still shaking his hips in front of me, when I tell him: "I think he is an Aries."

He stops abruptly.

"What's wrong?"

"It's just that Aries is such a strong-willed sign . . . They can even be selfish at times. I would say restless, even, and you, as a Libra, have already had so much upheaval recently . . ."

"But that's it, isn't it? Powerful and stormy." It's meant to be.

Tio nods. "Indeed . . ." He sighs and takes my face in his hands.

"I feel like an old aunt, giving you advice, and then when it's time to let you stand on your own two feet, I'm afraid you're going to get hurt. But I'll be right there with you, every step of the way, OK?"

I am on the verge of tears. This man, whom I've known for such a short time, is worried about me! I hug him tightly.

"You know, you really are incredible. Every girl should have a Tio to guide her and give her advice."

He laughs heartily. "Some kind of guru, eh? Hmm . . . I wouldn't look so bad in a turban . . ."

"More than a guru, a guide . . . An astrological guide . . . for broken hearts."

5

Libra on the Verge of
a Nervous Breakdown

It's official: I have nothing to wear.

Half of the contents of my closet are stacked on my bed and the rest scattered around the room, divided into piles. And I have absolutely no idea what I should wear tonight.

Following Tio's advice, it has been ten days since Luca's first message.

"You don't want to give in right away, Alice. Aries is a hunter. If he doesn't smell the scent of a challenge he won't have fun and I will lose interest. And you don't want me to lose interest now, do you?"

No, I don't want *him* to lose interest. So even though my "dance card" has been empty for several nights, I've invented four drink dates, two birthdays, a movie, and a dinner at my parents' house (the only true excuse, how pathetic).

Of course, Paola caught on a few days ago.

"Hello, Alice? What's this I hear about you being at my sister's birthday tonight? What are you up to? I thought that you wanted to go out with Luca . . . He says you're always busy. Since when are you so popular?"

I had to explain to her about Aries men and that I didn't want him to think that I was dying to go out with him.

"Yes, but enough is enough," she said at a certain point of my astrological spiel. "Besides, I'm sorry, but with all due respect to your clairvoyant friend, I know Luca and he's not like that. He's a sweet guy, strong but gentle. I mean, why don't you try being more spontaneous?"

I explained to her that Tio is an astrologer not Miss Cleo, and that so far my attempts at spontaneity, as she calls them, have always misfired.

In the end, I gave in. After all, a day or two couldn't make much difference.

The waiting period did not go to waste. In those ten days, I had subjected myself to a lifestyle change that made Demi Moore in *G.I. Jane* look like she was on vacation in the Bahamas.

My alarm went off at 6:00 a.m. every day so I could bend and flex along with an old videotape: *Firm and Burn with Jane Fonda.* Along with the kicks to give me buns of steel like Barbarella, I subjected myself to the purifying diet of Tibetan monks, which meant that I'd been feeding myself rabbit food for ten days. Now, my hips are a little bit trimmer and I feel more at peace with myself.

In short: I'm toned, I'm hot, and I'm ready.

But now I'm having a fashion crisis.

Should I be provocative and elegant, or casual and chic? Sophisticated woman or girl next door?

I sit on the bed and send an SOS text to Tio. Not even a minute later, my phone rings and I cling to it as if it were the last life preserver from the *Titanic*. "Hello?"

"Hi, gorgeous, how are the preparations going?" At the other end of the line is Paola, who must have felt the vibrations of my despair.

"It couldn't be going any worse. What should I wear?"

"Come on, what are you worried about? Wear something nice, without being over-the-top. You have to feel comfortable."

Right. With the phone pressed to my ear, I rummage through the scattered clothes and fish out my tight jeans. They look pretty good with one of those tight T-shirts. It's nothing earth shattering, but I could always dress up the outfit with some jewelry.

The trill of an incoming message makes me jump and my smartphone slips out of my hands. It's Tio.

Wow him with your sex appeal: high heels and a miniskirt. Aries is a carnivore. You have to dangle the goods in front of him while making him think you couldn't care less whether he samples them.

I admit showing up bundled up in jeans and a collared blouse wouldn't be the best option for enhancing my powers of seduction. I toss the clothes back into their respective piles and continue my search.

"Listen, Paola, what if I wore that sexy bodice instead, the one that looks very *Moulin Rouge*–esque?"

I immediately send a photo of it to Tio, who responds a nanosecond later with a thumbs-up emoji and many exclamation points.

"Are you crazy? That might work for a nightclub . . . and maybe not even there! To tell you the truth, that top has always seemed kind of vulgar to me. Come on! Plus you risk being glued to your chair by the fear that with the slightest movement one of your tits will pop out."

I write Tio a brief message:

No, won't work. Too restrictive . . .

"Listen, Alice, Luca is very easygoing. Wear a miniskirt if you want, but don't you think that he should focus his attention on you as a person rather than on your tits and legs? After all, when he met you, you were dressed normally and he was still interested."

As Paola continues her lecture on spontaneity, I read another message from Tio.

> **Remember, you must make him sigh. Aries is the sign of primordial instincts. He might give the impression of being a simple man, but in reality, he's a dormant volcano. His ideal woman is one who is falsely naïve. He likes to fight for the bone, like a dog, but he lacks imagination and you have to give him an idea of what that bone is made of.**

I get up and start tearing through my things like a crazy woman trying to take into account the suggestions of both my friends. When I check my reflection in the mirror, I am wearing a knee-length skirt with side slits, a high-necked but very close-fitting blouse, and shoes that are not too high. It doesn't work. I look like the modern version of Mary Poppins. I undress and start over again. High boots, miniskirt, top—and I'm all set for a shift in the red-light district. Next! Tank top, pants, and flat shoes: great. If I ever decide to go to a lesbian bar, I have my outfit picked out.

I collapse on the bed, and the only remotely positive thought that comes to mind is that all of this hustle and bustle is burning more calories than my Jane Fonda regime does in the mornings.

Yet another message from Tio arrives in a coup de grâce.

> **I forgot: being the primordial animal that he is, Aries loves bold colors, like red or yellow. And being a fire sign, they truly are his colors. I hope this was helpful.**

I place the telephone on the bed and resume my search, determined not to be distracted anymore, but three seconds later it starts ringing again.

It's my mother.

I answer because, in her mind, I'm still a teenager and she worries when I miss her calls.

"Mom . . . hi."

"Hi, sweetie . . . What's up?"

Here we go, the typical insanity of when she calls simply because she is bored.

"Sorry, Mom, but I'm just on my way out."

"You never have time when I call."

"No, I'm sorry . . . It's just that I have a date and I still have to get dressed."

Why did I tell her that? On the other end of the receiver there is silence for several seconds.

"With a man?" she finally asks.

I sigh. "No—I mean, yes—but he's a friend."

She sighs, too. "Guido! Alice is going out with a *man* tonight."

"Mom!"

"OK, what are you going to wear?" she asks next. Like mother, like daughter.

"I don't know yet, Mom. I was trying to figure that out."

"Why don't you stop by? You know we're packing up boxes to empty the house, and I found that beautiful polka-dot skirt in your closet and the blouse with the lace collar and the camellia brooch. Do you remember them?"

God help me.

"Mom, I wore those things when I was twelve years old." And I probably should have been ashamed of them even then. The polka-dot skirt and the blouse with the frilly collar probably explain why I never fit in as a child. Who in the world would want to be seen in the company of a Saint Honoré cake with measles?" "I'm sorry, I really have to go."

When the phone rings again and the display reads PRIVATE NUMBER, I think that I will never manage to get out of this house.

"Hello?"

"Alice, this is Carlo. I'm sorry to call from a restricted number but I need to speak to you. Please. There's too much happening all at once. I don't understand anything anymore." He attacks in bursts, hitting me with flurries of words. "I know that you're pissed off, because of Cristina, and the baby—I mean I can understand that you are jealous—and touchy—God, you've always been so impossibly touchy."

"Me, jealous? *Touchy?*"

"There. That's exactly what I mean. You see?"

"So, if I'm so impossibly *touchy*, what do you want from me?" I yell, practically strangling the cell phone.

"A little bit of understanding. Don't treat me like a prairie from Calcutta."

"Pariah. You mean pariah, idiot."

"God, you are awful when you play the wiseass. Why am I still wasting my time with you? Do you ever wonder why men run away from you all the time? Or is it always just your bad luck? Poor, unfortunate Alice, always meeting the wrong people. Well, maybe *you're* the wrong person."

Oh, hell no.

"That's enough! I don't need a lecture from a moron who doesn't have a shred of sensitivity. We are done. You keep me informed of anything important via the Internet anyway, right? I will wait until you update your marital status on Facebook and then post my congratulations on your wall. For everything else, chill out, and above all, stay away from me."

I throw the phone on top of the pillows and the room starts to spin around me. I look at the piles of clothes everywhere, and I'm no longer able to think: casual, elegant, serious, bold colors, simplicity, sensuality, charm . . . Carlo and Cristina, Tio, work, Paola, the wrong men, the wrong me . . . and I can't breathe. My heart is racing at a thousand beats per minute, and I can feel it in my throat. Is this a panic attack?

Thank God I have sedatives in the nightstand. I gulp one down and take five minutes to stretch out on the bed. Breathe, Alice. Breathe.

But a second later, the nightmare begins again.

"What the hell!" I exclaim, grabbing the ringing cell phone again.

As it turns out, five minutes has turned into almost an hour.

"Um, hey, Alice, it's Luca. I'm downstairs."

6

The Libra, the Aries, His Wife & Her Lover

T he car vibrates under my feet as I make my way down in the elevator. I reach the ground floor unscathed, only to realize that the vibrations aren't coming from the elevator but from the bass line of music that keeps getting nearer. In my driveway, I discover a flaming red sports car—which is where the deafening noise is coming from.

"Hi!" I scream, opening the car door, practically crouching to the ground to get in.

"Hey, Alisss, good evening, welcome," says Luca, butchering my name with the American pronunciation, Alissss.

I match him with a "Hey, Luuuke" and start laughing.

"Is everything OK? I was starting to think you had changed your mind . . ."

"No, I'm sorry. I got a bunch of calls that put me way behind."

"What?" Luca yells. Of course, if he were to lower the volume, we might be able to communicate without having to use sign language.

"Nice car!"

"Do you like it? It's my baby. I've had it less than a month."

As he slams the car in reverse, he is eager to inform me of its cylinder capacity, how fast it can go, and even the nightclub-worthy stereo system that he has unfortunately decided to install.

"Where are we going?" I ask him after a while.

"Ah yes. It's an amazing place in the Porta Romana area, naturally. They make a Negroni Sbagliato that is out of this world."

"Really? I don't really like Negroni, *sbagliato* or otherwise, but they serve food, too, don't they?"

Luca doesn't answer me; my words most likely fell on ears deafened by the roar of the car, car radio, and his own voice, going hoarse while singing the praises of the good life he is about to introduce me to.

In fact, the bar we enter is the epitome of Milan's drinking scene, filled with mid-November suntans and upturned polo collars, Dracula style. The atmosphere is very deliberate: dim lights, exposed stone walls, and six-foot-high flames that blessedly have metal casings.

"Luca! *Hello, brudder!*" As soon as we enter, one of the bartenders greets him with a high five and a bro shake.

"Hey, where've you been hiding? How's Anna?"

I step forward, waiting for him to introduce me, but instead he just mumbles something I don't understand to the bartender, which is not surprising, considering that the music is just as deafening in the club as it was in the car.

"What can I get you guys?"

"Two Negroni Sbagliatos. As only you can make 'em, *brudder!*"

He probably didn't hear me in the car when I told him that I didn't like Negronis, but now it seems rude to remind him.

"So, you and Paola met at the newspaper," I say when we're finally alone—just me and him and the roar of the speaker hanging above our heads.

He smiles at me and starts to talk about his job, about his colleagues and Paola. "I really respect her. She's really great for a woman."

I want to ask for clarification on that last point, but he's already moved on to telling me his dreams for the future.

The Negroni is really disgusting, but his story about free climbing in Malaysia isn't bad. And the one about diving in the Philippines. And trekking in Kenya, rafting in Colorado, kayaking in Ecuador, and hang gliding in Zimbabwe.

"Maybe we can get something to eat, what do you think?" I ask, with my ears buzzing, either from the background noise or from all that information about extreme sports practiced at the extreme ends of the earth.

As I approach the buffet counter, I feel my cell phone vibrate.

It's a message from Tio.

Well? How's it going? Is he able to look away from your neckline or is he already completely gone?

In the end, I decided to try and have it both ways, by wearing a red velvet dress (a decisive color evocative of an Aries's fire, in the words of Tio) that is flexible enough to allow me to move naturally (as suggested by Paola). Just then, to my horror, I notice that in my rush to leave I have failed spectacularly with my shoes. They don't match the dress or rather they do, but they don't match each other.

I put on two different shoes.

One is black, and the other has red stripes. How could I have missed that?!

I try to hide my red foot behind the other leg.

I answer the message by telling Tio about my horrendous mistake but he answers:

No worries, he's an Aries. He's not equipped with the ability to notice what is going on around him. You just have to hang on his every word and pretend to be eternally grateful for the mere fact that he is speaking to you.

I snort as I return to my seat.

Luca resumes his travel diaries with Easter Island, and then turns to New Guinea, where he was on a recent vacation with friends, bungee jumping. "... because it's such a *rush* to feel the force of nature like that. It's like—BAM! You get me? You feel everything. WHAM! You breathe it all in ..."

I nod, trying to give the impression of hanging on to his every word and every guttural onomatopoeic sound that he emits. "I have to admit: these things kind of scare me."

"These are sports for real men, but you could come watch me, sometime."

At this point, there's a lull in our conversation, and I get the feeling it's my turn to speak about myself. I talk about movies, my work at the TV station, and my interest in culture until I realize that one of two things has happened to Luca: either he has come down with an extreme case of squinting or he is staring at something behind me.

"Aha ... it must be ... well ... *cool* ... to work in a bookstore ..." he finally says, vaguely.

But at that point, the bartender from before, Mr. Negroni-Sbagliato-As-Only-You-Can, comes over smiling and whispers something in Luca's ear.

"Thank you, *brudder*," says Luca, clapping him on the shoulder. "Will you excuse me for a moment, Alisss?"

I watch him walk over to a six-foot-tall blonde, with a micro-skirt that modestly covers her thong and a skimpy sporty T-shirt.

Luca kisses her on the cheeks and then greets her companion, holding his hand in a grip that lasts at least eight seconds and makes the muscles of his jaw harden like the Incredible Hulk during his transformation.

When he comes back, his forehead is sweaty and his eyes slightly spooked. "Do you want something else to eat? Come on." He pulls out my chair like a true gentleman and accompanies me to the buffet table, leaning a hand on my waist and whispering in my ear with confidence.

"You look beautiful tonight. Have I told you that yet?"

No, in fact he hasn't given me a single compliment yet, and I just keep hoping that he's not going to notice my zebra shoe.

Suddenly, Luca is really sweet. He asks me what I would like to eat and serves me, following me the whole way. He even makes me try an olive, bringing his fingers close to his mouth and then immediately licking them, while staring into my eyes.

There, Tio, I think, *this Aries is not the boor that you made him out to be. He is sweet and polite, just like Paola said.* I begin to relax and let him take me back to our table, comforted by his warm hand resting on my lower back.

"Oh, I'm sorry, honey." Luca stops halfway and turns toward the table where the blonde and her companion are sitting. "Guys, this is Alisss."

The blonde smiles at me through clenched teeth.

"Anna."

Anna . . . As in Anna, his ex-girlfriend?

"How nice to meet you, *Aliss*," says Anna.

"It's actually All-ee-chay. The normal pronunciation is fine," I tell her.

She looks me up and down, judging me like a piece of meat. Damn, she is a woman and therefore genetically programmed to notice details . . . like my misfit shoe, for example.

She raises her eyes and instead of commenting, turns to face her thighs toward Luca, crossing her legs *Basic Instinct* style.

"Hi," says her friend, whom I discover answers to the improbable name of Wolf. "Come sit down for a second."

And since Luca doesn't have the slightest hesitation, I do so, rounding the table and pulling up a chair next to Wolf.

While we are served two more Negroni Sbagliatos, that once again I can't reject, it emerges that this was Luca and Anna's favorite hangout when they were dating. How sweet . . .

"I hope you don't mind, darling, that now I'm bringing Alisss here, too," he says reaching across the table to touch my fingers.

"Not at all, sweetie," Anna replies. "After all, I've brought Wolf here, haven't I?" She strokes Wolf's chin with the tip of her index finger.

"So, let's make a toast," says Wolf, who immediately calls one of the waiters and orders a round of shots.

In spite of her sensuality, Anna proves herself some sort of Viking when it comes to alcohol and successfully downs two glasses of grappa, one after another without putting a hair out of place. After the second, she looks at Luca and winks.

"You miss me as a drinking buddy, I bet. Do you remember Mexico?"

As they launch into a story about drunk Mexicans, I make my excuses and get up to go to the bathroom.

I'm starting to overheat and suddenly I feel very strange.

Locked in the toilet, I write to Tio.

It goin weeeel. Lucas is mice and took my band. But his X is her and we ere at her rable. What do do?

His answer arrives not even thirty seconds later.

**Are you drunk? Your message is almost incoherent. His EX?
Maybe he is testing you. He wants to be the conquest. But don't
give in. Be provocative, but keep your distance. Speak with
other men. Make him understand that he isn't the only catch
there. And stop drinking.**

I admit, my head is spinning a bit, but it's not like I'm not thinking clearly. When I come back, I see that the others are just outside the bar.

Suddenly I have a shot of tequila in my hand that I don't remember ordering, but I'm having fun. Anna is actually nice and even Wolf's not bad. Actually, he's pretty amazing. I don't know what we're talking about, but he really makes me laugh. He's a riot.

"Do you want another vodka? I'm going to get another round," he says, stroking my hip with his hand.

At this point, I'm no longer sure that he and Anna are actually together. In fact, what happened to her and Luca?

In the meantime, Wolf grabs me. Oh god, I can't breathe and my head is spinning.

"Want to go to my car and listen to some music for a while?"

"No, the only thing that's helping me right now is the fresh air on my face. I need to take some deep breaths."

"Let's go for a walk then. There's a little park right behind there," and without warning, his hand slides just above my butt.

"Alice?"

When I turn around, I am stunned, as if I've seen a ghost. "Raffaella?"

"I didn't know you come to the Cave," she says.

"I'm here with some friends, this is not my neighborhood . . . you?"

"Oh, I live around here."

And just then someone catches up to her and passes her a margarita.

I knew it. I knew I should have listened to Tio. I've drunk too much and now I'm having insane hallucinations.

"People are packed like sardines in there," says the man, who then turns around and recognizes me. "Alice . . . good evening."

So, it must be real: Davide Nardi is here, right in front of me. "Um . . . good evening."

Wolf finally removes his hand from my butt and stretches it toward them. "I'm Wolf."

Davide raises an eyebrow. He looks at Wolf and then at me.

Noting the ruby color of my dress, Davide cracks a smile and says, "So, that would make her Little Red Riding Hood?"

I burst out laughing. I had failed to notice that detail. This guy is such a hoot! I can't control myself.

"Alice, are you feeling OK?" Raffaella asks me.

"Wolf . . . Little Red Riding Hood . . . and the park . . . the hand on my . . . I mean . . ." Oh god, what am I babbling on about? "Actually, I was here with someone else."

"Oh, really?" Davide cranes his neck, as if he could pick out Luca without ever having seen him.

"Interesting shoes . . ." says Raffaella. Damn her. Now both Wolf and Davide are looking at them.

"It's . . . a new fad," I explain. "You know how fashion is, who knows what they'll come up with next?"

"Can I get you something else to drink, hon?" asks Wolf, turning into a human octopus and clutching at my side.

"Something without alcohol," Davide says decisively, pointing at his drink.

I start laughing uncontrollably again. Davide looks more than a little bizarre standing there in his black leather jacket, holding a glass filled with strawberries and a tiny umbrella.

Davide disappears into the bar, following Wolf, while Raffa and

I stay on the sidewalk, surrounded by the other patrons who are out getting air or smoking.

"Are you OK, Alice? You don't seem very . . . stable."

I give her a thumbs-up to let her know that I'm OK. "It takes a lot more, believe me. But you, what are you doing with Nardi?"

"Oh nothing, I'm just being nice. I took him to look at an apartment. He's not from Milan and he has to find a place to stay while he's here."

You mean a place for him to stay while he takes stock of the company and decides to get rid of us one by one.

"Come on, don't talk like that. Besides, he's actually working for the good of the network."

How did she hear my thoughts? I slap my hand over my mouth. Damn! I didn't just think it, I was talking out loud.

Just then, Davide returns to us with a bottle of still water.

"You absolutely must try this," says Wolf, who has joined us with a multicolored cocktail in hand. "It's a dream."

"Better not," Davide replies.

"Hey, there are my friends," Raffaella calls out. "Come on, Davide, I'll introduce you. This way, if you take the apartment, you'll already know someone . . ."

Wolf hands me the glass. At this point, it would be rude not to taste it, as he got it specifically for me. It's cold, and not half bad, and what's even better is how the world changes when you get some alcohol in your system. The people in front of me are multicolored shapes, and they're dancing.

There are even fireflies, countless yellow fireflies dancing in front of my eyes. Suddenly, I feel my legs cave in, and then, darkness.

7

Aries of Darkness

No, I haven't fainted. I am completely conscious, and I can hear everything going on around me perfectly. I may even be too conscious, because it seems to me that sounds are actually amplified. Unfortunately, however, I can't see a thing.

"I think I need to sit down for a second."

"Come on, my car is right here." Wolf pulls me tightly to him to hold me up as we make our way somewhere. He leans me against a car, and I can hear the sound of the door opening.

"Sit down, here."

Fuck, what if my vision doesn't come back? Shit . . . I might as well face it: I will never see a man again in my life!

I hear him giggle. "Come on, it will come back soon enough. Besides, why are you so worried about men? I'm here."

Oh Jesus, I was thinking out loud again.

Are those his lips I can feel on my mouth? "No, wait . . ."

"Oh, come on, just a kiss."

"I don't exactly feel at my most alluring right now . . ."

But he kisses me again and I feel his hand on my knee.

I gather my strength and get up. But, of course, I slam my head right into the car door and only manage a couple of steps before I collapse to my knees and have a close encounter of the third kind with the asphalt.

A pair of hands grabs me just under the armpits. "What happened?"

That is Davide Nardi's voice, and he's angry.

"I . . . I can't see."

"What the hell did you do? Did you give her another drink, you jerk?"

"I'm sorry, I didn't realize she was this far gone."

Someone lifts me from the ground, and my face is suddenly sticking to smooth and fragrant fabric. I realize it's leather; it's Davide Nardi's leather jacket.

"OK, you can go now," he barks.

"Wait!" I turn back toward Wolf and yell, "What sign are you?"

I don't hear his answer and soon after, Davide takes me away.

Damn, Debra Winger was certainly not blind when Richard Gere picked her up and carried her out of the factory in his arms in *An Officer and a Gentleman*. I feel like I'm at the movies when the idiot sitting in front of you gets up and makes you miss the most romantic scene. But this time I'm the idiot and I only have myself to blame for drinking enough to cause me to miss out on this fabulous, cinematic rescue. Tio did tell me to stop drinking!

"Who is Tio?"

"What?"

I feel Davide sit me down on a bench. He stays by my side as my head keeps collapsing onto his shoulder.

"You mentioned someone called 'Tio.' What a crazy name."

"Oh, why do I keep thinking out loud?"

"What?"

"No, yes . . . Tio is a friend of mine. He had warned me not to drink too much tonight."

I feel something wet and cool against my forehead and pull my head away.

"It's only a wet handkerchief," he explains. "Your blood pressure must have dropped."

"You're not laughing, are you?"

"Who, me? No, I swear . . ." But I hear it in his voice.

"I am at death's door; Hannibal Lector could make a delicious pâté with my liver, and you're laughing! But, of course, what else could I expect from someone like you?"

I feel him stiffen. "What do you mean someone like me?"

No, Alice, stop. What was in that cocktail, kryptonite? "I mean that your role requires you to see everything with a sense of detachment."

"I get it. How do you feel? How's your vision?"

I still can't see anything. Meanwhile, my stomach is incubating some kind of *Alien*. "I think . . ." I mumble, lifting my head. "I think I have to throw up."

I stagger as I get up, and he grabs me by the arm, brushing my hair from my face right before everything comes up.

"I'm sorry." I am the queen of making bad impressions.

As soon as I finish throwing up, the fog clouding my eyes rolls away. I still can't stand very well but at least I can see.

The moment I turn around, I find Davide in front of me, less than a foot away. Oh god, can I please go back to the dark? He's holding my hair behind my neck so I won't throw up on it. He looks tense.

I blink, and he realizes that I can see him now.

"Hello." He flashes a half-smile that twists his mouth to the side a little. Oh, why does he have to be so sexy when I still have the taste of stomach acid in my mouth?

I must be cursed. How do I always end up in these situations? And with Davide of all people? What is it about him? Where can I file a formal protest against fate?

Davide smiles and bites his lip. "You are crazy," he remarks. Then he lifts me up as if I were a can of spray paint, and sets me down, straight. He cleans my lip with a tissue and asks, "Better?"

As I nod, I burst into tears. I am a disaster, at work, with Carlo, and with all other men. I am alone, with zero prospects. Oh, god, all he needs now is a crybaby!

"Hey, why did you ask that guy for his zodiac sign?" Davide asks as he helps me to sit down again.

Should I tell him about Tio's theories? Because I really do believe that there's something in zodiac signs.

I explain that someone like Tio could really help clear things up for people. In a period of crisis like this, there's a real need for it. They should talk about it on television. And even offer a useful service to citizens, explaining relationships between people by using the alignment of the planets. I tell him that I have been trying it out for myself, and it works. I feel like the Marie Curie of zodiac signs, conducting field experiments with no protection. Real science is being done. Almost.

I hear him laugh. "An astrological guide, huh?" He crouches in front of me and lifts up one of my feet. That's when I realize that I am barefoot. My mismatched shoes are in his jacket pocket. He slips them on my feet, one by one, and for a moment I almost feel, to quote *Pretty Woman*, like I am "Cinder-fuckin-rella."

"Do you think you can walk?"

8

Libra Wednesday

I'm trying to keep up my relationship with Jane Fonda and after a Sunday spent napping to recover from my drunken escapade, today I get up early to exercise. I even arrive at work ahead of schedule. I have successfully freed myself from all unnecessary stress and anxiety.

The only thing bothering me is that my phone must be having connection problems, because I still haven't heard from Luca.

I still can't figure out what happened to him, although during my hangover yesterday, I was able to brood over it at length and, of course, get the opinion of my two best friends.

From Paola's point of view: I have properly exercised my rights as a woman, although perhaps I should have tried to understand Luca's point of view, think about what happened to him, and maybe find out if he needed help. She is sure that, if I had had the chance, I would have been empathetic to his problems, and this would have brought us even closer together. So, in her opinion, there has to be a reason for his disappearance. I should instead concentrate on analyzing how I felt when I was with him until he contacts me, because he will contact me. Paola chides my promiscuous behavior, because kissing one man and leaving with another—neither of whom were my date—is not my style and definitely doesn't give the impression of being a stable person interested in a long-term relationship. I don't fully agree with this point, given that Wolf planted one on me and I didn't kiss him back. And I'm not sure that Davide actually brought me home, but if he did, thank God, nothing happened . . . Or at least, I don't think it did.

From Tio's point of view: Aries hurt the tender feelings of the romantic Libra that I am, behaving in keeping with his rough nature and trying subtly to invert the roles and let himself be chased. He left me alone and has no excuses, neither as a man nor as a zodiac sign. It would be better if he were never to call again. My acting aloof gets a thumbs-up. To sum up, I made it clear to him that he's not the only man on this Earth, by kissing another guy and going home with yet another (again, this is a point I'm contesting). My behavior, according to Tio, was perfectly in line with the mood of a Libra: an air sign that is somewhat inconsistent. Even if Luca were to find out about the kiss and about my return home, it would be a point in my favor because he would see me as hard to get, and because I would avoid scaring him by making him think that I want commitment right off the bat.

I warm my face in the ray of sunshine filtering through the window, and for a second I stand mesmerized, watching Davide park his motorcycle, take off his helmet, and run a hand through his disheveled hair. I follow him with my gaze until I feel the tip of my nose against the glass. At that exact moment, I realize that there's no way to avoid him . . . unless I manage to camouflage myself among the ornamental potted plants.

I sneak down the corridor, flattening myself like a ninja against the wall, and I try to duck into the first office I find, but the door is locked.

"Alice!"

Caught just as I put my hand on another doorknob.

"Um, good morning." God, what should I call him now? Mr. Nardi? Davide? Darth Vader?

"Everything OK? I mean, are you all right?"

I wrap my arms around my chest. "Yes, fine, thanks."

"I'm really sorry I didn't get in touch yesterday."

Now I'm the one looking bewildered. Suddenly I feel uneasy, because I can tell there's something in his eyes, something I don't remember.

"No problem," I mumble, staring at my shoes.

He sighs. "But I wanted to talk to you. I mean, it would have been the right thing to do after the other night . . . before we saw each other at work."

Immediately, I feel the blood drain from my cheeks. What does he mean, "after the other night"?

All right, yes, I made a complete ass of myself with him, blackout drunk and vomiting right in the middle of Milan, but the way he puts it and with that fire in his eyes, it seems like quite a different story . . .

The truth is that I don't remember anything after being *Barefoot in the Park* with him.

Oh god, maybe we spent a passionate night together and now he feels guilty because he thinks he took advantage of me.

Davide cracks a smile. "Anyway, I'm sorry I didn't call to make sure you were OK, but I didn't have your number."

I examine him again from head to toe and let out a sigh of regret for remembering absolutely nothing. "Well, that . . . we can work on," I say, flashing a smile, and adding, why not, a wink.

He frowns. "Sure, but there's no need. Meet me in my office in an hour, will you?"

I would not have expected this turn of events. Of course, Paola would not approve, and I should tread carefully, given his position at the company. I am playing with fire. Sleeping with the enemy! I must take the opportunity to explain that it was all a mistake, that I was not myself because of the alcohol and so on. Oh god, thank goodness I showered this morning.

As I head back to my office, I stop and turn again. He's already halfway through the door.

"Davide?"

"Yes?"

"What sign are you?"

He smiles and winks at me.

"Excellent! That's my girl."

. . .

For the next hour, all I can do is check the clock, approximately every three minutes, and try to ransack my brain for some detail about my acrobatics between the sheets with Davide. Nothing.

Raffaella enters the office, more beautiful than ever. "Hi, sweetie. Have you recovered?" she says, and the heads of my two coworkers pop up from their desks and stare at me.

"What happened?" they ask.

"Oh, nothing, I just wasn't feeling too well."

"Alice is a fish," she explains, elbowing me. "You should see how much she drinks."

Welcome to a meeting of Alcoholics "not so" Anonymous. "Oh, no, just a couple of glasses . . ." I murmur, hoping to shoot it down.

Raffa doesn't seem to listen to me. She sighs, looks around, and for a second, has an expression of melancholy.

"Is something going on?" I ask her.

"Nothing." But she smiles as if she has a secret. "Actually, it's something great . . . but I can't talk about it."

When I look at the clock, I realize that there are just ten min-utes until my appointment with Nardi. Davide . . .

I run to the bathroom with my heart dancing the Macarena. I need to freshen up and calm down.

As I'm about to go out, Tio's horoscope arrives.

The day begins with the Moon in your sign, but it's no guarantee of tranquility. Tension is high, both from a business and an emotional point of view. News is on the horizon but the wind that brings it doesn't exactly correspond to your expectations. It promises to be an interesting month in your job, but today it is specifically your feelings that put you under pressure.

Oh, Tio . . . you can't imagine what is about to happen.

I head upstairs. My heart is thumping in my ears.

I reach Davide's door and put my hand on the handle, trying to build up the courage. "May I come in?"

Davide is standing in front of the window. And when he turns around the sun casts golden highlights through his hair.

Then Raffaella and Mr. President also turn to look at me.

"Oh, I'm sorry, I didn't mean to disturb you."

Davide takes a step forward. "Please, Miss Bassi, take a seat."

I swallow and fix my gaze on Raffaella. Even she doesn't seem too sure what's going on.

Then, it hits me: They're going to fire me!

The reality is that I've made a fool of myself, I've shown my worst sides: irresponsible and reprobate.

I take my place and await judgment.

"Davide has spoken a lot about you, Miss Bassi," begins Mr. President.

Oh really? Let me guess, instead of calling me Sunday, Davide called Mr. President and told him about my behavior. How sweet . . . "Yes, but I can explain. It's not something that happens to me every day."

"I imagine, and a more detailed explanation was exactly what we were hoping for. As you know, we can't invest money in people without a guarantee."

Clearly, he is talking about the salary that he is going to deprive me of.

"Mr. President," Raffaella interjects, "it seems a bit reckless to me. Simply based on some barroom chat . . ."

Damn, I never thought our friendship ran this deep.

"Raffaella, I'm not saying that your plan isn't good, but it's very expensive and the network can't afford it right now," says Davide.

Wait, now I am totally lost. Please, someone explain what we are talking about.

"In fact," continues Mr. President, leaning on my shoulder. "Alice's idea is much more on target. It's young and fresh, and no other network has ever done it. It's experimental and completely in line with the image that we want to create to attract a broader audience."

I make eye contact with Davide, and it seems as if his lips are just barely forming the hint of a smile. "If you are prepared to work hard for the next couple weeks, we can be ready to shoot the pilot episode of *An Astrological Guide for Broken Hearts* at the end of the month."

9

Working Libra

On average, I have gotten four hours of sleep each night this week. The rest of the time, I spent here—where I still am—in the Delta studio.

I feel like I'm in an episode of the *Twilight Zone*, and suddenly knowing someone's zodiac sign is more important than knowing someone's blood type after they've had a car accident. "We need five units of Capricorn, nurse, or we'll lose him!"

The atmosphere is electric, overflowing with adrenaline . . . and with sweat. The truth is, we have reason to be on overdrive, because in the blink of an eye, we have had to create a complete television program, the sets, and everything that goes into it. It's become so bad that any time we may have for our own lives, which for some includes the small matter of personal hygiene, has reached an all-time low.

Today, I am sporting a beautiful braid, which makes me feel like Lara Croft and hides the fact that I won't be winning a L'Oréal competition anytime soon.

Hair notwithstanding, I have made an effort, wanting to make a good impression for the first show that bears my name as a creator. I'm wearing a nice gray suit and brand-new Christian Louboutin shoes, which cost me almost all of my newly earned bonus. Sadly, while my wallet shrank, my feet continue to swell.

From the production room, Luciano yells, "Alice, look, the guests are here!"

The network can be blamed for this, as it decided to add the genius element of "reality" to the program. In addition to the big-name guests—experts in the astrological and other fields—there will be twelve competitors, one of each sign, and we will follow their progress week by week. When it comes to fresh and modern ideas, we really know how to stand out.

"Alice! Damn it, we're missing the Steadicam! I know you're a 'writer' now, but we do need someone to monitor everything."

"Ferruccio, please, don't you start, too!"

"I would gladly never have started. At this hour, I would normally be at home watching a movie. But instead, we are all here to do *your* show."

I invoke the Zen calm that the yoga class from last year was supposed to teach me, and I wonder if I missed the fundamental classes. "Wax on, wax off," I repeat to calm myself down. In a half hour, the theme song will be starting. "Ask Enrico," I respond curtly. After all, isn't he the production manager?

Ferruccio laughs in my face. "Good one. If only I could find him!"

I walk away, promising to look for Enrico.

"And remember to print the schedules!" yells Luciano.

With the steel of a bionic woman, I speed away, ignoring the pain from the blisters that are forming on my foot.

I bound up the stairs and have almost reached Enrico's office when I catch him at my three o'clock, red-handed, standing in front of the vending machine, stuffing his pockets with snacks.

When I call out to him, he jumps, dropping his contraband: four juices, three chocolate snacks, two cracker breads, and a packet of cookies with diet marmalade. Then he grinds his teeth: "YOU! What are you doing here? You should be in the studios ... Don't you get that after ten years here?"

No, Mr. Miyagi would not be happy with me at all as I draw myself up to my maximum height and yell that perhaps *he* is the one who needs to check his job description. I've had enough of being told that everything is my fault. "Wax on, wax off," my ass.

Enrico throws his haul onto the windowsill and points at me with his chubby finger, covered with a makeshift bandage fashioned from Kleenex and masking tape.

"You're the one who dragged us all into this mess with your program, so that we have to work day and night. I don't even know what my house looks like anymore. All you care about is making a good impression on the management, while you leave me to organize everything. As if I hadn't already spent enough nights here, sweating blood for this company!"

Enrico is almost as blue as Papa Smurf and I am terrified that I will have to take a shot at CPR or, God forbid, mouth-to-mouth.

"Enrico, calm down. Everything will work itself out, but I need you to give me a hand. I'm sorry, we're all tired. I understand—"

"No, you don't understand. You really don't understand the damage you have done." He walks away toward his office. "I'll be right down. You go ahead," he says, taking out the key from his pocket and putting it in the lock.

I run behind him. "Wait! I have to print the schedules. I'll do it in your office."

"No!" he cuts me off. "I'm out of ink!"

Five minutes later, I'm back in the production room, throwing schedules at people like Frisbees. I (and my feet) pray to god that

Tio is in makeup, but the room is just teeming with shouting zodiac signs.

The makeup artist gives me a desperate look, then narrows her eyes and makes a face. "Raffaella tells me this program is your doing…"

Yes, yes. Okay. It's me. You've found me out. I'm as vindictive as Keyser Söze, and I plotted all of this at your expense purely because I hate you.

Before scurrying off again, I spy Enrico approaching the production room and run over to tell him about the missing lens. When he turns around, I realize that he has a half-closed, swollen, bloodshot eye. He yells, "Why hadn't you told me sooner?" then runs into Ferruccio's office.

At this point, I am operating on autopilot. My only objective is to find Tio, but I know exactly where he might be: *Mal d'Amore*.

As much as I've begged him to give up his agreement with the soap, Tio has whined that he is and always will be an actor, and he wants to act.

When I enter the Alpha studio, dim lights illuminate the scene of a room where Tio, in bed, is tossing and turning, as if he's having a nightmare.

Like the true professional that I am, I calmly wait for them to finish, then I approach the director and tell him: "Excuse me, I am the creator of *Astrological Guide*." With certain people, it is always better to state one's title, plus I really like saying it.

"We're done," he says curtly.

Happy to have asserted my authority, I go help Tio pick up the clothes that his character has scattered on the ground.

"*No es bueno para mí, Salva.*"

I am holding a sock, retrieved from under the cot, when a warm and mellow voice slides over me like velvet on bare skin.

The Latin timbre makes me look up sharply and slam my head against the corner of the wood, cursing Mr. IKEA and his family for seven generations. When I turn around, still in the elegant position of all fours, I find myself in front of a pair of legs wrapped in suede pants.

An olive-skinned hand moves toward me, and instinctively I grab it, noticing the forearm that bulges, showing off the sexiest vein on the planet.

Then my horizon extends beyond the waist of the unknown. *Somebody up there likes me*, I think, eyeing a flat and muscular stomach worthy of a stadium wave. The soft, dark hair rising toward his navel makes me drop my jaw like I am in a cartoon, and his abs . . . *The abs!* So, it is not just an insidious invention for Dolce & Gabbana publicity. The six-pack exists! God exists!

Feeling miraculously restored, my rundown concludes on a face with a strong jaw, dark eyes, bushy eyebrows, and hair better than Daniel Day-Lewis's in *The Last of the Mohicans.*

I release a postcoital sigh that earns me a couple of coughs from Tio who says, "We need to go, otherwise you'll hear it from Enrico."

I blink. "Enrico . . . who?"

"Yes, Alejandro, let them go," says the director.

"You're still here," exclaims another voice behind me. "Alice, there you are! I've been looking for you for a half hour!"

When I turn around, I see Raffaella who struts toward us. "Fifteen minutes before we go live! I've prepared the guests, told the zodiac signs what order to enter in, and checked the graphic and movie clips with the tape room. If only you could be of any help . . ."

And the unthinkable happens. The beautiful Alejandro breaks away from me to look at her with a smile that would melt a glacier.

"*Hola* . . ."

Raffaella joins us and answers him in perfectly formulated Spanish.

He laughs and runs a hand through his hair, then shoots me a dirty look. What in the world did she say to him?

Tio pulls me by the sleeve.

"Be right there," I say, staying on the sidelines to stare at Alejandro and Raffaella like the Little Match Girl.

At that moment, Raffaella must realize that there is an annoying third wheel between her and the Antonio Banderas of the network, and she turns, wrinkling her nose at me.

"Excuse me, Alice," she whispers. "I know it's not nice, but as a friend, I have to tell you . . . You don't smell too good. You should go wash up."

I should . . . I immediately take a step back, as if fifty centimeters were sufficient to ensure my quarantine.

At the door, I cast one more look at Alejandro's back and sigh. His muscles are resplendent under the spotlight. It seems unfair that an overheated man is able to be, and in fact frequently is, sexy and virile while a woman should be genetically devoid of sweat glands.

But I may have a solution to my problem. In my desk drawer, there is a bottle of unopened perfume my colleagues gave me for my last birthday. Perhaps there is a light at the end of the tunnel!

10

The Curse of the Jade Scorpio

After I snap back to reality, I schlep back upstairs and Enrico yells: "Alice, what are you still doing here!"

"I . . . I forgot something."

He closes the door and flattens himself against it just as I am crawling along the wall on the other side. His eye is still red and swollen, and there is an ink stain on his cheek. We hear a crash coming from inside his office and Enrico jumps. "Oh damn, I must have left the window open. You go ahead, but be quick!!"

I sprint away, hoping not to leave behind a chemical trail.

I open my desk drawer and squeal as if I've found the Holy Grail. I quickly rip off the plastic and subject myself to a decontamination shower. And now I am coughing.

It's like Pine Sol combined with Trident gum—topped off with my sweat, the smell could easily be patented as a weapon of mass destruction.

Out of desperation, I sprint back to the production room, hoping that the effect will cause the smell to wear off, but instead I just feel more uncomfortable, especially when Tio approaches only to take a step back, motioning that we will speak later.

"One minute until the theme song," croaks the voice over the intercom.

Tio starts off the show like a pro, orating about horoscopes with such unrelenting confidence that not even Margherita Hack would dare contradict him. The only slip-up during the first segment was made by Marlin, who after briefly glancing at her printed material, introduced the "Skeptic Guest," a member of CICAP, the Italian Committee for the Investigation of Claims on Pseudo-Science by calling him "Doctor" and asking if using his "checkups" he has discovered any signs of the zodiac that are particularly prone to diseases.

In a clumsy attempt to save her, Tio changes the segment order, and instead of introducing Aries, he follows his train of thought and begins with Scorpio, who he claims would be most in need of a good physical at the moment.

"This year, Saturn is dominating the heavens, and it came into Scorpio a few months ago. This planet reveals the weakness of the sign and its bad behaviors. In particular, it could exacerbate an already distinctive trait of the native Scorpio: pessimism. It could also spur them on to new choices, new paths, and new challenges. For those in relationships already having problems, there could even be a breakup. This zodiac sign must learn to communicate more and ask for help when it needs it."

I breathe a sigh of relief and stretch my arms above my head, but I immediately pull them down, for fear that my new recipe for nerve gas will cause instantaneous genocide in the production room. As I stealthily check that no one has fainted, at the other end of the hall I spy the *Mal d'Amore* macho man, Alejandro.

His penetrating gaze meets mine, and he smiles, taking a few steps forward. I curse the fact that when I finally have half a chance with a smoking hot guy I reek of "*Cheval* No. 5," so I am almost relieved when Raffaella stops him in his tracks. I take the opportunity to slip away to the nearest bathroom to decontaminate my armpits.

When I leave the bathroom, I am quite pleased with myself and ready to dazzle the gorgeous Alejandro with the amazing properties of liquid soap.

As I pass the lighting room, I hear a noise, imagining that it might be him setting up some equipment. Instead of Alejandro, I find my colleague Sergio standing up suddenly after zipping up a large bag.

"Oh, hey, Alice. Do you need something?"

I get back to the production room and find we are on a commercial break, and Tio is standing outside the studio getting some air. When he sees me, he pulls me aside and smiles at me. "Well?"

"Bravo. You were fabulous."

"I was referring to how your friend, the Scorpio, is doing. Didn't you get it?"

"You completely changed the lineup to tell me about . . . Alejandro?"

"No." He raises an eyebrow. "Not Alejandro. Enrico."

"What?"

He takes me by the arm and drags me away. "Look, I know I'm an expert on zodiac signs, but you have a knack for missing what's right under your nose, which is so typical of a Libra. He' s up to something. And I can tell you that he's not doing so hot. With you, I just needed one look to know what sign you were; didn't you think I would figure out that he's a Scorpio after knowing him for a month? By nature he is rather grumpy because Mars is his dominant planet. He tends to hide his feelings because he doesn't like to look weak and therefore prefers to be the first to attack. If you haven't noticed, your boss has been out of his mind lately, all revved up and flying off the handle over the slightest setback. Ergo, he is a Scorpio, and Saturn is giving him a rough time. Now we just have to find out exactly what kind of 'rough time' we are dealing with."

Hearing the countdown for the return to the studio, I send Tio back to his place. I return to the production room and can't help but look for Enrico, but he hasn't come back yet. He was only supposed to be printing something in his office, but wasn't he out of ink? That was supposedly why he wouldn't let me in the room earlier. When I get up to go look for him, I feel a bit like Jessica Fletcher, albeit a few years younger and with ten times higher heels.

"Alice . . ."

Hearing that voice automatically makes me go weak at the knees. Davide's office door is half open, and he is looking at me from his desk. It's so late I never would have imagined anyone would still be up here.

"Hey, um . . ."

"How's it going?"

"Good, yeah . . . good. Tio is very well prepped. And Marlin is . . . well, Marlin is beautiful."

He snorts. "But how are you? You look tired."

Why do I feel hurt by this?

"I was running around a lot today. You know how it is, launching a new show."

He grumbles and rubs his face with one hand. If I seem tired, he seems to have the weight of the world on his shoulders. "No, to tell you the truth, I don't know how things go in television. This is the first time I've worked in this environment."

"What do you mean? You've never worked for a television network?"

"I'm a reviewer. My job is to evaluate a company's workforce and understand its functions and its flaws . . . with detachment." He gets up, stretching his back. "At times, it seems like nothing ever changes except the place: Rome, Paris, Barcelona . . ." He shrugs his shoulders.

"Kind of like being in a blender," I comment, thinking of all the people that he must have met, all the Alice Bassis who have come before me and all those who will be part of his future. That thought worries me and makes me tighten my grip on the doorknob. I look him in his eyes and feel like I am going to disappear.

He laughs. "A blender really captures the idea. I am practically homeless."

"What about the apartment you looked at with Raffaella?"

"It didn't work out. They don't allow dogs."

"You have a dog?"

"Somebody's got to keep me company."

In that moment, his telephone rings and he looks at the display and closes his eyes just before he answers. "Hello?" He raises his index finger at me, as if asking me to wait, and leaves the office saying: "At work. Yes, still."

I sigh. What am I doing in here? What am I doing with him?

From the hallway, I can still hear his voice: "I told you, it's a long assignment. I don't know. No. Not this weekend."

I smile because his desk is a mess of papers, coffee cups, pens, pencils, and various knickknacks, and the chaos of objects makes him seem a little more human and a little less Terminator.

Then my attention is caught by something familiar: my name. Under a pen, and next to Sergio's file, is mine, complete with a horrendous photo featuring helmet hair that makes me look like a cross between Doris Day and a Playmobil figure. God, how embarrassing that Davide saw it.

I wonder if I am trying to prove that he isn't actually evil. Although he has chosen a job that puts him in contention for "most hated man of the year," I am able to catch a glimpse of *him*, beyond all of this: a single man who can never put down roots and keeps running away from himself.

I shoot a glance into the hall, but he is far away so that I can't even make out a word. I have to get back to work, find Enrico, and return to the production room. Loitering there between his office and the hallway makes no sense. It just doesn't.

. . .

"Enrico?" I have my fist raised to knock, but I jump backward when I hear a Tarzan-like scream. Without thinking twice, I enter and stop dead in my tracks as I see what looks like a gruesome crime scene from a horror film, one featuring a graphomaniac serial killer intent on expressing his existential malaise on the walls using the blood of his victims. "My god, Enrico, what . . ."

Then my eyes catch the movement of something else that quickly detaches from his leg and sneaks away.

"What was that?" I ask.

"I told you to stay down in the production room," he snaps.

I look anxiously at the walls, terrorized by the idea of finding "all work and no play makes Jack a dull boy" repeated a million times.

I frown and look again at Enrico as he raises his pant leg and massages his leg. His calf is purple and he has a bite mark on his shin. He snorts and turns his back to me saying, "Riccardino, please come out. Be a good boy, come to Daddy."

"Riccardino? Did you bring *your kid* to work? That's against the rules!"

Enrico turns to glare at me. "How dare you speak to me like that! If it weren't for you and your damned show, I wouldn't be in this mess," he yells, almost foaming at the mouth. "You had to come up with all this crap. An *Astrological Guide* to my ass!"

"Enrico!" I shout, looking around for the child, who should not be hearing this language.

Enrico bites his lip and turns around. "Riccardino, don't repeat that, OK? Do your dad a favor."

"I want Mom."

The little voice comes from behind the filing cabinet. "Hey, little one. There you are." Riccardino raises a head of golden curls and looks at me with eyes even bluer than his father's.

"Oh, how cute!"

Someone else knocks at the door and instinctively I push the child back behind the cabinet while Enrico runs to open it. "Davide . . . did you need me?" I hear him say.

"Yes. Enrico, I'm sorry, I need you to go down to the studio with me. There's something I need to talk to you about. Something serious."

The filing cabinet is pushed against me with force, hitting me in the knee. "Ouch!"

Enrico glares at me while I hear Davide ask him: "Is there someone else here?"

"Um . . . No, just Alice."

"Ah, well, she can come, too."

"No!" Enrico scowls at me. "Alice can't come now. She has to stay here and deal with something."

I open my mouth to protest, but he doesn't give me the time.

"Because Alice *owes me.*"

He is about to close the door on me when I ask him, "Enrico, what sign are you?"

He turns around and stares at me with contempt. "Fuck off. I'm a Scorpio."

So Tio was right, yet again. Like a true Scorpio, Enrico is battling the Mephistophelian Saturn and bringing me down with him.

What do I do now? "Look, Riccardino, what a nice little car. Wanna play with the car?"

He snatches it from me and starts to beat it on the floor. "I wanna break the car!"

"No, come on, don't do that." I try to remove it from his hand. "Give me that car . . . come on, give it to me!"

But instead of giving me the car, he takes the opportunity to smash it against my head with all his might.

"Shit!" I bring my hand to my mouth, and I have tears in my eyes from the pain. But he's stopped.

"Is shit like poopoo?" he asks me.

"Um, no. I mean . . . I didn't say shit, technically . . . I mean I didn't actually say that word."

"Shit!"

"No!"

"Shit poopoo, shit poopoo, shit poopoo!"

"That's enough!" Suddenly I get a stroke of genius. "How about watching some TV?"

In my infinite discussions with Paola, we have determined that television is very morally harmful, and we have always despised those parents who are incapable of doing anything but sedating the minds of their children by placing them in front of stupid programs. Should I feel guilty as I furiously search for the remote? Like hell. It's not like he's my own son, right?

Unfortunately, I turn on the TV and realize that it is only transmitting images of the Delta studio, and all we can see are the outtakes from *Astrological Guide* because they have cut to commercial.

"That man is completely naked!" exclaims Riccardino pointing his finger.

I'm sitting at the desk and when I look up at the monitor, I see that Alejandro is walking in front of the cameras and he is still shirtless. A moment later, Raffaella appears, rests her hands on his abs, and pushes him away.

"Oh fu—"

Riccardino looks right at me and says confidently, "Shit."

I sigh, the screen goes black, and after the musical interlude the show starts up again.

"To charm a Scorpio," Tio says, "you must be mysterious. Even in the best relationships, always expect a storm just around the corner. To keep him captivated, you must always be elusive. But Scorpio is also one of the most dangerous signs of the zodiac, and if he should think that you had wronged him, he would hunt you down and make you pay."

Oh, to hell with Enrico, Tio who sent me to look for him, and everything else.

"I'm so thirsty!!" says Riccardino.

On Enrico's desk, there are several empty boxes of fruit juice, but there is still one unopened. "Do you want this?" I ask him, stuffing a straw in his Minute Maid.

He then climbs onto me and starts to drink heartily. Of course, when he's calm, he's really cute.

He puts his curly head on me and sighs, relaxing. I do the same, leaning back in the chair and enjoying the warmth emanating from his little body, and it starts to spread through my body, too.

No, wait. Not my entire body.

I lift up Riccardino and raise my eyes to the ceiling railing against Saturn's curse . . . and against the child's pee on the skirt of my business suit.

"Why the hell don't they put a diaper on you, little hydrant of Satan?"

In response, Riccardino bursts into tears, and the only solution is that we go wash up and change clothing. Lucky for him, I find a bag with his other clothes.

Not far from the studios, there is a fully equipped bathroom for management, with a shower and a hair dryer. I head in that direction, dragging Riccardino with me.

"Let's pretend we are boats!" he says, opening the sink faucet and spraying water on me.

"Let's pretend that you're a fish and I'll put your head under water and see if you can breathe," I answer as I start removing my clothing. At this point, I know that not even my blouse will escape unscathed if I keep it on while I wash it, and, since there is a shower, I might as well take the opportunity to remove all the day's delightful fragrances.

After rinsing my clothes, I hand over the hair dryer to Riccardino with a task.

"Now you're a cowboy and you have to point this gun at the clothes, which are dangerous bandits. OK?" This way he can at least help dry them while I take a quick shower.

While I soap myself up, I keep looking over my shoulder. Behind the opaque curtain, I see his shadow fidgeting, and I pray that he doesn't even think about pulling a *Psycho* and throwing the hair dryer at me as a joke.

When I finish, I wrap myself in a towel. But as soon as I turn off the water, I realize that the room is quiet. Too quiet.

When I pull open the curtain I almost have a heart attack. He's not there. The door is wide open, and Riccardino is gone. What's worse is that my clothes have also disappeared. All of them. The only thing left is a single shoe, Cinderella style, but in my case, I don't even have half a pumpkin to work with.

"Riccardino!"

Nothing. Even when I lean out in the hallway, the infamous child is nowhere to be found. Instead, I catch sight of something on the floor. I know it is practically a suicide mission, but the alternative is staying trapped, naked, in the management bathroom, so I run to retrieve my bra, strewn on the ground by Tom Thumb.

I'm already bending down when I hear voices. I pull the bra out of their path just in time to slip into a closet as Davide and Enrico pass directly in front of it.

"Good conduct is the most important thing, Davide. Stealing material is unacceptable, and if he's made a mistake, he must take responsibility for his actions."

If only Davide were not there, perhaps I could have caught Enrico's attention and gotten some help. But what would I say? "Hey, Dad, I lost your son"?

God, if he only knew that Riccardino was doing a solo marathon through the corridors of the studios, wandering around like Lady Godiva would be the least of my problems.

As Davide and Enrico move farther down the hallway, I suddenly hear Riccardino laugh. Damn him, he's enjoying himself, wreaking havoc like a Teletubby version of Attila the Hun!

The door of the production room that we use for the newscast is open. I step out of the closet and move closer to the door.

"Riccardino? Are you in here? Come on, don't push your luck. Come out now."

I move through the dark but stop when I catch a glimpse of a shadow running back and forth.

"Riccardino!" I exclaim.

I see him in the shadows, but he speeds past, throwing me to the ground and grasping at the door.

When I get up, fumbling in the dark, I discover that in his flight, the Killer Baby has lost another of his trophies. Praise the Lord; it is my skirt. Yes, it's still wet, but at least I no longer risk showing the world my backside (or my front side, which would be even worse!).

A second later, I feel like I'm going to die when I see Davide and

Enrico cross the hallway. Davide stops next to the column behind which I am hiding, and I pray that he is not blessed with X-ray vision.

"Davide . . . ?" calls Enrico, who had moved a few steps ahead.

"Oh, it's nothing," says Davide. "I just thought I heard a kid's voice."

"A kid?" Enrico laughs hysterically. "Here? A kid? That's just crazy!"

"Yes . . ." Davide turns toward the hallway that winds around the studios. "There at the far end."

I wait for Enrico to lead him away and then I follow Davide's directions. He was right. Now that I'm closer, I hear him, too. "Riccardino?"

I see him, but what I find is terrifying. He is lying still, on his back, like the child from _The Ring_. When he turns around he says, "I wanna give you a boo-boo!" And then clings to my calf like a Rottweiler.

After what seems like an eternity, I find myself panting and writhing on the ground like a lame horse, but with my blouse safely back in my hands. The score is Riccardino 0, Alice 1.

As I drag myself away hobbling, with a bare left foot, I fasten the buttons of my blouse and think of all the ways that I can make him pay.

When I turn the corner, however, I bump smack into a concrete wall that I am certain wasn't here before. A wall that grabs me and holds me close, putting its hands on my butt. A wall with rippling muscles and the powerful, masculine, virile scent of leather.

Alejandro.

The grip on my buttocks gives no sign of loosening up.

He looks into my eyes and says, "_Lo siento mucho._"

"I . . . feel it _mucho_, too," I reply, as long as it seems there is a balloon between us right now.

"Alice!"

Enrico's thundering voice has the effect of detaching Alejandro's hands from my butt cheeks and causing me to stagger backward.

"What are you . . . ? Where is . . . ?" Enrico turns white as a ghost, then bites his lip because he definitely can't ask me about his sweet little baby in front of Davide.

That's right. Davide. Nardi glares first at Alejandro and then at me without saying a word.

"Umm . . . everything is . . . under control," I say, tugging at my blouse as I try to pull myself together, and I realize I've fastened the buttons incorrectly. "I was just talking about the program, with . . . Alejandro here, and I was asking him . . . um . . . what sign he was."

"Sagittarius."

"OK . . . great . . . interesting."

"Discovering someone's zodiac sign, and then their horoscope, is an effective way to start to understand a person," Tio is saying in the studio. "On this show, we're here to give you some tips. Do you want to tame a Scorpio? This is a sign that loves extremes, so you could try spicy food or a very sweet cream pie . . ."

I think that for Enrico, at this moment, a necklace of garlic would be more useful.

And just then, Luciano pans out to show the entire studio, and I have a revelation.

Leaning against the large screen behind the guests' seats, lies my lonely missing shoe.

"Cut to commercials!" I yell.

"I can't, there are still at least ten minutes left," says Luciano. "What's the matter?"

If my Christian Louboutin is in there, Riccardino must be, too!

I ignore Luciano's shouts and, trying to make as little noise as possible, I slip into the studio to look around. There are cameramen, the studio assistant, the guests, Tio, and Marlin . . . but no

Riccardino? He might be small, but somebody is sure to notice him under their feet. Unless . . .

When I spot him, I am astounded. He has climbed the platform that runs around the floodlights, almost fourteen feet off the ground.

If he were to fall, maybe the world would be spared all kinds of trouble in the future, but I wouldn't live to reap the benefit.

Riccardino sees me, too. In answer to my desperate gesturing, he holds up the last article of clothing and waves it: my underwear.

As I start to climb the ladder, I don't know if I'm more afraid that he'll crash to the ground, that he'll drop the underwear on the head of one of the guests, or that someone will look up and realize "commando" doesn't just refer to my climbing skills.

Riccardino is in his element up there, and does a miniature version of the *Phantom of the Opera*, dropping down the ladder on the opposite side of the studio.

I, however, manage to let my foot slip and end up practically counting the rungs from top to bottom with my chin. I stifle a couple of rightful but very un-ladylike utterances and enter through the service door to collect the panties that Riccardino has left behind.

"Alice?"

Maybe this is a nightmare. Maybe I'll wake up and discover that I haven't even gotten to work yet and none of this has happened. Instead, I am standing in front of Davide, while holding my panties.

"Would you care to tell me what's been going on here tonight?"

What else could I say other than, "It's not what it looks like . . . I can explain?"

His eyes narrow. "Aren't you going to put them on?" he says, alluding to my underwear.

I bite my lip, and he sighs and turns his back to me, granting me, bless him, a hint of privacy.

"So, you really couldn't wait?"

I blink. "Well, no, Enrico . . ."

"Enrico?" He spins around, and his neck turns blood red. "First that King Kong creature and now Enrico?"

"Alejandro? No, no, no . . ." I'm going to have to explain everything to him from the beginning, hoping that Enrico won't kill me and that Davide is not on the Dark Side of the Force and about to reprimand us both for hiding a minor in a dangerous workplace. When I've finished, he stares at me as if I just revealed that Mr. President likes to dress up as a nun in private and get spanked.

"He stole your clothes?"

"After he peed on me, yes."

He rubs his face with a hand and makes a face. Then I notice that he has bruised knuckles.

"Are you hurt?"

"It's nothing, just a scratch." Between the two of us, we'd make great dialogue writers for *Mal d'Amore*. I stare at him as he takes a few steps and then turns back toward me. "Are you coming?"

"Where?"

"To look for the kid."

. . .

"How did you decide to work in television?"

We are walking through the sets of *Mal d'Amore*, passing by the offices of the show's powerful steel magnates to reach the emergency hallway.

"Well . . . actually, I would have liked to work in film," I tell him.

"And what films do you like?"

I avoid his gaze. "Oh, well, obviously the great directors. You know, Forman, Kubrick, Kiarostami . . ."

"And the truth?"

"What do you mean?"

"Those are not really the movies that you love. I can tell when you're lying, Alice. I can read it on your face."

"OK, you win. I love romantic comedies, filled with misadventures that always finish with a happy ending that makes you feel that all is right with the world."

"Such as?"

"Well, *Ghost*, for example. It's a beautiful love story."

"Sure. He dies . . . What could be more perfect?"

"*Pretty Woman*."

"Very romantic. She's a prost—"

"*Someone Like You!*" I interrupt him.

"Like *me*?"

"No . . . I mean, that's the title of another movie. *When Harry Met Sally, Notting Hill . . . Dirty Dancing*."

"They all seem a bit dated. Is there nothing in theaters now that you would like to see?"

I shrug my shoulders. "When I watch them again, I feel like a girl. What can I say, I've always had my head a little bit in the clouds. It's my dad's fault."

"What do you mean?"

I go to open a closet door to look for Riccardino, but it must have been off its hinges because it immediately starts to topple over.

"Watch out!" Behind me, Davide grabs it with both hands, preventing it from ending up on my head, and I find myself trapped between his arms and the closet.

"In the sense that," I say, trying not to think about the warmth of his body and the beating of his heart against my back. "He chose my name: Alice. He calls me Alice in Wonderland. I think Alice in La La Land would be more suitable."

I turn around and see that he is smiling.

"And you?"

We cross what appears to be the aisle of a shopping center, with shelves full of colorful products.

"Well, not David and Goliath. They just named me after my grandfather."

"I didn't mean that! I was trying to ask why you do this job . . ."

Davide, suddenly serious, shifts his gaze to the next set. "Let's try over there." Instead of answering my question, he enters another set and examines it like a crime scene, taking care to avoid looking at me.

"I'm going to say he's not here either. He is small, but there's no way he could have slipped through the cracks in the floor," I comment, earning a glance and a snort.

"Are you always like this?"

"Like what?"

"Sarcastic."

I shrug my shoulders. "I don't think I can be anything else."

"No, it's nice! I mean, I like it, but . . ." He crosses another door, leaving that "but" hanging. *But what?* I look at him quizzically, and he sighs again.

"It's hard to keep up with you."

Uh-oh. One less point for Alice.

"It's not always easy to keep up with you either," I say, but without being aggressive, "a career man, in an important position. I mean, a girl might feel uncomfortable." I chuckle, adding: "But you are a man, after all. You probably used to play with other kids like I did . . . the things that make us all human."

But I see his jaw harden. "Um . . . no."

He doesn't say anything more and turns his back. When we have covered practically all of the sets without finding a trace of the child, he holds the door open for me to let me pass, and I get the feeling that something has ended, that a spell has been broken. And, in fact, we are soon joined by Enrico, who gives me a grim look and then bites his lip, staring at Davide as he asks me, "Why aren't you in the production room?"

I don't know what to say. Enrico doesn't know that Davide knows. I know that Davide knows, but I also know that he shouldn't know what he knows. But does Davide know that he shouldn't know what he knows? My head is spinning!

"I called her," says Davide, causing me to breathe a sigh of relief. "But now she's all yours, if you need her."

It doesn't mean anything, but that "all yours" makes my stomach clench.

"Did you find him?" I ask Enrico as soon as the coast is clear.

"No, I didn't find him! Damn it, Alice, how the hell did you lose him in the first place? If something happens to him, Emilia will kill me. And I will kill you, don't doubt that."

"Why couldn't your wife keep him at home?" I growl.

"She said that I have to spend some time with my son. And that she needed a break."

"But you need to work, Enrico. She should understand that. You can't bring a kid here; it's way too dangerous. What about a babysitter?"

"Emilia's gone, Alice. She took off to spend the afternoon at the beach with her friends. And all three babysitters said no."

"You don't say? Does nobody appreciate a nice game of 'I tie you up and stick pins under your fingernails' these days? What has the world come to?"

We split up again to comb more areas, and when I ended up near the production room, Luciano leans over the video mixer and stops me.

"There you are, Alice." For a second I worry that he wants to give me a lecture, too, but instead he nods toward the phone. "Nardi called. He wants you in his office. He told me to tell you that he found it. I don't know what, but he found it."

I charge the stairs two at a time. Now the little pest is going to get it.

When I throw open the door, however, I am taken aback. Davide turns toward me, without getting up from his armchair in order to not wake Riccardino, who is sleeping in his arms like a little angel.

"I found him next to the snack machine. He was already asleep, with his little hand tucked in the cabinet door."

All these words are buzzing in my ears because all I can think is that there is nothing more captivating than a man with a sleeping baby in his arms.

He stands up. "I could use your help . . ."

Only when he reaches me do I notice that one of his hands is planted inside the child's mouth, firmly between his teeth.

"Oh, oh god!"

"He won't let go, and he doesn't seem to have any intention of waking up. I don't even know how he did it, since he was sleeping."

I shrug my shoulders. "It must be a reflex, like with sharks." I pinch Riccardino's nose and less than three seconds later, the boy's mouth snaps open, releasing his prey.

"You're a woman of many talents," comments Davide, passing the child to me and massaging his hand. "Be careful."

"I dare him to try that with me," I say with a wink. "I'm beginning to think that the witch from Hansel and Gretel had cause for what she did." I try to shake off a lock of hair that has slipped onto my face and makes me want to scratch my nose, but with Riccardino in my arms I can't get it; I keep blowing and blowing as it bounces up and down. Davide tries to help me, brushing my cheek with his fingers. As I feel red blotches burning into my face, I turn around and go out into the hallway.

"Thank you for finding him. And for calling me and not Enrico. For . . ."

"For not being the monster I'm supposed to be? Despite my job?"

"No . . ."

"Well, that's what you were asking me before: How could anyone do this kind of job? Alice, I try to save companies, not destroy them. I want you to understand that. Really, it would mean a lot to me."

"Sure. Of course, I understand," I manage before hurrying away, because in truth I really don't understand anything.

. . .

When I get to the production room, the show is over and almost everyone has left, but Raffaella is still there and flashes me a big smile.

"Enrico told me that you had problems tonight. Don't worry. I handled everything here." With her hand on the doorknob, she turns back to me. "Have you heard?"

"Heard what?"

"Sergio got fired. I'm afraid that the slaughter has begun." She pats me on the shoulder. "Who knows who will be next?"

She walks away, and I feel like I'm in a bubble. I hear Davide's voice begging me not to be angry with him because it is nothing personal if he has to fire someone. Suddenly, I flash on an image: a memory from tonight when Davide answered that phone call and I was left alone in his office. At the time, not thinking about his role in the company but casting him in the lead role of one of my usual pseudoromantic projections, I had gone over to the desk and seen Sergio's résumé—right next to mine.

Who knows who will be next?

Outside, it's raining heavily. I hadn't even noticed. I run toward my car, because the only thing that I want is to drive, turn on the radio full blast, numb myself with music, and not think about what is going on. I don't want to think about Sergio, who no longer has a job; about Davide, who sent him packing; or about myself, who as usual didn't have a clue what was going on.

But when I reach the car, I realize that once again I've been an idiot, because I left my purse with my car keys and everything else in the production room.

I go back in, slamming the door violently. I am furious.

I've had it with Davide, because he lied to me, because he's not the person he seems; and with myself, because I keep interpreting every tiny thing as if I were wearing rose-colored glasses. I am so angry that I am out of breath. My blouse is soaked through to my skin, clinging so horribly that the only option is to remove it.

I've already done that when I realize that I'm not alone. Standing at the door to the production room, Alejandro doesn't say a word but stares at me with his dark, distant Latin eyes. I don't say anything either, but I approach him without removing my eyes from his.

With a fluid, tested motion he takes off his shirt, revealing those competition-worthy abs. I need this. I need to lose myself.

His lips have the salty taste of my despair.

11

Into the Wild Sagittarius

You did *not* do that!"

"Paola, it was just a kiss, it's not like I made a porno on the production room counter."

Honestly, I am gloating as I tell her, because yes, it was just a kiss, but a kiss as scorching as the Gobi Desert.

I felt like the beautiful, uninhibited women in American movies, the kind that walk into a bar and don't even have to make an effort. Just one of their passionate, confident looks will instantly earn them a free drink, a man for the night (who of course would turn out to be their soul mate in any good romance film), along with a wedding gown, a country house with a pool, the latest Williams-Sonoma has to offer, and maybe even the best in orthopedic mattresses.

"You're not exaggerating?" asks Paola, who, like a good best friend, is at the control tower, initiating my landing maneuvers. "Alice, listen, I'm happy that you experienced something so . . . so passionate, but I don't want you to have any delusions about this guy. A guy who goes around half naked like an ape with a six-pack you could grate cheese on, and who jumps on top of you before you've even exchanged a hundred words, with full intentions of unleashing the anaconda . . . I don't think that's his way of looking for a soul mate."

"You're making this sound like a trip to the zoo," I say, snorting. "And besides, I wouldn't have been able to go all the way."

"Thank God, Alice. I'm happy that you showed at least an ounce of self-control and that the irreparable didn't happen."

The "irreparable," as she calls it, would have been at most a nice diversion for my nether regions that are now in early retirement and wouldn't have said no to a carousel ride or, to continue the Tarzan metaphor, a swing on the vine.

"Yes, *Granny*, that, too. But it's more because I have to clean up the area. Tomorrow, I have an appointment for a full wax, and then, if I find myself in the firing line again, it's every man for himself," I reply, teasing her.

On the telephone with Paola, it's easy for me to play the fabulous femme fatale who has men falling at her feet at the snap of a finger, but in reality, I've never been able to snap my fingers. Maybe that's why I've had to pull every trick in the book to get even a poor excuse for a boyfriend.

Given my results, maybe I should really practice snapping.

When I stamp my card on Monday morning, I am still rubbing my thumb on my index finger, in an attempt to produce a snap worthy of the name. More than anything else, I do it to release tension, although Tio's message should have put me in a good mood.

Good morning, Libra

You are bursting with energy and zest for life and this is a disaster for the people around you. You can thank not only the

Full Moon in Libra, but also the conjunction between Venus and Uranus that favors relationships and new friendships.

Be wary, however, of the Square Moon in Negative Transit with Neptune that leads you to give in to delusion, to abandon reality for a dream. Uranus in conjunction with Venus could cause you to fight with a loved one or even make you impulsive in your romantic choices and in drawing conclusions. However, the Sextile of Mercury with Pluto seems to indicate that you are on the right path to assert your personality and affirm your strength, especially in the work environment, where Saturn will back you up, encouraging concentration and allowing you to handle even stressful tasks with tranquility.

I close my eyes and take a deep breath, hoping to fill my lungs with strength and determination. However, when I let my breath go, I also exhale all the good intentions Tio has tried to instill in me. As much as I would like to abandon myself to the fantasy of being a superwoman who never asks for help, I can't ignore the layoff that could be right around the corner, and I can't avoid seeing Alejandro and facing the embarrassment of our Wednesday-night rendezvous. Then there's Davide; I must face Davide.

The only person around right now is Conchita, who is emptying the trash, dusting the desks, and watering the plants. It occurs to me that she may truly be the only one around here who does any work.

"Hey, Conchy, do you know where everyone else is?"

She shrugs and then makes a gesture of bringing an invisible glass to her lips, with her pinky carefully lifted.

"Toes," she says. And when I shake my head because I didn't understand, she adds, "Café."

As I cross the hallway toward the cafeteria, I hear a growing buzz. When I push open the revolving doors, everyone is there. They are toasting with coffee and fruit juice.

"Congratulations!" Enrico exclaims, giving Carlo a pat on the back and a warm handshake.

"Congratulations, Cristina!" says Raffaella, handing over an enormous package.

This is not your average "good job" professional toast. I have crashed the baby shower for Carlo's future offspring.

"You are all amazing and too kind. Thank you, friends," says my ex-friend, so sugary sweet that I want to vomit.

As Cristina starts to unwrap the package, Raffa sees me and suddenly, as if in slow motion, lifts her hands and brings them to her mouth. "Alice!"

Everyone turns to look at me. Carlo takes a step forward but stops dead in his tracks after a death stare from his soon-to-be wife and soon-to-be mother of his child.

"Um, Alice, welcome," says Cristina. "And thank you," she adds, indicating the beribboned package.

Raffa steps toward me, surrounded by the Secretaries of East-wick from upstairs. "Actually, Alice wasn't part of the gift," she says, then turns toward me with an understanding look. "It seemed kinder not to tell you about all this," she added only to me, confirming that I was purposely not invited to their lovely little party.

All that I am able to come up with in response is, "Excuse me."

I take a step backward, and in a desperate attempt to reach the door, someone grabs my arms.

"To tell the truth, Alice did know about this gathering. I told her when I asked her to help me pick out a gift." Davide drags me forward. "In fact, we decided to get it together. Here it is."

I stare into his eyes while that annoying gnat Cristina breathily gushes.

"Oh, wow, thank you. You are too kind. Right, Carlo? Aren't they so kind? Both of them. Davide and *Alice*."

"Thank you, Davide. And Alice," says my ex-boyfriend. "Thank you for giving us a . . . mini acoustic guitar."

"Um, I imagine that Carletto Junior will enjoy it . . . in a few years," says Cristina.

I see Davide blush. Davide Nardi, the fastest firer in the West, who probably just put my name at the top of his lengthy hit list. Incidentally, it's not like everyone has let up on their death stares since Davide came to my rescue. If you're born the Grim Reaper, you can't suddenly start calling yourself Lancelot and attempt to be the most chivalrous knight of the realm.

"I don't know about you, but I need a coffee," I tell Davide to remove him from the awkward situation with Carlo and Cristina. It's the least I can do to repay him.

"I'd love one," he says, following me to the counter.

We stand together in complete silence as the barista makes our coffee.

"How did . . ."

"Do you know . . ."

We speak over each other, just as the cups hit the saucers.

"Sorry," I say.

"Go ahead." He shakes his head, still not looking me in the eye.

"I just wanted to ask if you knew how the first episode of *Astrological Guide* went."

"Oh, sure. Well. I think well, but we are going to check the share later with the president."

I sigh and gulp down my coffee, hoping that this is really the case.

When I see Davide frown and look at a point over my shoulder, I instinctively turn around, and I see Conchita in front of me, with her mop in one hand and a yellow rose in the other.

"For-ju," answers Conchita. "Brang now. For-ju."

"I think she wants to say that they brought it for you just now, Alice," explains Davide. "Thank you, Conchita."

Davide slips the flower out of the woman's hand and gives it to me, but I remain frozen, with my eyes interlocked with his, because at that precise moment an arm finds its way around my waist, and a pair of soft, warm, *Latin* lips land on my neck. A voice behind me whispers: "*Mi amor . . .*"

If it weren't for my current situation, perhaps I would start laughing, imagining myself as Morticia Addams and responding to the pinch on my butt by saying, "Thank you, Thing!"

But there's nothing to laugh about. Not while I'm looking at Davide, anyway. Rose in hand, Davide stands there long enough to watch Alejandro dancing the *lambada* against me at nine in the morning, then puts the flower down on the counter.

"Well, I have to go," he says, gritting his teeth. "Have a nice day, Alice."

12

Libra Girls Are Easy

Back in the day, I was a big fan of Agatha Christie, but never in my wildest dreams would I have thought my life would someday start to resemble a thriller . . . And yet, I find myself grappling with the *Mystery of the Yellow Rose*.

It's not a very original title, but here's the gist: I haven't the slightest idea who sent that rose to me.

I admit, at first I assumed it was the work of *Steel Jeeg*, given that the handsome Alejandro materialized practically in sync with the rose, but he denied it immediately.

"Hello, Mom?" I ask, when I hear her voice at the other end of the telephone.

"Hi, dear, what's up?"

"Um . . . Did you or Dad send me flowers at the office?"

"Guido, someone sent Alice flowers and she doesn't know who!" yells my mother.

"They made a mistake!" cries my father charmingly from the other part of the house.

"Why does it have to be a mistake? I can't get flowers?" I whine, hurt.

I hear my father in the background: "If someone sends you a flower or two, it's because he's not sure what to do, but he wants to go to bed with you."

I sigh. "OK, I have to go. Thanks for the poetry, Dad."

When I hang up, I feel a strange shiver run down my spine. What if this is the first move of a stalker?

This really is the limit. Here I am, without even the slightest hint of a boyfriend, and someone falls in love with me and starts stalking me by sending roses. If this guy had some guts and just made himself known, I'd probably at least give him a shot.

"Who knows what sign he might be . . ."

At lunch, I try to distract myself from the imminent threat of a stalker by eating with Tio.

"Come on, you received a flower, not a human ear!" he teases.

"Yes, but I want to know who sent it."

"Because you are as curious as a monkey." He looks around the cafeteria. "Nardi? I see him as a secret admirer."

Davide. I lift my gaze toward the mezzanine level of the cafeteria. He's at a table with Mr. President and the head of HR.

"I don't think so. He seemed surprised when Conchita showed up."

"Conchita? Or Abdominal Man?"

I haven't seen Davide again since this morning. I should be happy about Abdominal Man's—I mean Alejandro's—attentions, but thinking about that moment makes me feel a little uncomfortable.

"Speak of the devil . . . and his biceps appear."

Tio's words make me turn to stare at the revolving doors through which Alejandro appears, surveying the terrain like a gunslinger in a saloon.

At the table next to ours, the assistant from *Mal d'Amore*, Mara, beckons him over, and he approaches with a cheetah-like gait, fluid, languid, and full of sex appeal.

Except he doesn't sit in the place that she freed up by moving her bag. One step away from the chair, Alejandro shakes his mane and deviates toward me, eyeing Tio like a competing stallion.

"Aliz, *mi amor*, there you are." He takes my hand, delicately removes the salad-laden fork from my fingers, and plants a kiss on my knuckles.

"I eh-search *mucho*. I miss you . . ."

Then Alejandro pulls my hand toward him, in a motion that suggests we need to leave the cafeteria. Now.

"*Ven conmigo, querida.*"

Swayed by the Spanish timbre of his voice, I feel almost as slinky as a cheetah myself as we walk out.

. . .

"Why don't we put it to a vote," I say, raising my hand. I'm sitting opposite Tio, staring quizzically at the cell phone on the desk between us.

"It's a *no* from me, Alice. Absolutely *not*," says Paola from the other end of the line.

"So, in your opinion, I should go out with Alejandro tonight like *this . . . without* waxing?!"

"You asked me and I'm telling you. If you don't wax, it won't even remotely cross your mind to give it up on the first date. It's a tactic, Alice. With men like that, all it takes is a half-smile and you've lost your underwear. Have some sense!"

I snort, looking to Tio to rescue me.

"NO," he says crossing his arms across his chest. When I show him my puppy dog eyes and pouty lips in my last attempt to win him over, he leans back in his chair, putting more distance between us.

"You've already kissed. Then he asked you on a date, and you made the mistake of saying yes right away. Now you need to make up for it in some other way. Alejandro is a Sagittarius; that is the *Homo eroticus* of the zodiac. It's enough to know that Sagittarius is always focused on sex: If he's not doing it with someone, he's thinking about doing it, or he's doing it on his own. Of course, when you do get a Sagittarius between the sheets, you will discover he is an exceptional lover, fully endowed, every woman's secret fantasy, a mystical experience par excellence."

"TIO!" we hear Paola exclaim from the telephone.

"Sorry, Paola . . . But in the end, they are not big fans of lasting relationships. Therefore, it's better to build up their interest before you let them reach their goal."

By the time Alejandro comes to pick me up, I have put together an ensemble of stiletto boots with a high leg, prudish '80s denier stockings, and a miniskirt.

However, Alejandro seems ready to disprove every hypothesis conjured up by the two conspirators I still call friends. First of all, he doesn't jump on top of me like Paola told me to expect. He doesn't even try for a quick grope during the customary kisses on the cheek, like Tio told me to expect. In fact, he is even kind enough to open the car door for me, something that Carlo never deigned to do in five years of dating.

On the way, he talks a lot, mostly about himself, about Seville and Spain. He asks if I've ever been there and what I thought of it. I am more and more inclined to believe that those two don't understand him one bit.

"So, you see, when I eh-saw you *otra vez* . . . and you . . . You muss excuse me, because this is not my way. It's that I like you, Aliz. And I take advantage of you. *Lo siento mucho.* And *esta noche lo que quería,* what I wanted to do, is eh-say eh-sorry."

His idea of *eh-sorry* meant going to a bar, which in his opinion, a "simple and spontaneous" girl like myself would like. Of course, with my leather leggings and heels, I don't feel so simple and spontaneous tonight, or even steady enough to walk through the long grass as we try to reach the lights down below. I avoid a sprain by stopping to contemplate the colored lanterns waving in the breeze.

"They are so beautiful," I say, to catch my breath.

"Maybe I eh-should have tell you where I take you *esta noche,*" he says, smiling at me. "I don't want for you to hurt yourself . . . *Espere* . . . Wait." He bends to his knees and, with no effort at all, lifts me up in his arms and finishes crossing the remaining three hundred feet of field.

If I were to attempt to describe the palpitations of his heart and mine, the scent of his hair flowing in the wind and tickling my cheek, the heat emanating from his alpha male body and all my turmoil as a result, I would risk sounding like the swooning heroine of an Austen novel. Let's just say that I enjoyed every single stride of that moonlit walk, and when he sets my feet down on the rough wooden planks of some sort of dance floor en plein air, I am still wrapped up in a dream.

"What is this?" I ask him, happy that his arm is still supporting me.

"*Aquí bailamos.* Flamenco, tango . . . Dance *de mi tierra.*"

The only problem is that I can't move an inch—and it's not just because of the high-heeled boots. I've always been stiff as a poker.

"*El momento* I eh-saw you, I want you in my arms . . . *Quiero bailar contigo,* Aliz."

How could anyone say no to someone who puts it like that? I tell myself that if Jennifer Grey could do it, I should be able to do it.

It goes without saying, Alejandro is a dancing god. I, obviously, am not. I trip, but he doesn't mind. He helps me as we move, correcting me sweetly, whispering in my ear what I should do. And suddenly I am dancing, without even trying.

We end up flushed, me pressed against his sweaty body. Our hearts beat crazily and we look into each other's eyes as if we've already made love. That is the feeling that I got dancing with him, touching him, feeling his secure hold. We made love in the most sublime and platonic sense of the word.

We dance again, this time to slow and sensual music. Again there are caresses, his lips against my ear and his warm breath on my neck.

And he kisses me.

He does it suddenly, stopping in the middle of the floor and in the middle of the dance. In spite of the music, I hear him sigh when his eyes meet mine, with a look that is definitely unsuitable for minors, and he takes my face in his hands.

"I don't know how much time is passed from the last time I feel this."

I nuzzle my cheek against the palm of his hand.

"Aliz, *mi vida* was *imperfecto* . . . I keep running, running, from *estado* to *estado*, *continente* to *continente*. *Un hombre* eh . . . seeking desperately for eh . . . something. *Y eres tú*, Aliz. *Eres tú, mi amor.* Make love to me . . . *por favor* . . . *ayuda a un hombre moribundo.*"

How could I not help a "*moribundo*"? God, I want to be in his bed already.

But I can't! Thanks to Tio, Paola, and my untrimmed forest.

I flash him a smile, kissing the point of his nose.

"Excuse me just a second . . ."

I slip away, rummaging through my purse and calling Tio's number—and when he doesn't answer, Paola's—while I wait in line at the bar.

"Hello, Alice? How did it go?"

"Paola, damn it!"

"Honey, you're making me worried. What did he do to you?"

"What did he do to me? What *didn't* he do to me? What *can't* he do to me . . . not to mention what I will do to you tomorrow! Alejandro is . . . simply divine . . . we are in love . . . and I can't go to bed with him because you stopped me from waxing."

"Alice, this is exactly what you must avoid at all costs. Be strong. There'll be other chances. After all . . . if he really loves you, he will wait."

"You don't understand: I'm the one who can't wait! I'm telling you, either I'm going to find a razor or I'll remove these hairs one by one with my teeth, and you will have that on your conscience."

"No, Alice! I forbid it. No shaving!"

"Yes. I'm shaving now!" And I will never in my life listen to either of those two again.

13

Libra on a Hot Tin Roof

I'm in for a sleepless night; unfortunately, not because of a tall, dark, and handsome man with a six-pack straight out of a fitness magazine, but because of another yellow rose.

As it turns out, the worst bars in Caracas don't allow under-the-table distribution of toiletries like hotels do. So, since removing every hair with a cocktail umbrella would take the entire night, I decided to let it go.

Sure, I could have told Alejandro to come up to my house and at least looked for a razor, but because, as usual, I listened to Paola and Tio, my apartment looks like a set from a postatomic horror movie. I made up an excuse and have accepted the fact that the only steamy thing in my night will be a cup of chamomile tea to sedate my desires.

I walk out of the elevator on cloud nine after one of those kisses that knocks you completely off your feet . . . and then I see it.

On my doormat is a rose identical to the one I had received in the office.

I bend down to collect it and as soon as I lift it up, a shiver runs down my spine. This time, there is a note. And it has just one word: *Remember?*

Panic. What am I supposed to remember?

OK, Alice, you really may have a secret admirer. Holy cow! I mean, really, deep down, aren't I someone who believes in the unlikeliest romantic situations?

The problem is that I've always thought about my life like a romantic comedy. What if it is actually a thriller? All this time I've been thinking that I am Julia Roberts but maybe I am actually one of those extras that no one cares about who dies ten minutes into a movie.

Between my unsated passion for Alejandro and the prospect of being a stupid cheerleader in a horror film, it took me a while to fall asleep.

. . .

The next day, my day off, I decide I am in need of pampering and, let's face it, grooming. I need a beautician who will allow me to undress without fear of being mistaken for the missing link between men and apes.

After the spa, I walk through the Sempione Park to get to the tram back home.

I allow myself a moment to savor the prospect of no longer being single. It's true; my relationship with Alejandro is just beginning, but it has all the signs of growing and becoming something truly incredible. Perhaps we could go on vacation to Spain this summer; we could even decide to get married there.

Who would have ever thought that I would marry a Spaniard? Cool . . . and very Melanie Griffith of me.

I feel my cell vibrate and sigh as I pull it out. It's Alejandro. We have been sending romantic messages since this morning. It's only to be expected; after all, we're in love.

He writes:

How can I stop thinking about you?

I answer:

Just give in and think of me.

Short and direct. Go Alice. You're making him happy without dragging on too long and making him think that you're hanging on his every word.

Him again:

Work without you is torture . . . *¿Dónde está mi vida?*

I sigh and respond:

Getting ready to hold you.

Another buzz. I open it anxiously.
This time it's Tio. Ugh.

Don't think that I don't know what you are doing! Your Moon is conjunct to Neptune, and this prevents you from seeing things realistically and facilitates your abandonment to dreamlike and delusionary states. Furthermore, there is a Sextile of Mercury stimulating your already natural attraction to mystery . . . and you haven't answered me since this morning. You're Not Fooling Me: I know you're up to something! Remember that Sagittarius is as much a master of seduction as he is of cut and run. I'm not saying they are not sincere when they tell you they love you, but that tomorrow they could say it just as sincerely to someone else. Like I've told you, we need an Ascendant to really be sure. Find out what it is and we'll speak again.

Damn Tio and his astrological third eye. Now that he's met Paola, I'm sure that he'll go blab everything to her. I really don't think he's understanding Alejandro very well.

He said he was going to help me with men, but he never approves of anyone. I mean, Sagittarius is supposed to be a sign that is compatible with me. He mentioned it more than once, and when I rejoiced that I'd finally met someone that might work, he dragged out this story about also needing the Ascendant. No! Now he's pulled the rug out from under my feet. What do I know about Alejandro's Ascendant? I even tried to ask him, but he answered with three question marks, which means that he's never even heard of it.

I decide to cut through a meadow, and today I am not even bothered by the couples I see rolling in the grass at dusk. I no longer feel excluded. Soon I, too, could be rolling around this meadow.

Just as I am imagining the perfect '80s movie moment, kissing Alejandro silhouetted against a flaming red sunset, two things happen.

The first is a meteorite that hits me on the neck and throws me off balance.

The second is a cargo truck of flesh, paws, and drool that crashes into me, throwing me to the ground and launching my smartphone into the air, along with Alejandro's last message:

Tú eres elegante y hermosa.

And I find myself, *hermosa* and *elegante*, face-planted on the ground.

As I try to get up, a long, warm tongue laps at my cheek, causing me to spring backward.

"Wait!" yells a voice behind me. "Good boy, Flash. OFF!"

I feel strange, like that tingling you get when someone kisses your neck, especially when you don't expect it. It lasts a microsecond, and I'm not sure if I recognize him because I turn around or if I turn around because I recognize him. All I know is that Davide is in front of me.

He runs up to me. "Alice, are you OK? Are you hurt? Let me see."

"No . . . I'm fine, don't worry about it."

"I'm sorry. Flash is oblivious to anything around him whenever we're playing catch."

Meanwhile the phone buzzes again, a sign that it wasn't broken by the fall. Thank God. I was already worried about having lost touch with Alejandro. Tragedy averted.

"Come on, let's go clean you up. Don't faint," Davide says. "It's just a little blood."

Blood?

BLOOD!

I look at my arm. There is a cut that runs from my wrist almost all the way up to my elbow. And I'm still bleeding.

I fear the creature could mistake my arm for a steak. "Good boy, Cujo, be good."

"His name is Flash. Don't be scared. He's as good as gold."

Another buzz from my cell announces a new message. I give a quick look.

What are you doing? Why aren't you answering me?

Oh god, it's true. I didn't answer him.

"He's a Great Dane," Davide says while he puts my arm under the water fountain. "He needs to run, and sometimes we come here to play ball." More precisely, with the punctured leather ball with the consistency of concrete that took me by surprise.

With my arm still dripping with reddish water, I quickly type:

I was deciding what to wear for you . . .

I turn to Davide, who looks at me with a raised eyebrow. "It's not broken, is it?" he asks, pointing to the phone.

God, why am I blushing? "Just checking. No, it's not broken, luckily."

"Good. I'm sorry about the fall," he says, glancing at the dog. "Come on, to say sorry, Flash and I will buy you an *aperitivo*."

. . .

We order a platter of cold cuts and two glasses of white wine. Davide insists on paying, frowning when I go to take out my wallet. "Don't even try."

I look down, flattered. And I feel vaguely guilty when the phone buzzes yet again.

Te imagino dressing for *mi*, putting your panties . . .

I blush and bring the glass to my lips.

"With all these chance encounters, you must think I'm following you."

The bubbles rise to my nose and I start to cough, covering my face with my hand.

In my mind, the image of the yellow rose appears. What if Tio had been right when he said that he could see Davide as my *Cyrano de Bergerac*? In fact, he does know where I live, since he brought me home that time.

"Calm down! I didn't say that I am. I said that perhaps you might think so. I ended up taking a house here."

"Ah . . ." I ask myself why Davide always has this hallucinatory effect on me. Then my cell phone buzzes again.

¿De qué color es tu lingerie, querida? Make me dream *hasta la noche.*

Oh god. For a moment, I start to daydream and I see Alejandro taking off his shirt. Except that, as soon as he slips it over his head, it's no longer him, but . . .

Davide is still in front of me. "Are you OK?"

I take another gulp of wine and force myself to respond as I type something to Alejandro. "Oh yeah . . . sure . . . so what were you doing here?"

He keeps looking at me and frowning. "I just told you. Alice, are you sure that you don't want to go to the emergency room?"

"No, no. I'm good."

Davide shrugs and sips his wine. "Actually, what I meant to say was that I am happy that I ran into you, Alice. There are some things I would like to explain."

The buzzing of the phone distracts me again. It buzzes, two, three times. Alejandro is going crazy for my underwear descriptions. When I look up, I see Davide snort and fold his arms across his chest.

"Sorry. Keep talking. I'll just be a second."

"In part, it concerns work. Well, no, not really, not exactly . . . Yes, work has something to do with it, but the thing is that I feel the need to clarify something with you. It's something that's happening, and I wanted to ask you . . ."

The messages from my Latin stallion are now delirious. He's even mentioning some particular tortures that he will subject me to under his tongue. Damn. How do I reply to that?

"So, you were speaking about the show?" I sigh, after sending a string of emojis worthy of a teenager.

But Davide is getting up. "It doesn't matter," he replies, drily. "I'm sorry to have kept you. You obviously have things to do. We'll speak about it in the office."

14

A Very Little Sagittarius

I don't understand why Davide left in such a hurry.

I especially don't know why I'm still thinking about him, even now that I'm with Alejandro. I am really in a bad way if, when I'm with my B-O-Y-F-R-I-E-N-D, I am racking my brains about what someone else said or didn't say.

In this regard, I always get the impression that I'm missing something with Davide.

But I can't think about that now. I will worry about it tomorrow. Right now, I have to concentrate on Alejandro.

He was working late today, so, in direct defiance of Paola and Tio, I went right to the little apartment that he rents not far from the television studios.

I ate something first, as he told me to do, because he was going to be late. That way we wouldn't waste any time.

While Alejandro is taking a shower, I give myself a quick once-over.

"*Mi amor.*"

I feel a shiver down my spine and his wet mouth on the back of my neck.

I dedicate all my attention to him: his arms, his biceps, his mouth, and his kisses.

Shivers. I feel shivers all over. In the excitement, I feel like the heroine of one of those soft porn novels that's always at the top of the charts. Except I don't want shades of gray, or black, or white; I want to experience every moment in glorious Technicolor.

I devote myself to Alejandro's abs, which seem to come directly from a glossy magazine, and I run my fingers over them like the keys on a piano.

Alejandro's hands run over me, undress me, caress me, followed by his hot tongue and the cold drops of water from his still-dripping hair that fall in my eyes.

I inhale deeply, taking in his intoxicating smell. I look for the perfume of leather that they always describe in romance novels when a man undresses—the scent of a man—but I only smell shower gel, which isn't even Scots pine, but berry scented. What does it matter when I am about to experience the most mystical, stratospheric, fulfilling, and unique sexual experience in history? He could smell like gingerbread, and I wouldn't complain.

In the Mr. Zodiac competition, Sagittarius came first, ahead of the others by several *lengths*. That's what Tio said. The signs say that I will have as many orgasms as there are stars in the Big Dipper. Hooray!

He spreads my legs and stands over me, only then dropping the towel from his waist.

He looks at me. I look at him.

Virginally, I bat my eyelashes, sliding my eyes over his powerful neck, his virile chest, and that six-pack that could cause a fainting epidemic, and then ...

Oh god, it must be an optical illusion, caused by overworking those muscles just above, but the effect is like one of those sneezes that as it first starts to tickle your nose seems like it could bring down a house but then extinguishes in your throat with a wheeze.

I frown, but only for a second—I was always taught that it's rude to stare—and I bring my eyes back to his, smiling gracefully.

Who knows, perhaps Alejandro is like Sting in his heyday, having sex for five or more hours, and a single glance from him is all it takes to reach a climax. Let's hope, I think to myself, still staring as he approaches.

Come on, Alice; even if he's not Rocco Siffredi, it will still be a fantastic experience. You're in love!

15

Guess If the Sagittarius Is Coming to Dinner

My romance has lasted for two weeks now. When I look into Alejandro's dark eyes, I lose myself; he can speak to me about anything and I hang, breathless, on his every word.

We make love, too, although it's not the most important element of our relationship.

I feel so lucky to have found him. I am so happy that tonight we decided to go to my parents' house. When I called to say I would go over for dinner, I intimated that I had some really big news.

The pretext is the famous boxes, the ones full of my things that Mom and Dad packed before repainting the house.

And Tio will finally have to change his mind about my Sagittarius, because tonight he practically invited himself to dinner, so he will be there, too. I must say that he's been very kind. He borrowed a Fiat Doblò from a friend so we can easily load all my things. This also means he has instantly found his way into my dad's heart—he loves organized people.

My personal astrologer follows my dad and shows an interest in painting techniques, asking questions worthy of an art expert faced with the imminent restoration of the Sistine Chapel. My father smiles. Tio can win people over in a heartbeat. He can read anyone with his astrology. So much so, that it seems you have known him forever. Or more like he has known you forever, since he barely speaks about himself.

I glance at the clock. Alejandro should be here soon.

"Your friend is really nice," says my mom, at the stove. "He's handsome, too." She gestures toward the living room.

Instinctively I cast another glance at the door. Well, yes even without all the greasepaint they use to transform him into Marcus Alvarez, I admit that he is easy on the eyes: long legs and broad shoulders, the kind you always see in those gossip magazines that my dad consults during long moments of spiritual retreat in the bathroom, the guys who change their women as often as they change their clothes. But Tio is not like that. In fact, he doesn't even seem interested in love.

He catches my furtive glance and pulls a face, before blowing me a kiss.

For a second, I wonder if it's possible that he is the one sending me the yellow roses. That wouldn't really make any sense, since we talk every day, and he's done nothing but help me try to find the man of my dreams.

Speaking of roses, I didn't tell Alejandro about the latest one that arrived yesterday morning. He is *un hombre latino*, after all, and jealousy is as much a part of his DNA as his dark eyes, amber skin, broad chest, and . . . Oh well, you can't have everything in life. I think, if given a choice, I would have preferred that *that* were his dominant trait, but that particular feature must have been a recessive gene. What rotten luck!

Anyway, perfection is scary, isn't it? I'm glad that there is something there (or not there) that makes him human. Much better ...

Since it's getting late, and Dad is already pouring the drinks, I decide to escape down the hall to call Alejandro. The phone rings four or five times before he picks up.

"*Hola, amor,* where are you? *¿Abajo?*" I ask hopefully.

At least three seconds of silence. "Um, no ... I'm on the highway."

I frown. "What do you mean?"

"Aliz, *lo siento mucho,* I cannot be there. They call me for ... work. I go to Vigevano."

"What!"

"*Lo siento,* Aliz. *Otra ocasión. Besitos. Besitos.*"

He hangs up, without giving it a second thought. *Besitos. Besitos,* my ass. He ruined the surprise. I could still tell Mom and Dad that I'm dating someone, but it's not the same thing.

"You see how much of a Libra you are?" says Tio, when I explain the problem to him. "You are a perfectionist, and once you get something in your head, you can't stand being made to review and correct it."

"And here I was thinking I had some kind of mental disease. Instead, I'm affected by a form of acute Libra-itis."

"Hey, I'm here. Am I not enough for you?" He puts his arm around me to console me and gives me a kiss on the forehead.

"Kids, *aperitivo* time!" my father calls us to order.

The problem isn't really that Alejandro can't make it tonight. The fact is that it always triggers something strange in my head when things don't go according to plan. And, I wasn't too nice to Alejandro the other night.

I'd had a rough day. I had seen Davide, who is now giving me the cold shoulder. The third episode of the *Guide* had suffered a drop in viewing figures. Maybe that's why Davide is so nervous; after all, he was the one who pushed for my program with Mr. President. I might end up on the network's blacklist after all.

In short, all I wanted was to be cuddled, for Alejandro to hold me in his arms, more tenderly than passionately.

"How are you? Better?" asks Tio.

I shrug. "I guess, sure. Maybe I'll feel even better not making the announcement tonight."

"Oh, it's the *announcement* now, is it!"

"So to speak."

He gives me a suspicious look. "Alice, are you really OK? I don't mean just now because Alejandro's not coming to dinner, but in general. Are you sure you're OK with him?"

"Weren't you the one who said Libra and Sagittarius were compatible signs? Very compatible?"

He sighs. "Sagittarius is undoubtedly a compatible sign, but often individualistic and even all-consuming. And above all, he's a free spirit, who loves new conquests and doesn't settle down easily. You have clearly been charmed by the *huge* qualities of his sign." He winks at me, like someone who is incredibly well versed on the topic and has studied it at great length.

I bite my lip because I don't want to discuss intimate matters, but the truth is that that small detail—ha!—that Tio had told me about a Sagittarius was still at the back of my mind . . . In this case, it sure is small, but I think it's important in a relationship. "Maybe you let yourself be too influenced by zodiac signs in judging people. Everything doesn't always match up. I can assure you."

"So, is this a serious relationship? I mean, isn't it a bit early to, say, introduce him to your parents?"

"I'm happy, Tio. That I can say despite the relative *length*"—I cough—"of our relationship, I mean."

Why do I keep thinking about sex? Sex is, after all, of little importance. In the long run, it's feelings that matter, right? Yet, to make a long story short, I keep thinking about it.

Given Tio's comments on the enormous capabilities of the Sagittarius, I'd like to ask him if this particular exception to the rule could be due to perhaps his Ascendant?

"Well, yes, the Ascendant is an important part," says Tio, when I turn around and ask him the question. "It's like the mask we show to the world, which largely determines the way others see us, their first impression. Before the twentieth century, it was considered even more important than the Solar Sign because of its influence."

I think about the way Alejandro and I make love. And ask myself what could the demonic Ascendant be that makes things so difficult?

"Well, it's not like one should necessarily overdo it," I reply.

"Come off it!" he exclaims, slapping me on the back. "No one believes you. Sex is a fundamental part of the life of a couple. Otherwise..."

"Otherwise what? Is this one of those macho, sexist speeches?" I blurt out. "You mean to say that if someone is 'small' and can't satisfy a woman, he can't have a serious and rewarding relationship with someone? For your information, I am very, very happy. Very. Can you say the same? Where are your girlfriends? Maybe you're the one who has something to hide!"

I see his expression darken.

Luckily, my mother intervenes, appearing in the kitchen doorway.

We all sit down and I cast a hard look at Tio, even though I know I shouldn't be mad at him and that he's not to blame for what I'm going through.

"I know we usually only do this at Christmas," announces my mother proudly, "but tonight, we have a guest, and if I'm not mistaken, there's something to celebrate, right? So, I made a typical

family dish: eel." She smiles winking at my father. "Guido found me
a *nice, big* one."

I close my eyes, wondering if this isn't a conspiracy.

The truth is that I am racked with guilt. In reality, it's not a complete disaster with Alejandro, but that is only because, at a certain
point, I throw in the towel and think of someone else . . . Davide.
There, I've thought it. Mea culpa.

"Aren't you happy, Alice? You love eel," says my mother when I
pass her my plate.

"Oh, yes," I repeat. "I love it."

"And your boyfriend, how's he doing?" When my father asks
this question, I turn abruptly to him as he adds, "Does he eat eel?"

A moment of glacial embarrassment follows, where Tio looks
at me, I look at him, and I understand. For my parents, the star of
Guess Who's Coming to Dinner is Tio, not Alejandro, about whom
they know nothing.

"Guido, you're such a spoilsport. You should have waited for
them to tell us!"

"Oh, I like eel, a lot," answers Tio through his teeth. "It's sublime," he adds, shooting me a glare. "As for love, I fear that there's
been a mistake. Alice doesn't consider me anything more than a
good friend. She's a Libra, after all, and like everyone in her sign, she
longs for an all-encompassing and perfect love."

"Oh, Alice has always been a perfectionist," says my mother rue-
fully, shaking her head. "She should learn to find happiness in little
things."

Tio raises an eyebrow at me with the cunning and cruel air of
someone unwilling to forgive. "Exactly. That's what *her boyfriend*
keeps telling her."

16

Just a Question of Horoscope

It's been days since I've received my horoscope. I keep checking the spam folder on my messages, but the reason they're not arriving is not because of a system error; it's because of a human error. Tio is mad at me. No, I'm mad at him. Paola called us a pair of idiots for dragging out this game of competitive silence.

Today, though, one of us has to give in. We're filming the show and we have to behave like serious professionals who can put aside their personal disagreements.

"Alice, we have a problem," says a colleague entering the production room while I'm checking the video recordings.

"What's wrong?"

"Marlin doesn't like the lineup."

"What do you mean she doesn't like it? Does she want it printed on scented paper?"

"Good one. No, *she* wants to do the interview with our skeptic guest, the astrogeologist."

I knew this moment would come, the moment I would have to cross the threshold of the dressing room and come face-to-face with

Tio, or at least with his face through the mirror. I'm sure he saw me, and that's why he's pretending to be immersed in his copy of *Book of the Zodiac*. In the other chair, Marlin takes the gesture as a personal affront and responds by picking up a bottle of makeup remover and squinting her eyes in an attempt to focus on the inscriptions in Japanese on the back.

"So?" I ask, looking from one to the other, without success.

The only one who turns toward me is Erika, the makeup artist, who shakes her head and shrugs her shoulders. Poor thing; I don't envy her having to cope with the two of them.

Marlin slams the bottle on the table like a Supreme Court justice. "I've fronted *Good Morning Milan*, *Vacations Together*, *Thursdays by the Fire* . . . and now? I show the guests in and then I have to sit on my ass the whole time? What am I, a hostess? If that's what you think, Alice, you're making a big mistake! I know how to interview a fucking *theologist*."

"Astrogeologist."

"Same thing."

Obviously, I can't leave Andrea Magni, the famous astrogeologist, in Marlin's lacquered clutches after it's taken a lifetime to convince him to come on the air.

Tio turns to Erika without lowering the newspaper. "Sweetie, could you tell our writer that she can't let a famous astrogeologist be interviewed by someone who thinks that continental crust is a type of pizza."

Marlin opens and closes her mouth, outraged. "You want to pay more attention to your own *crust*! You haven't heard the last of this," she mutters, calling Mr. President's private number and disappearing into the hallway to whine at the phone.

Erika turns toward me with a bewildered look.

I raise my hand. "Excuse me, Erika, could you tell Tio he should be more courteous to his colleagues?"

"Erika, forgive me," says Tio with an affected tone. "Could you please relay these exact words to our distinguished writer?" He looks at me through the mirror and growls: "Look who's talking!"

"Erika," I say, ignoring the poor girl's desperate look. "Could you remind Mr. Tiziano Falcetti that if he weren't the first to pass judgment on other people's private lives, none of this would have happened?"

He slams the book on the counter in front of the mirror. He detests being called by his real name. "And, Erika dear," he replies, pausing for effect, as if pulling back the string of a bow to take aim, "tell *her* that if she had never come to me crying about her and her boyfriend's miserable sex life, I would never have dared to speak my mind. If she doesn't like my advice, she should quit bothering me and just stand in front of the mirror and tell herself whatever she wants to hear."

Erika quickly shoves all the makeup scattered on the counter into her bag. "I'm done," she says, reaching the door.

"Erika!" My voice comes out so shrill that I don't recognize it.

I don't turn around, but I can still see her reflection as I stare right at Tio. "Please tell Marlin to come see me. We have to discuss what she's going to ask Andrea Magni in the interview."

I couldn't let Tio have the last word on this. Who does he think he is?

Too bad he'll never find out Alejandro's Ascendant—I'm sure he's as curious as a cat. For the record, it's Capricorn. I know, because I asked my mother-in-law on the telephone.

Tio is not indispensable. From now on, if I want something done, I'll do it myself. I downloaded a great app on my phone. For less than six euros per week (5.99 to be exact), I have real-time news and updates on my map of the skies. Let me see. As soon as I start it, I hear a tinny new age arpeggio and a few seconds after inserting the data, a message appears on the screen from my new trusted astrological service:

Character Traits of a Sagittarius with a Capricorn Ascendant.

The article is long and, I imagine, very detailed.

Cheerful peoples, athletic and full of energies, who love travels and independence.

In spite of the shaky grammar—you can't expect a database to write like Ernest Hemingway—it seems to me an apt definition. How wonderful.

Good hereditary health. Their parents might have a beneficial influence on their financial situation. Inherited lands or legacies.

This also makes me very happy. It's not that I want to pry into his financial affairs, but it would be fantastic to have an estate in Spain.

Endowed with fluctuating emotion, they are often instability, shady, lazy and create a double life. In worse cases, addicted to alcohols and drugs.

I don't understand how in a few lines he has transformed from Dr. Jekyll to Mr. Hyde. And then ... drugs? Oh god!

Serene and reassuring peoples.

Well, I'm definitely reassured now ...

Little probability of inheriting.

And now no estate in Spain, it appears. The Lord giveth and the Lord taketh away, in the blink of an eye. When I turn around, I am facing a man who looks like he really doesn't belong here.

"Allow me to introduce myself. Andrea Magni," he says, offering me his hand. "Miss Bassi, I presume?"

I restrain myself from curtsying. "Nice to meet you. Yes, you can call me Alice."

"My heartfelt thanks for your invitation to the program," he says, bowing his head and briefly breaking into a very British smile.

"Oh. Sure. You're welcome. Actually, we should be the ones thanking you . . . Um . . . Most sincerely, for agreeing to join us."

I point to one of the chairs, to have him complete a release form, but he pulls out my abandoned seat and motions for me to sit back down. "After you."

I watch him fill out the card with his information, and I'm astonished when he fills in his birthday, because the year is the same as mine.

"So, your show preaches the merits of astrology?" he asks.

I nod as a shiver runs down my back. I know all too well that speaking to a scientist about astrology is tantamount to waving a red flag at a bull. After all, he's a Taurus, judging from his birth date. And I've just given Marlin permission to interview him. God, this could be a disaster.

"Yes, you know how it is. Our program is geared toward a large segment of the public who are not experts on scientific matters," I say, by way of a justification.

"Of course," he replies. "Usually television doesn't bother teaching the common man about scientific issues. If it did, we would have more alert and aware minds, but instead there is always just a load of garbage."

"And this is the very reason we want to inform them. By speaking about horoscopes in a more serious way than usual."

"I'm afraid 'serious horoscopes' is an oxymoron. Though, I find nothing wrong with reading them purely as a form of entertainment.

Obviously, you and I are well aware that it's all a load of nonsense aimed at deceiving pitiful minds."

Uh ... Yes, well aware. "That's why I would like to only hint at your aversion to astrological theories and give more space to science, which as you've rightly pointed out, is grossly neglected," I conclude, holding my breath.

"Thank you. I would be delighted to be able to leave the public with the impression that not everything is as disingenuous as horoscopes and that some of it would be worth exploring further. I'm confident that people would be interested in carbon dioxide emissions released from the ISON comet or enthusiastic about the super-Earths discovered in the Tau Ceti system, just twelve million light-years away from us. As a science, astrogeology is pretty *stellar*, as young people say these days." He grins, pleased at his joke, and stands up, and I do the same to accompany him to makeup. Except, when we turn around ...

"Good morning," the astrogeologist says affably, stretching out his hand. "Andrea Magni, and you are?"

"Professor Tiziano Falcetti," replies Tio, tight-lipped. "The 'charlatan' running this dump."

"Doctor Magnet!" At the door of the dressing room Marlin emerges, sheathed in a latex jumpsuit that leaves nothing to the imagination.

"By Jove!" exclaims the astrogeologist, who perhaps under his earthly crust has a throbbing core of physical passions in addition to his astrophysical ones.

"Good evening, Dr. Magnet. I am Marlin and I will deal with you ... in the interview." She takes him by the hand, and he doesn't even bother to correct his name. "Come, come. While they make you beautiful, we can have a good talk about catatonic plates. Or do I mean tectonic plates? The ones in continents. They move. Did you know that?"

No, I don't need a psychic to foresee disaster.

Aware of the imminent defeat, all that's left is to do everything in my power to win back the only person who can save me. I am ready to make amends, to take a pledge, to "cross my heart and hope to die" that I will never contradict him for the rest of my days.

"Tio." I flash my best set of puppy dog eyes, but he turns around, raises a hand, shakes his head, and walks away.

I feel truly alone for the first time in months.

"All right, now I'm angry," begins Ferruccio, the lighting technician, wiping his brow. "I mean . . . where the hell is Mr. Heartthrob, your Spaniard?"

"He's not my Spaniard!" I obstinately insist, although I'm not fooling anyone. In a place like this, it's impossible to have a secret liaison. But Ferruccio is right; Alejandro is supposed to be on call with us tonight.

I'm happy because at least we'll get to see each other. Even though we didn't discuss it, I'm expecting to go home with him after the broadcast, which is why I took public transportation today. That way we can speak about us, about our future.

Racked with anxiety about work and my love life, I read the notes from my horoscope app.

Family difficulties, or strict father and Spartan education. Mentally ill mother.

Oh god, is that why I feel distant from him?

They tend to have their own definition of honesty. Possible feet problems and trouble with the law.

I frown. In fact, with all the dancing, it's no wonder that he would get sore feet. But trouble with the law? Does this have to do with the drugs from before?

Very respectful of ethics and moral.

I poke my head in the studio of *Mal d'Amore* to look for him. I need answers, because instead of settling my doubts, this horoscope is multiplying them.

Led to fall in love with a foreign person.

There it is. In black and white! I almost, almost forward the message to Tio, but think better of it.

"Excuse me!" I yell, getting the attention of the assistant for *Mal d'Amore*.

"Mara, isn't it?" I say, trying to be nice. "Do you know where I can find Alejandro?"

"That's the question we're all asking! What has become of Alejandro?"

Does she mean *all* of us, men and women, or just all the women? Because it really changes the meaning. She must be jealous. I've seen how she was looking at him.

I turn around for a second and see that she is staring at me with empty eyes. She opens her mouth, but then bites her lip, and goes back to the script that she was checking.

I take the opportunity to go to the bathroom.

Existence marked by trials of a chronic nature. Operations, stays in nursing home. Death from intestinal disease.

I am still staring at the words on the tiny phone screen, wondering why I ever thought *Ghost* was a good movie. Like hell do I want to be in Demi Moore's shoes. But I would feel like a real bitch if I even thought about leaving Alejandro because I was afraid of his health problems.

I rinse my hands quickly and go out, only to bump directly into him, my elusive Spaniard, who in fact is taking a step back and pushing the door of the men's bathroom to be sure that it is solidly closed.

"Everything OK?" I ask.

"Yes. I was just in the bathroom."

I look for a second at the closed door, then at him. He seems paler than usual. Is he hiding something?

Perhaps that's how it all begins. His bowel problems, I mean. "Can I do something?"

"No, Aliz. Don't worry."

I try to walk beside him, as we move toward the studio, but his legs are longer than mine and goes too fast.

I am not imagining things. There is something up and I must find out what it is.

When we reach the studio, it feels almost like I'm standing in front of a firing squad.

In the front row is Tio, who on this occasion has decided not to stay in the studio and is leaning against the door of the production room, his eyes burning holes in my back. Then there's Mr. President. He's here for Marlin, of course, not for me, but he will be the first to eat me alive if his protégée makes a slip that tarnishes her image, or that of the program or of the whole network. And then there's Davide, leaning against the plasterboard wall, hands behind his back, lips pressed into a hard line.

I feel like there's something wrong, something bothering him, although he is perfectly controlled, as always. A distance has grown between us over the last month or so, but it's not about that, not tonight. He looks right through me without really seeing me. He is not focused; he's not here right now.

I look for Alejandro, hoping to at least find backup in him for this trial that I am about to face. He's in the production room, but he turns his back to me and speaks quietly to Raffaella. She brushes aside her hair, stroking her neck.

The announcement crackles through the intercom that there are thirty seconds until we go live. I grab the microphone, press the button that allows me to speak to the studio, and tell everyone to take their places.

The green eyes of our star pierce the screen, and she smiles, winking at the camera, taking her time to walk toward the stool, swaying her hips.

At the very least, the introduction is impeccable. Miraculously, she pronounces his name correctly and even his profession, perhaps aided in both cases by the astrogeology book in her hand.

The trouble, however, begins immediately after the first question. "Why study the composition of the planets?"

A very simple question, in short, for those who are satisfied with a no-frills response. But Magni has more extensive educational objectives, and I see Marlin falter under the barrage of big words like *geomorphology, petrography, magnetosphere, hydrocarbons, magnetic fields, orbital parameters . . .*

For a second, I think the poor thing is going to faint. But then, she suddenly seems to rouse at the word *universe*, which has made it even into her meager vocabulary—although more frequently in association with the word *Miss*. She bats her eyes, telling him that she always feels overwhelmed by the immensity of the heavens, which she finds so romantic precisely because it is infinite and unfathomable.

Yes, she actually says *unfathomable*. I am shocked, but Magni doesn't let himself be impressed by Marlin's lexical prowess.

"My dear, the Hubble variable, which is none other than v equals H times d, tells us the veloc onity of displacement of one galaxy compared to the others, where v is the velocity of distancing in the direction of our line of sight, d expresses the distance of the galaxy from Earth, and H is a proportional constant whose value, alas, is still rather uncertain but should fluctuate somewhere around sixty-five kilometers per second for every megaparsec of distance. At this point, I think it is clear to everyone, that the constant gives us the rate of expansion of the universe, which therefore, in a certain sense, is perfectly measurable."

"Poor Marlin," comments Raffaella. "Hung out to dry. Why did we do such a thing to her?" She shakes her head and shoots Mr. President a clandestine look. "I would never have allowed it," she comments, while her gaze flickers for a nanosecond just on me.

I return to staring at the control monitor, where Magni and Marlin are on full display.

"... as the physics of the degenerate matter imposes a mass limit on the white dwarf, called a Chandrasekhar Limit. In the most common type, carbon-oxygen, exceeding that limit, usually because of the transfer of mass to a binary system, can cause the explosion of a nova or supernova."

Marlin brushes a strand of hair from her cleavage. "Poor thing, though, a dwarf and yet obese!"

I cover my eyes with my hands, not that it will do me any good.

"Cut to commercials," I hear behind me. "Something long, if possible."

Davide has broken away from the wall and, standing next to my chair, leafs through the lineup with a wrinkled brow. "Bring the news forward," he says, pointing his index finger on the paper.

"But that's two segments ahead. We still have a half hour," I fumble, lifting my gaze to his.

"We need time to get organized," he says, staring at me with those eyes, dark as chocolate, that suddenly flash, because now he is smiling. At me. "We can do it, Alice. You and I, together."

I blink; my blood is rushing up and down through my body with reckless abandon.

"And Tio," Davide adds, turning to Tio, still leaning against the door with his arms folded. "Come on."

While I speak through the headphones to the studio assistant, telling him to cut to commercials, the other two disappear into the adjacent editing room. From the glass wall, I can see Davide sit down at the computer and Tio tell him something as he takes his place at his side.

I don't know what they have in mind, but I don't have time to think about it, because I am bombarded with insults from our own red dwarf, who clicks into the production room on her eight-inch stilts.

"Someone want to tell us what the hell is going on? The countdown read that there were still seven minutes! Why did you go to commercials?"

"My dear, everything was going incredibly well. And, let me tell you, tonight you look like a million bucks," intervenes the president. "Come with me, Doctor Magni, I'll get you a coffee."

"Alice . . ."

Davide. He's so close to me that I have to raise my chin to look him in the eye. Hasn't he noticed he's invading my personal space? I can't say that it bothers me though. He smells nice, and the heat emanating from his chest has a reassuring effect.

"What's up?" I stammer.

He doesn't say anything. He keeps looking at me with that magnetic smile of his, and then takes a pair of headphones from the dashboard of the production room and puts them on me.

Suddenly, I hear notes in my head. It's that song, "Reality," from the movie *The Party*.

In the chaos of an absurd evening, I can't believe that I feel like

I'm at a thirteen-year-old's birthday. I meet Davide's gaze and wait for him to wrap his arms around my waist to dance, but he doesn't. Instead, he takes a step back and brings a transmitter to his lips.

"Do you hear me? Testing, testing. Check . . . one, two . . . Alice, do you hear me?"

I hear him perfectly.

There is no music except in my imagination, and the reason why Davide threw those headphones on me has nothing to do with Sophie Marceau and her first kiss.

I nod, but he doesn't pay attention to me and slips back into the editing room. He waves at me through the window.

"Can you still hear me now, honey?"

I move a couple steps closer to the window. Then I see that the headphones also have a microphone with two buttons. I press one, and Davide winces, removing his headphones. The receiver produced a whistle that was probably much louder for him than for me.

"Sorry," I say. "Do you hear me?"

"Yes, Alice. Now, listen. Here's the idea. We are going to create a bridge. We'll give Marlin a wireless earpiece, hidden behind her ear, on the frequency of your intercom, so that you can tell her what to say to interview Magni without screwing up."

"But I'm not an astrogeologist!"

He raises his hand to silence me. "You will repeat what I tell you."

"Why don't you just speak to her directly?"

"I'll need time to do some Internet research. I'm not an expert in astrogeology either, Alice. You'll have to pay attention in case he changes the subject suddenly, and I'm too busy reading to realize."

"One minute to go. People in the studio!" cries Ferruccio.

With difficulty, I break Davide's intense gaze to nod toward the director. "I'm ready."

"Are you sure?" Davide's voice spills thick and warm directly into my ear.

I turn around again to look at him.

"You have to be my woman . . . behind the woman. Are you ready, Alice?" He raises his hand and presses it against the glass, as if he wants to touch me.

Looking at him is like an earthquake in perfect stillness. I am tongue-tied, and I end up standing there like a deer in the headlights, while in my head the notes of Richard Sanderson's "Reality" magically begin to play again.

"Ten seconds, Alice!"

My fingertips slide onto the glass just as Davide removes his hand and turns to sit at the computer.

"Welcome back to the studio," says a beaming Marlin.

I press the button of the headset that allows me to talk to her. "We apologize for the technical problems."

"We apologize for the technical problems," she repeats, adding her flirtatious smile to then continue according to my instructions: "But for those who are still with us, we will be continuing our fascinating interview with Dr. Andrea Magni."

"The famous astrogeologist," I suggest in the headset.

"Who, on closer inspection, should also be famous for his *physical* attributes, not just because he's so *astrophysical*," she adds, before asking him the question I've suggested.

In my headphones, I hear a beep and then Davide's voice: "Did you tell her to say that? Do you like this guy?"

"Of course not!" I say.

"Of course not!" repeats Marlin, smiling at Magni.

I hasten to cut off communication with her while Magni raises an eyebrow.

"Klutz," whispers Davide, with a smile in his voice.

"You're the one distracting me," I say pouting, this time thank heavens pressing the right button.

When Magni expresses his doubt as a scientist on the actual effectiveness of astrology, Tio, who kindly has agreed to return to the studio, is prompted by Marlin—that is by Davide, and then me, and hence by Marlin—to counter with his point of view.

"Thank God," I say to Davide in the headphones. "We can kill two birds with one stone."

"Let me guess who you would kill first," he replies.

Now he's even joking with me. He seems strangely elated, as if he really likes this game, his prior apathy almost completely forgotten.

"You, Mr. Nardi, are not being honest," I tease. "Tell the truth, you're having fun doing *The Truman Show*."

"Oh, Alice, it's you who's fun, not *The Truman Show*."

Meanwhile, Magni says that astrology did indeed precede astronomy, but only because it was created in very dark times for science.

"Well done," Davide says into the headphones. "Brava. See, we're a great team!"

I blush. Fortunately, I have my back to him, so he can't see me.

"I've always wondered," Magni taunts, "why, in order to determine the zodiac sign, and hence the character of a person, astrologists take into account the moment at which you are born and not the moment of conception. After all, that is the origin of life. Do the stars have no influence on the fetus? Is it shielded by the mother's shell?"

While Tio responds that it is the separation from the mother that creates individuality, I again hear the beep in the headset and prepare to take mental notes about what Davide will suggest for Marlin.

"Because for many people it would be difficult to determine

the exact moment of conception, don't you think? Astrologers are clever," says Davide, in a more hesitant voice, as if he were testing the waters, given that a little while ago I hadn't answered him.

I press the button to talk and argue. "Whose side are you on? Do I really have to tell her that?"

"Hell no! I was saying that to you. These horoscopes are all nonsense, right?"

"Nonsense or not, I find a certain correspondence between the characteristics of a sign and the characteristics of a person. Then, of course, we have different experiences. What sign are you? Let's see!"

Except that I pressed the wrong button again and Marlin repeats the same thing.

"Oh god!"

"Um, I would be a Taurus," says Andrea Magni in the studio.

"You did it again, didn't you?" Davide chuckles into my earpiece. "You pressed the wrong button! Oh, Alice, you really are . . . the most fun that I've had in this place. You are special."

Another beep and his voice again. "But don't say that to Marlin, please."

When I take off the headphones during the closing theme song, my ears are buzzing.

"Well done, well done everyone," says the president, walking over to Davide. His eyes also seem tired, but he doesn't draw back when the president puts a hand on his shoulder and takes him away to talk.

It is destiny that a mystery remains between this man and me, I tell myself.

Then there's Alejandro. I mean, we have our problems, but we are a nice couple.

Tio is smoking a cigarette with Andrea Magni, and I hear them laughing amiably. They make a strange couple.

Ferruccio is fumbling with lamps and cables, and Alejandro has removed his shirt to reveal his chest glistening with sweat. The fifteen feet that more or less separate us seem to stretch out like in those nightmares where you can never reach your goal.

"Shall we go home together?" I say to Alejandro.

His shoulders sag. After a few seconds, he tells me, "*No puedo, Aliz. Lo siento. Otra ocasión*, eh?"

"Is something wrong?" I hate my squeaky supplication, the pitch of my voice rising, like a naughty child or a fly banging against the glass to get out.

When he looks at me, Alejandro has a blank expression that I can only bounce against, without getting answers. "*Bueno*, Aliz. Let's say I call you."

His answer stuns me into silence. I head to the bathroom and rinse my face with cold water. When I look in the mirror, I have some kind of déjà vu.

Mara, the assistant from *Mal d'Amore*, her eyes, her hard and empty expression. Her disappointment.

That's the question we're all asking! What has become of Alejandro?

My phone is on the sink, and the still lit screen shows a glimpse of the last sentence that I read on the profile of his sign.

Strong sexuality. Psychological blocks in the sexual sphere. Multiple flirtations and lack of sincere attachment. Poor sexual interest.

Somehow, I make my way outside.

"Are you OK?" asks Davide, just behind me.

"I'm OK," I repeat on autopilot, as if I were addressing the question to myself.

"Don't worry about the show; everything went well. The president was very pleased. And even Marlin's screwups . . . Well, it all gets viewers."

The show, the share, Marlin, Tio, who's gone without even say-ing goodbye, Alejandro who no longer has reason to. I feel empty.

"Want to talk about it?" he asks softly, hesitant. I look him in the eye and manage a shy smile.

"You always ask about everyone else, but you never talk about yourself," I reply, and it almost seems like an accusation.

"As you can see, I'm not very interesting. There is nothing re-markable about my life, except for a large dog, a rented house, and constant moving."

"How did you end up with such a big dog?"

Davide thinks for a moment, as if he can't decide what to tell me. "It happened . . . on a job."

"That's it?"

"What?"

"That's all you can tell me? I'd like you to tell me more about it."

He raises his arm to look at his watch. "It's past midnight, Alice. Perhaps another time OK? I'll walk you to your car."

"Don't worry about it. I don't have my car tonight. I'll call a taxi."

"Why don't you have your car?"

"It's past midnight, Davide. Maybe I'll explain another time."

"I'll take you home then."

"Why?" I growl with eyes filled with tears. I don't know who I'm angrier at, Davide and the wall he keeps putting up, or Alejandro and the door he has just closed. In any case, I hate architectural barriers.

Davide, however, hasn't stopped looking me up and down. "Be-cause one should never leave a woman in trouble," he finally says.

"I'm in trouble? I don't think so." I pull out my wallet and show him that I have more than seventy euros in cash. "I have enough for a taxi and probably enough to go back and forth three or four times between my house and here."

He raises his hands. "I'd like to take you home, Alice. I would like to do it to thank you for tonight."

When I don't answer, he adds, "I would like to talk to you."

By the time Davide's car stops outside my house, I've learned that Flash belonged to his last employer. When the man died, his wife didn't want to keep the dog.

"Rather than have Flash put down, I wanted to take him with me. What can I say, I was fond of him," he explains, turning off the engine.

"What a horrible person."

"You're wrong. She's not cruel. It's just that Flash always scared her."

I still don't find it right that one can kill an animal so indiscriminately, but I stay quiet and am happy that Flash has found another master. "I'm pleased that it's a story with a happy ending."

"You love that. Stories with happy endings, I mean. Your romantic movies."

I shrug. "Life is something else, though. A happy ending is never guaranteed."

Davide takes my hand and his fingers tighten around mine. "No. The happy ending is never guaranteed."

"Love is always much more complicated than in the movies. In the movies, it's usually clear from the beginning who the protagonist is going to end up with. There are no doubts, just some misunderstandings."

"And there are no betrayals." Davide sighs, returning to stare at the wheel. "Have you ever cheated, Alice?"

The question comes sharp as an arrow. I ask myself if perhaps he's trying to gauge my moral integrity. "No, never."

He nods, and for a couple of seconds all we do is look at each other, the light of the streetlamp drawing the outlines of our faces against the darkness.

There is a world of questions, of invisible words, that makes the space between us so dense that we cannot cross it. His body eases toward me, like an astronaut in space, until his face is so close to me it seems almost unreal.

"Good night, Alice," he whispers, before planting a kiss on my cheek.

17

No Country for Old Libras

$\mathcal{B}$eing dumped is certainly not the end of the world. This is hardly my first time, and I've survived it before. On closer examination, this insignificant fling with Alejandro doesn't even merit consideration.

All too often, those who have been dumped have the tendency to hide, lower our eyes, deem ourselves unworthy of a kind word from anyone. But who said that we are plague-stricken people with no dignity? It's those horrible heartbreakers, the love tourists, the sentimental discount professionals, who should be ashamed.

So instead, this time, I have decided to be a phoenix and rise, reborn from my ashes. You just wait and see.

When I walk through the door of Mi-A-Mi Network, teetering like a tightrope walker on my high heels, I do it in the most conspicuous way possible, waving and kissing everyone I meet, with a radiant smile.

However, when I arrive at my desk, I think I literally turn white as a ghost. This time there is not just one yellow rose, but an entire luxuriant bouquet.

"Who sent these?" I shout, grabbing the card.

Just one sentence again: *I miss you.* And no signature.

Oh no. This time I'm going to say no to the rose maniac and yes to an Alice who is not won over by easy compliments. I take the entire bouquet and dump it in the trash.

Now I feel good. I am a new woman, free and lighthearted.

"Oh," says Enrico approaching me. "Hi, Alice. Davide came by looking for you earlier."

Forgetting about the thorns, I stick my hands in the trash to retrieve the bouquet of roses and lay them carefully on my desk, only to stare at them, puzzled.

Well, it's useless to keep denying it. I like the man. A lot.

Outside his office, I quickly catch my breath.

"Hi, Davide. Enrico told me that you wanted to see me."

He gets up from the desk. "Alice," he says, his eyes dancing close to a smile. "Hi . . . You look good."

"Thank you. And thank you for . . . well, for everything. For calling me, for bringing me home the other day. For caring. And, for telling me . . . Anyway, I hope that Flash is OK." *Oh my god, Alice, stop this verbal diarrhea immediately!*

After all that, he just mutters, "Yes."

Couldn't he make just a little more of an effort? I mean, I know I am awkward, but he's not so perfect himself.

I gather the courage to break the tension. Davide seems so indecisive—anxious, really—so I ask, "Is this about the audience for our show?"

"Yes . . . I mean, no. The ratings were pretty good. I would say that our experiment was a home run."

"Really?" *Our* experiment . . . We look at each other and I notice his expression change slowly. His smile fades, and his eyes cloud over with a distance that I would like to fill by taking a few steps forward. But it's as if both of us are frozen.

"Anything else?" I manage to ask him, my hand pausing for a second on the doorknob.

Please, Davide, speak. Tell me something. Stop me.

He sighs and bites his lip as he moves around the desk to be closer to me.

"There is something else I wanted to talk to you about."

When he takes my hand, his is cold; his pulse is racing, and mine soon catches up.

"Yes," I whisper. I could lose myself in his eyes.

"Alice . . . I owe you an apology."

The violins stop playing; the birds stop chirping and instead get tangled in my hair. All of a sudden, I've lost the fairy-tale feeling and I don't understand what's happening. Or why he feels the need to apologize.

"Is this about work?" I ask, terrified that he's about to tell me that I've just earned an indefinite holiday.

He shakes his head. I step back slowly, finding my back against the door, my hand in his and my heart threatening to burst through my ears.

"I wanted to . . . I have to ask your forgiveness for my behavior. I need to tell you something. I mean, I think that I've behaved badly toward you . . . You are a beautiful woman, you're kind and intelligent. Who wouldn't be attracted to you?"

What the hell are you talking about, Davide? I think, but in reality, I'm not capable of moving more than an eyelid.

"The other night when I drove you home, there was a moment . . . I almost lost control. That wouldn't be fair; you didn't want that. You were in pieces. And I . . . well . . . I wanted to apologize in case I gave you, you know, the wrong impression. We work together and there are other reasons . . . So, I'm sorry. So sorry."

When I close the door behind me, there is just a faint click, but to me it sounds like an eight-story building just exploded.

I head toward the stairs.

Just then, Cristina comes out of her office. "Excuse me," she says, rubbing her prominent belly. "Have you spoken with Carlo recently?"

"No," I reply, half turning around. I have as much desire to speak with her as I do to take a hammer to my finger.

"Oh . . . I thought you two told each other everything."

That used to be true, but Cristina and the baby have changed everything. I wonder why. After all, it's not Carlo's fault if he has rebuilt his life before I have. I'm really just envious because he has something that I don't.

When I return to my desk, the yellow roses are still there, only the buds are a little floppier than before, echoing my mood.

"You're becoming very popular," Tio says as he approaches. "What are you sulking about?"

"Sure, *Cosmopolitan* wants to interview me as one of the ten most abandoned women on the planet," I say to Tio, trying to smile.

"If you're referring to the cowboy in the tight shirt, you should consider yourself lucky. He wasn't the guy for you. When will you listen to me?"

"And where *is* the guy for me, Tio? Where is it written that he actually exists?" I sit down and slam my head on the desk a couple of times, before letting out a deep sigh. I don't want to tell him about Davide. It seems too complicated to explain, and above all I don't want to hear him tell me, yet again, that I've got the wrong person, that he's not the man for me.

"Hey," says Tio, patting me on the shoulder. "It's true, you are a little unlucky in love, but . . ."

"A little?" I ask with a groan, lifting my head slightly, before crashing back onto the desk. "A little is like saying that the atomic bomb had a *few* victims."

Tio, however, is not discouraged by my complaints. "But the last word still hasn't been spoken. So far, we haven't really taken this seriously. What happens when the going gets tough?"

"Let me guess ... You choose something simpler?"

"Wrong! The tough get going."

18

Some Like It Taurus

Standing in front of my desk, Tio keeps staring at me suspiciously, then he reaches into his shoulder bag and pulls out a scroll that he unravels in front of me, and I have the impression that we are preparing to do battle.

"And what the hell is this?" I ask him, staring at the convoluted patterns, lines, and symbols in different colors.

"This, my dear," he says with all the emphasis of an actor playing the role of Merlin, "is your natal chart."

"My what?"

"Remember when you gave me your date, time, and place of birth, and all of that? Well, I've drawn your astrological chart." At the sight of my puzzled, blinking eyes, he sighs. "Jeez, this is a reproduction of your birth chart; how the stars aligned at the precise day and hour you took your first breath."

"Wow," I murmur.

"The three key elements to understanding a natal chart are houses, signs, and planets. There are twelve houses in astrology, each one representing an area of life: money, love, communication, creativity, health, death, friends . . . Don't sniff at this, go with me."

"It's complicated," I reply, scratching my temple.

"And life isn't?"

I snort and go back to staring at the map.

He continues: "From here, we start to see which houses the planets are positioned in at the moment of birth. When a house contains more than one planet, for example, it is emphasized. And if the planet is located in the sign that governs it, its influence is even stronger."

"Um, let's see," I say, trying to focus. "Which is my house of love?"

"Love is in the seventh house. It's called the House of Marriage and Partnership," he tells me, tapping his finger on the chart.

I stare at the paper. Then at him. Then at the paper again. And back at him. "Are you kidding?"

"Why?"

"It's empty," I reply, crossing my arms over my chest. "What happened to the planets? Why is there not even one inside there?"

Tio shrugs. "Well, it can happen. It's not extremely"—he gives me a half smile—"serious."

"Of course, it's not 'extremely' serious. My house of love is as empty as a black hole in outer space, but that's just fine. Nothing to worry about!" I raise my hands, exasperated.

"Calm down, really, it's not a terrible thing. Not having planets in your House of Marriage doesn't mean that you'll never have love. You have a lot in your career house. And you have Venus near your Ascendant. It means that you are a fascinating person and even diplomatic, with an aptitude for the arts. It could mean a bit of confusion and even disappointment in terms of love, but we have to be optimistic."

I whine. I knew there was something fundamentally wrong with my love life, and now it turns out I have confused planets and my astrological chart looks like it was painted by Picasso.

Tio puts his arm around my shoulders to console me. "We should never be discouraged. You are a beautiful, kind, and intelligent woman. There is absolutely no reason why you shouldn't find someone. Except that, like I said, you always choose the wrong men—perhaps because they are charming and mysterious, which is only natural, given your astrological chart. Consider someone else, someone who seems the opposite, perhaps."

I sigh and sink into his arms.

He gives me a kiss on the forehead, whispering in my ear, "You really are stubborn, who knows when you'll catch on."

"Sorry to interrupt you," says a voice behind him.

As Tio quickly moves away, I see Andrea Magni at my desk.

"Good morning," I greet him, aware that my tone is questioning. "Did you need something, Mr. Magni? Is there anything I can help you with?"

"Oh, I was passing by and I wanted to say hello and thank you again for your kindness."

"Would you like a coffee?" Tio asks him.

"Well, by Jove, how can I refuse?"

"Come this way, Mr. Magni," I say, starting for the door.

"Oh, you can call me Andrea. Alice, isn't it? Please." He holds the door open to let me pass. "Ladies first."

There's no denying it. He's a real gentleman, an old-fashioned guy.

He's even friendly with Tio, despite their diametrically opposed opinions. He insists on paying for the coffee and asks us some questions about the program.

"I was able to review the recording," says Andrea. "Our discussion was heated but never descended into banal vulgarity. Even your point of view, Tiziano, was well argued, in spite of every-thing."

Yikes! I don't like that "in spite of everything" at all. I look at Tio, expecting one of his digs, but he simply says: "Thank you, you are very kind." He leans against the coffee machine and smiles. "You are very telegenic; has anyone ever told you that?" Then he gives a little cough and looks at me. "Isn't that right, Alice? Weren't we just saying that this morning? That Andrea looked very good on tape . . . and the ratings were out of this world. We should have him back, don't you think?"

Oh god, we said nothing of the kind, but it doesn't cost me any-thing to humor him. "Of course."

"Your offer is very flattering, Tiziano. As is your compliment."

"Well, we could think of some interesting little entr'acte like changing roles, um . . . an analysis of your zodiac sign and astrologi-cal chart. You're a Taurus, aren't you?" He keeps looking at me. "The Taurus has a rather peaceful way of life. He is selfless, calm, and generally very . . . faithful."

"Oh!" I shift my gaze from Tio to Magni and then from Magni to Tio. And I understand. Tio is suggesting that I consider someone like Andrea, a quiet type, a creature of habit, someone who is not impulsive. I sigh and look at him. Well, he is a handsome man. Why not try to get to know him?

"That sounds great. It would be worth discussing." I look at the clock. "Unfortunately, I have to get back to work on some other things right now." I take a deep breath. It's not like me, I know, but I say: "Perhaps we could discuss it over dinner?"

Tio's head spins abruptly toward me. "At . . . dinner?"

I don't pay any attention to him and look at Andrea.

"Oh, well, of course. I'd be delighted. Will you be joining us, Tiziano?"

I snap my fingers. "Tio unfortunately has a commitment tonight, but given that this concerns Wednesday's broadcast, it's rather urgent that the two of us meet to discuss it," I say biting my lip soon after.

"Well, in that case . . . it seems appropriate to . . ."

"Alice, you should really think about this," whispers Tio, looking at me with wide eyes.

Now what does he want? He's the one that suggested I consider people who I wouldn't normally go for. I can try, right?

. . .

"Alice, listen, don't you think that I should come with you?" This will be the seventh call that I've received from Tio in less than two hours. "I could say that I skipped my appointment; it doesn't matter."

"I don't see why you have to do that. I know you're worried that I'll be disappointed again, but I assure you, no irreversible damage will be done. It will just be an evening for us to get to know each other better. After all, you're the one who suggested it. You said that I always choose men who are too dark and complicated. Andrea seems the total opposite. He's definitely not the type of man I would be interested in."

"Exactly! Let it be!" he yells, directly into my eardrum.

"But did you see his astrological chart? Of course you saw it; you did it this afternoon." And I've practically memorized it. "Do I have to remind you about . . . what was it? The Moon-Uranus Tropic?"

"The Trine."

"The Moon-Uranus Trine that says that we possibly have a strong compatibility on the physical front. But that's not all. How about the Mars-Jupiter Sextile? I took note of it. Although we don't have the same interests, we complement each other and understand each other very well."

"Alice, listen to me, really. There are other factors to consider, apart from astrology."

"Help me understand," I say, growing angry. "You've been complaining for months that I should trust astrology and now, when in black and white there's a man who is potentially perfect for me, you say that's not the only thing to consider?" I growl into the receiver, then spot Andrea next to the front door, stiff as a rake. I arm myself with a reassuring smile as I end the conversation with Tio, saying, "We will keep you updated on any developments. Don't worry. Have a nice evening."

On the elevator ride up to the bar, I risk a neck strain to look at him. He's not bad at all.

Once again, he compliments the show, saying that he had fun and how nice Tio is. He asks me if I've known him for a long time. I tell him that our relationship only began a couple of months ago.

"Oh, um . . . relationship. You're dating," he says.

"Oh, no, no, no, no! I mean our relationship as friends. There is no *relationship* in that sense."

Rather direct, Mr. Astro-playboy. There is certainly the Tropic of Taurus at play here, that Moon-Uranus Trine that attracts us.

The bar is quite full, but thanks to his periscopic height, Andrea spots a free table on the terrace. Romantic!

"The temperature is around seventy degrees tonight, so you should not therefore undergo any thermal variation that would lead you to experience the symptoms of a cold," he says, pulling out my chair gallantly.

"It's too bad that there is so much light in the city that you can't see the stars." I sigh, sitting down. I stare into his eyes and force myself to imagine what a life together might be like, with him and me.

"Technically, the reason why we can't see the stars is not the presence of light sources, but Earth's atmosphere."

I say goodbye to my fantasy and nod repeatedly until Stephen Hawking here concludes his romantic explanation of the heavens. Then I sigh and bury my head in the menu.

"The buffet is excellent here, you know. There's practically everything, from appetizers to desserts."

We order; me, the usual spritz and him, a citron juice.

He has Chiron in Taurus, and this makes him respectful of his physique and very attentive to his diet, and you can tell, but really, a man of almost forty drinking citrus juice with a straw? Perhaps a drop of booze might encourage the conversation a bit, I am tempted to say after a quarter of an hour spent trying to follow his speeches, but perhaps because I lack the necessary scientific foundations, or because the only foundation I have now is alcohol, my eyes start to close and I'm on the verge of yawning.

"Can you excuse me for a second?" I get up and reach the bathroom. "Hello? Tio, damn it!" I scream.

"Calm down, what's happening?" he answers lazily from the other end of the phone.

"Tell me it's a joke! I can't be destined for a man who has the sense of humor of a computer. I want heat, passion, and loving glances."

"Calm down. I've got your back."

"But how?"

"Leave it to me. And—"

It's no good, I can't stand it. "Please, don't say, 'I told you so.' I hate it when you do that."

"And I hate that I told you so, honey."

"Mmm . . . I love you."

"Me, too."

I end the conversation and rinse my neck and wrists with a little cold water to wake myself up. OK, enough alcohol for tonight; I need all my energy to prevent my head from falling onto my plate.

I return to the dining room and head for the terrace, but when I reach the French doors, I stop, unable to believe my eyes. Andrea is still there at the table, laughing and chatting animatedly with someone. Then Tio turns to me and waves.

19

Libra in Pink

There are days when you think you're kaput, finished, nothing more than an old wreck to be thrown away. You wish that a potato sack would become the height of fashion, and you nostalgically yearn for a time when families arranged marriages and that was the end of it. Even with the worst luck, you would be taken in by a convent.

Then there are days like today.

This is my favorite day of the month, which Paola and I have named our Sacred Day.

Today is the day we go to have our nails done by Karin.

The Sacred Day is a day for women, by women, with women. It is dedicated to beauty, relaxation, shopping, chatting. It's a break, without men, that allows us to speak freely about our problems and about things that really do matter to us.

"So?" Karin asks me, putting the last touches to my pinky.

"So, he was *so* boring that I could hardly keep my eyes open," I say, putting my hand under the heat lamp. "Good thing Tio came and sacrificed himself for the cause. He spoke to Andrea about the show for the rest of the evening. He's a darling."

"Enough already, Alice, OK?" my manicurist friend reproaches me. "You find all the weirdos out there! I remember when you told me about that idiot . . ."

"Alejandro?"

"No, the other one."

"Luca?"

"Luca? That's new. Who is he?"

"Not relevant . . . let's move on. Do you mean Carlo?"

"Come on, that's ancient history! I mean the one you were dating last year."

"Oh, you mean Giorgio!"

"For the love of God," exclaims Paola from the sofa.

She never approved of Giorgio. She found him too melodramatic, too over-the-top to be truthful, which, in fact, turned out to be the case.

"May I remind you that he had major memory problems, especially when he should have remembered that he was dating you and couldn't just take his pants off and hop into bed with anyone he wanted." Paola puts down the newspaper and sighs. "Alice, enough with the problematic, the indecisive, the forty-year-old children, the bloodsuckers, and the manipulators."

I pull a face. "OK, OK! The post-Carlo phase has been a bit stormy, but hell, I'm getting over a difficult relationship."

"Alice, it's been more than two years of 'getting over it.' Not even a magnitude eight earthquake takes that long to get over."

"And this Tio?" asks Karin. "He must really like you." Paola shakes her head and stifles a laugh.

I huff and return to fixing my nails, hoping that the pink color and, most of all, the glitter will help improve my mood for the days ahead.

"It's easy for you to talk, Paola, now that you've found Giacomo. But it's not that simple. Take Andrea. Perfect astrological chart, zodiac sign, ascendant, planetary arrangement, and compatibility, and . . . ? Nothing. We didn't click. Not even the slightest interest."

"Doesn't surprise me!" she says.

"You don't think I'm smart enough for an astrogeologist?"

"I think you're the one who would never be interested in a guy like him," she explains, turning yet another page to discover that bangs will be in again in the fall. "Sparks don't always fly just because everything is perfect."

"Do you want me to set you up with one of my boyfriend Federico's friends?" Karin interrupts my sad musings. "He just told me about an interesting guy that goes to his bar. If I'm not mistaken, he's some kind of artist, very cool guy. If you want . . ."

"What sign is he?" I ask, and she takes out her phone.

"Alice, stop!" Paola scolds. "This is not how you'll find the man of your dreams."

"So how will I find the man of my dreams, Paola? Where will I find him, in a cereal box?"

She closes the newspaper and looks at me. "And Davide? What happened to him?"

"I think that we can add him to the long, long list of: 'Men who have rejected Alice.'"

"Why don't you start a list of 'Men rejected by Alice'? I think that sounds a little better. And now would be a good time to start it."

I know she's right, but I can't shake the feeling of rejection that I get every time something goes wrong with a guy.

"Davide?" says Karin, ending her telephone call. "I want to know everything. Who is he? What does he do? What sign is he?"

Paola sets down the newspaper. "Yes . . . What sign *is* he?"

I admit defeat, shaking my head. "I haven't the slightest idea."

"Age?"

"No clue."

Paola chuckles. "Damn . . . We can't play with Chinese horoscopes as well!"

20

Love in the Time of Aquarius

I'm really proud of myself.

Today, instead of succumbing to a tedious solitary Sunday, surviving on leftovers and falling asleep in front of the TV, I made a decision and did something I've never done before.

I went to the movies. Alone.

Why should the movie theater be exclusively for couples and families? I am passionate about movies; I should feel free to go whenever I want and not miss movies that appeal to me just because I have no one to go with me.

Of course, I called Tio first, but he was already busy.

And Paola, but she was at lunch with her mother-in-law, and in a certain sense I didn't envy her.

Then my parents surprised me by not even being in Milan.

Happy to have gotten away with it this time, I decide to reward myself with shopping. Just as I'm skipping from window to window, I find myself in front of a scene that would almost be too absurd for a movie.

I stop dead in my tracks in front of a café, undecided whether to go in or not, because I have no idea what I'll do with myself if I do venture inside. Sitting there, alone at a table, is Carlo, and he is clearly crying.

I don't know what to do. As close as we'd been all these years, recently there has definitely been a barrier between us. I would like to put an end to it now, but unfortunately, I've never had a knack for these things. Instead, what really is part of my DNA, is the Red Cross syndrome, which is an epidemic among women of my generation.

Carlo is a few inches away from me, playing with his cup, staring at it intensely, as if it could predict his future. His tears have dried, but his eyes are still red. It's as if he's in a bubble, a world of his own; I'm scared to burst it.

Suddenly, he raises his head, as if he senses something, but he doesn't turn toward me. His gaze shoots toward the bathroom door, which was just opened by a girl in light colors: her T-shirt, pants, and eyes all have the faded blue color of forget-me-nots.

I'm about to step forward, but she precedes me, sitting opposite Carlo and taking his hand. Then the girl stands up and Carlo follows. She tries to pass him but he catches his arm around her waist. If there were fog, it could be the end of *Casablanca*. They look into each other's eyes, and nothing else exists before Carlo closes the distance between them with a soft and desperate kiss that makes my knees melt.

Just a minute!

That can't be Carlo, also known as Carlo my ex-boyfriend-who-in-the-blink-of-an-eye-has-impregnated-someone-else-and-announced-their-wedding-on-Facebook? No, in this precise moment he by no means seems like a father-to-be, and above all, the woman he is kissing is not pregnant.

The lovers release their embrace, and the girl looks intensely at Carlo before turning her back and leaving, brushing right past me.

Why, oh why have I gotten myself into this mess?

But Carlo doesn't say anything and turns his back to me, returning to sit behind the now empty coffee cup.

"Um ... Hi ..."

He doesn't even look up as I move in front of him, but I notice an almost imperceptible shake in his shoulder. I sit down.

"What are you doing here?" he asks me in such a low voice that it takes me a few seconds to understand the question.

"I ... I saw you ... I mean, I was outside ... You were alone and I came in to say hello."

"Well, hi," he says drily, without even looking up.

"Do you want to tell me what's going on?"

"Why should I? You will never stop meddling in my business, will you? And anyhow, don't you have eyes? Tell me what it looked like to you!" He looks up to gaze fiercely at me.

"I assure you that it wasn't my intention to spy on you. It was just a coincidence that I was passing by here; I was at the movies ..."

Carlo narrows his eyes even more, squinting at a point behind me. "So, there's someone else, too? Paola?"

And I'm the one who meddles in other people's business!

"Don't worry. I went by myself," I say, not without a good dose of bravado.

"No way! That's not your style. Please. You would never."

"You think I'm incapable of going to the movies alone? It's not rocket science."

"In our five years of dating, you never moved a muscle unless I did ... or you were with Paola or another one of your friends. Please."

"What do you know? It's been two years since we were together. I could have changed. I have changed."

"Ha. People don't change. *You* don't change. That's the terrible truth."

Of course, when he wants to, Carlo has a sense of tragedy that makes Hamlet seem like a stand-up comedian.

"You don't know; we're not dating anymore."

"I know what I see. A girl trying to be a 'career woman,' wearing push-up bras and high heels."

"Does it bother you that I look feminine?"

"You didn't give a damn about that before."

"No, Carlo. It was you who didn't give a damn. I accommodated you. I changed when you said that only stupid people cared about putting on makeup or taking care of their appearance to go to work. Instead, I realize that people who wear makeup feel good about themselves, and that's why I go for a manicure every month, see?"

I show him my hands, with the brilliant pink nails, but for some reason, I suddenly feel very stupid for having done it, and for being there in that café talking about our long-dead and buried relationship, after seeing him kiss a stranger.

"Oh, of course, nails! That's a huge commitment. I guess that's why you don't have time for friends anymore."

I ignore his jab. I am used to his ways, especially when he's angry.

"We all have the lives we choose for ourselves, Carlo."

"Really? Do you think you can always choose?"

Suddenly the air around us seems to have the consistency of a dense jelly. We are imprisoned inside of it; and it takes a superhuman effort to force out any words at all.

"Don't you want the baby? Don't you love Cristina?"

"Don't pretend you didn't see what you just saw, Alice. How could I kiss another woman if I loved Cristina?" he hisses. "You don't understand; you can't understand. I . . . I love her."

I turn briefly toward the door, as if the girl were still there, her echo still reverberating in the air along with the trail of her perfume.

"Are you sure you're not just getting cold feet about the commitment you're about to make? I mean, a baby is a huge responsibility."

"What do you know about it? Nothing. You haven't asked me anything. You simply disappeared when I needed your advice and support the most."

I look down at my hands, but the glitter and pink nail polish make me feel even more uncomfortable now.

"I felt . . . betrayed," I can only murmur, although I know that it doesn't make much sense. But I remember all too well how awful I felt when I found out. It was like he was moving on with his life when I still wasn't able to. I had felt like a jar that was fast approaching its expiration date and destined to be left on the shelf.

"Oh, give me a break, Alice. We haven't been together for a long time, and it was a good thing that we split up. We didn't really love each other."

I look at him again, more intensely than before. "What are you saying?"

"That now I know what love is. What I feel for Sonia is true love. I've never felt it before, not for you, and definitely not for Cristina."

If he had just picked up his teaspoon and shoved it in my heart, it would have hurt less.

I spent five years with that man, five of the best years of my life, during which time I thought I had found The One; the man I wanted by my side forever, to be my husband and the father of my children. With one sentence, he just erased everything. He has just canceled out the most important relationship that I've had, reducing it to nothing more than a joke.

"Sonia is . . . well, it's a complicated relationship," he starts explaining, as if nothing had happened. "To begin with, she doesn't entirely trust me. The baby is a problem for her."

"Well, hello! Smart girl!" What did he expect? *Darling, I love*

you, but I'm about to marry someone else. Oh, and by the way, she's
pregnant.

Carlo looks at me with contempt. "I can't expect you to understand. You've always been quite superficial, like the rest of the world."

"Oh yes, and of course you are such a deep, sensitive individual!" I blurt out, suddenly remembering what Tio had said about his
horoscope and why it would be impossible for a Libra with a Pisces
Moon like me to be with an Aquarius with Gemini Ascendant like
him. Aquarians by definition are the contrarians of the zodiac. You
say something is white? You can be sure that even if it was white
to him a minute ago, now it's black. He hates conforming to the
masses. Carlo is definitely defying conventions with his love triangle. And then there's his Moon in Aries . . .

"It's your Moon in Aries that makes you impulsive and erratic,
you know. Probably contributes to your being a bit of a Peter Pan,
making your imminent bond with Cristina feel like a noose around
your neck."

"What the hell are you saying?" He slams his fist onto the table,
and the cup jumps in the air. "Have you lost your mind? Aries,
Moon, horoscope? I'm telling you that my life is ruined, and you
come out with this crap!"

"Oh, but of course, you are the intelligent one, going around
playing Inseminator and then whining like a baby about your horrible fate."

"I expected a little more intelligence from you, Alice. I was
wrong. I was wrong about us, too. It took me five years to realize it
back then, but now all I needed was five minutes."

Of course. Anyone who doesn't see things his way is accused of
lacking intelligence.

"I needed your friendship," he says.

I can't believe he still has the balls to speak about friendship when he didn't think twice about using words that cut like knives. At that second, I understand that I've always idealized him, and now I feel like I'm seeing him for the first time. Not as the strong, intelligent, charismatic man he was when he was courting me. This time I see a temperamental child who doesn't want to grow up and is afraid of responsibilities.

"I don't know what to do," he says again, holding his head in his hands.

Anger overwhelms me like a sudden tide. I understand that I've never been special for him. But it doesn't hurt, because I realize that he is not special for me. Not anymore.

It's one of those times that I regret not having a mustache, a quizzical eyebrow, and a gravelly voice. But I have the line, and it's perfect, ready and waiting since 1939.

I look into those eyes full of anger and I bite my lip, hesitating for just a second, before I say, "Frankly, my dear, I don't give a damn."

21

Bread, Love, and Astrology

Look here." Ferruccio indicates the bags that have just been unloaded. "We're missing number four; it had the spotlights to illuminate the dungeons for the fire signs' trials. What are we going to do?"

Thanks to the ratings from the Tio/Magni duo, we have a new sponsor, as well as an avalanche of rave reviews about a possible breakthrough in the quality of our show. We also earned a very cool trip to a medieval castle to record part of the next episode. My god, I almost feel like I'm in Hollywood. To emphasize my status as a brilliant TV writer/producer, I'm wearing a dark blue suit that is very Armani-esque, and I have embodied a professional, efficient, strict, and yet still very feminine attitude. I love this job.

"What's going on?"

The voice behind us makes all three of us turn around.

There. The only flaw of the day: Carlo is the one who oversees productions outside the studio. Being forced to deal with him after what we said to each other the other day is about as pleasant as repeatedly slamming my finger in a door.

"Apparently you men forget your responsibilities quite easily," I add, throwing a sharp glance at Carlo.

He knits his brow. "Why do we need to bother remembering them, when you women love to remind us ad nauseam?"

I open my mouth to reply, but Alejandro beats me to it. "I eh-swear it was there, Aliz. I remember, I put with bags, no?" Alejandro whines, stroking his six-pack, trying to reassure himself.

Oh no, honey, that doesn't work on me anymore. "I don't care if you saw it. What's done is done. Over. In the past. What can you tell me about the present? Where is that bag with the lights?"

"Um . . . *quizás* . . . I leaf them . . . they no in any of the cars."

"Fine," I say, becoming the good cop. "That scene is in the afternoon so you have plenty of time to go get them."

"But . . . is more than two *horas* for this!!"

"I'm sorry; we need those lights."

"*Bueno,* I go." Alejandro shakes his head and walks toward one of the cars.

"Um, no, sorry, sweetie. Ferruccio needs you here now to set up the first scene, with the earth signs. You can go during the lunch break."

"But . . ."

I raise my hand and delight in a thought of the *pollice verso* of the Roman emperors when they decreed the death of a gladiator with the flick of a wrist. Do I feel guilty as I watch him walk away with sunken shoulders thinking about the farm where the rest of us will eat lunch without him? Hmm, let's see . . . Nope, not a bit.

"I am not going to put those horns on my head!"

Silence is something that we city folks have no problem shattering.

"What's wrong now?"

As I look up at the sky, still clear and bright, Marlin emerges from the castle wrapped in a magnificent velvet and brocade gown, with her green eyes and auburn hair shining—you can see why people go crazy over her.

"I refuse to be filmed with a pair of horns on my head," she exclaims, heading straight toward the motorcycle Davide has just arrived on.

Man, he's sexy! Um! I am a strong, professional woman.

My showdown with Carlo a couple of weeks ago made me realize that I need to change my tune so that I am not strung along anymore. I have grown, improved, and focused.

"Welcome, Davide. We are preparing for the first shot. The signs are in makeup and Marlin is trying on dresses. Darling, you look magical!" I exclaim, pretending to notice her right at that moment. "You look like a goddess—that dress really shows off your waist! Have you lost weight?"

"Do you think? These inserts are really slimming."

"Do you know what else is really slimming? I know it's a bit strange, but at the time all the most important women wore them." I take the Viking helmet from her and mold it onto her head. "*Voilà!* Stunning. You look so tall with this."

I exhale while she walks away happily, muttering that she could put it on after all.

"You were fantastic. I could never have done it," says Davide.

"So . . . why are you here?" I ask him.

Well done, Alice: detached, professional.

Now he's the one to look away, probably intimidated by the gaze of the new and improved Alice.

"I know the owners," he explains tersely, unzipping his leather jacket.

It's no surprise that this is the first I've heard of it. Getting information out of Davide is like pulling teeth. Can you imagine the effort it would take to be with someone like that for life?

He ruffles his hair again and walks by me. His black jeans hug his thighs and butt tightly.

"Mmm . . ." I sigh. Yes . . . what an effort.

What we need to shoot today has the old-school flavor of *Family Double Dare*, one of those good old game shows where the contestants, divided into teams, must undergo tests of strength, skill, and ingenuity, possibly making fools of themselves and of the human race in general. To achieve this, we've divided the representatives of the zodiac signs into four teams.

One of the first things that I've learned, as a new convert to astrology, is that each of the signs is presided over not only by a dominant planet, but also by one of four elements: earth, air, fire, and water. In this way, depending on their element, all contestants will undergo trials that are more or less appropriate to their team, earning points for victories and losing points for defeats.

"We will begin with Tio's presentation and then follow the game with the cameras," says Carlo.

The game is a sort of race that he, the camera operators, and the assistants will have to follow at close range.

Since this contest favors the earth element, the qualities it requires are rationality, collaboration, and reasoning. Theoretically, Taurus, Capricorn, and Virgo, the signs ruled by this element, have a character advantage, especially when compared to the fire signs, Leo, Aries, and Sagittarius, who, being more passionate and sometimes bullish, are already making fools of themselves by squabbling over who should go first and who should be team captain.

As I take my place by Carlo for the shooting, he grabs my elbow and pulls me aside. "Will you cut it out? You're acting like a jealous girlfriend. We are here to work, not for a field trip."

"You're one to talk!" I answer, pushing his hand aside. "If you haven't noticed, my name is on this show. It's like my child, and I follow through on projects I have started. I don't think that you can say the same."

He's about to come back at me, but I raise my finger to ask him to wait while I dig my vibrating phone out of my pocket. The caller ID lists UNKNOWN NUMBER. I stuff the phone back in my pocket so we can start the competition.

"Anyway, quit it," resumes Carlo. "It's bad enough that you told Cristina to come with us. In her condition, she shouldn't be under stress, as you know. I don't know how she let you talk her into it."

"I see, it had to be me who convinced her to come?" I was actually just asking myself why he brought her along; ever since we arrived, she's been clinging to me like a limpet.

In fact, as soon as the game begins, she hovers behind me like a condor.

"It's all Carlo's fault," Cristina mumbles. "If it weren't for him, the two of us would have been great friends."

I admit it; the weasel and I did get along for a moment there. But when she got her claws into Carlo, I became the uncomfortable skeleton in her man's closet, and she became the uncomfortable other half of my best friend. So, friendship was out of the question.

"Who knows. Anything could have happened," I answer. I can't let Cristina crack my armor, after all the effort I've made with Carlo, Alejandro, and Davide.

"I'm just so emotional . . ." she says, clinging to my arm in tears. "The baby . . . I mean . . . I have constant mood swings and I get obsessed with things . . . I think . . . I am so tired."

After a pause, she continues, "It was mostly my fault. But it's stupid to be jealous, right? Because you're not in love with Carlo, and he is going to marry me."

I look back at her and her eyes are desperate, pleading. What she's actually telling me is that she suspects that Carlo and I are still seeing each other behind her back. I would like to go over to Carlo and shake him, tell him to grow up, once and for all.

Meanwhile, the four groups have almost reached their goal and are competing for the key to the treasure chest at the end of the path, searching like mad in the slime and drenching Alejandro in mud as he squats to shoot them. As it starts dripping from his eyes to his lips, I see him stiffen and hold back a grimace. I, on the other hand, am holding back a grin.

"Carlo is just worried about the future," I say, turning to Cristina. "Try to be patient."

At the whistle that ends the race, her "thank you" is lost among the joyful cries from the Air team and the complaints of Alejandro, smeared with mud from head to toe.

22

The Gemini Connection

I find Tio on the road in front of the gate, excitedly waving at an Alfa Romeo tossing up gravel in its wake.

"Are we expecting someone else?" I ask.

"Andrea," he says, half to me and half as a greeting to the driver of the car that stops next to us.

Andrea Magni rolls down his window and lifts his sunglasses, greeting us.

"What is Andrea doing here?"

"He was at a conference nearby, and I asked him to join us for lunch," Tio explains.

I wanted to tell Tio about Carlo, but now he's running toward Andrea.

"Wait, Tio!"

He slows down and smiles at me.

"I wanted to talk to you before we break for lunch."

"I'm here," he says, and I look at Andrea, waiting for us one hundred feet away.

"Yes, but . . ." I'm still not sure it's right to blab Carlo and Cristina's problems to a third party, and I especially don't want to tell them to a guy who could turn them into mathematical equations, confusing me even further.

"I have an ethical problem . . ." I begin, grabbing his arm. "What would you do if you discovered that someone you always thought you knew, someone you loved—as a friend—has become . . . how shall I put it . . . *promiscuous* . . . You always thought that your friend was going in one direction and had made a certain choice, but now you've discovered that was not the case."

I look at Andrea, who is coming closer to us, and I speak frantically because I don't want him to reach us in the middle of my speech.

"I mean, as much as you love him, you just can't accept his behavior and you don't know whether or not it's right to talk to other people about it, because they might behave differently toward him when they find out who he really is."

Now that I've said it, I feel relieved. It's a weight off my shoulders, and I truly believe it was right for me to be vague and respect Carlo and Cristina's privacy.

When I look up at him, however, Tio remains frozen, having moved a couple of steps behind me.

"Well?"

"Well, that seems rather hypocritical of you," he replies.

"What?"

"You should try to understand your friend instead of condemning him. Who are you to judge other people's feelings? Maybe he wasn't totally honest with you because he was afraid you wouldn't understand and end up pushing him away, which would have been much, much worse than living in the shadows where at least your friendship was secure."

What is Tio talking about? I am so stunned by his senseless attack that I can't even open my mouth.

Andrea tries to stop him by putting a hand on his arm, but Tio turns and walks away, pushing him aside rudely.

My mind turns to Karin's words about the fact that Tio really likes me, then my mother's insinuations, all the affection he always pours over me, and his persistence in finding a boyfriend for me, then dashing my hopes by saying that man is not the right one.

For a moment, I seem to hear Paola's voice.

Tio is in love with you, Alice.

Oh damn.

If Tio really is in love with me, this is a serious problem. I understand just how serious as soon as I set foot in the entrance of the castle, catching sight of a man standing there, looking at a picture of a gentleman in a large wig. It could be a scene from a period film, like *Pride and Prejudice*, when Elizabeth accidentally interrupts Mr. Darcy's contemplation of his ancestor's portrait. Except the gloves tightening behind his back are motorcycle gloves, and he is wearing a pair of black, ripped, badass jeans.

Davide spins around and drops one of his gloves to the ground in surprise. There is definitely something up with him. I would call it amazement, anxiety, or perhaps even melancholy. Maybe these are the three sides of the Bermuda Triangle that attract me to him.

As usual, he looks at me and doesn't speak.

"Is there something wrong? You are as pale as if you'd seen a ghost."

"Me? Oh, well . . . the fact is that I was imagining just that."

"What?"

"You, walking through that door."

"Oh . . ." I smile, even though I don't really know what he means.

"You are strange. Has anyone ever told you that?"

"Constantly. And you?"

"Constantly. I was thinking of writing it on my ID." We both laugh.

"See? That is precisely what makes you so unique," he says suddenly. "You are so brilliant. You are beautiful, friendly, intelligent . . ."

OK. Stop everything. To say I was a little confused at this point would be an understatement.

"I mean, I was hoping that you would come in here because I have to tell you something."

I smile at him. "Tell me."

His lips part; his tongue moistens them, and then his teeth bite on them for a second . . . This is why I have to clarify things with Tio. Even if, unfortunately, he were to have a crush on me, which I dread that he does, I cannot, simply cannot . . . Just as it would never work with Andrea, Alejandro, or Carlo, it could never work with him. And it's not because of incompatible horoscopes, his sign, his ascendant, or some dancing planet that capriciously became transverse at the moment of our birth. It can't work because I am in love with someone else.

Walking through that door, looking at Davide's back, it suddenly became very clear to me, as if it were written in big, bold letters before me.

I have fallen in love with Davide Nardi.

And I am scared shitless.

I love the way his strength vibrates under his calm appearance. I love everything that he sets eyes on, because his gaze envelops it and cradles it gently, and I love every word that passes his lips, in that smooth but rough voice, like an intimate caress between the two of us.

"I am a jerk," he blurts out.

"Sorry?"

"Bringing you here was a mistake. What the hell was I thinking?" As he drags me out the door, I hear him repeat, "Asshole, asshole, asshole!"

"Do you want to stop for a second? We can't leave. *I* can't leave. I have to work. I have to find Tio . . ." As much as I would love to go away with him, I can't abandon the set or leave Tio like this, without having resolved things, or at least having tried.

Davide isn't listening to me. He fastens his helmet, almost feverishly, his gaze determined not to meet mine while he opens the storage compartment of his motorcycle, pulls out a second helmet, and puts it on my head.

"Wait, I'll fix it. This one has a loose clasp," he says, fiddling with the strap under my chin. "I need to talk to you, Alice, but I have to do it far away from here, immediately. Please, come with me. Now."

The tsunami raging in his eyes overwhelms me. I am reeling in the muddled flow of words and emotions: logic and fairness versus feelings and desires.

I nod.

He looks me in the eye again, terribly serious, raking in the air, as if to gather his courage. He starts to put on his gloves but realizes that he only has one in his hand.

"Wait, you dropped it in the entrance." I run toward the doorway, and the helmet makes my head dance like one of those little dogs with a spring for a neck. I return, waving the glove, victorious, but Davide is no longer alone.

I catch sight of his beautiful derrière, but this time I don't lose myself because my attention moves swiftly to the woman I see speaking to him. The woman who has parked, if one can call it that, the horse she has just dismounted alongside Davide's motorcycle.

A motorcycle and a horse make for quite a strange pair. On the other hand, this woman, ethereal in her beige riding suit, and Davide, rugged in all-black, go together like night and day.

Looking at her, I am reminded that fate is a cruel mistress and that, try as you might, elegance is something that you are born with.

We mere mortals would have a blouse covered in sweat stains, bird's nest hair, and a noticeably flushed face, at least, but she looks absolutely flawless.

"Barbara, let me introduce you to Alice . . . Alice Bassi. Um, the creator of the show, actually. Alice, this is Barbara Buchneim-Wessler Ricci Pastori . . . who has kindly opened her home to us today."

"Nice to meet you, Ms. Bu-ka-inen . . ." It's impossible not to stumble on that last name.

"And I am delighted to meet someone from Davide's work." As she shakes my hand, her eyes never leave Davide, and her lips uncover a row of teeth as white as the driven snow.

Maybe it has something to do with the name? It's not like you can be called Blu-cher-God-Knows-What and not walk around like you have a stick where the sun doesn't shine.

Oh god, I despise her. She's too perfect to not make me feel like crap. How can I compete with Barbie Frau Blucher-Fritz-Rich? And then there is that look that she shoots at Davide while she lays a hand on his arm with the grace of a geisha.

"You already know each other, then," I say, imitating her and resting a hand on Davide.

"I worked with Barbara's husband before I was hired by Mi-A-Mi Network," intervenes Davide, moving toward his bike and leaving us both behind.

HUSBAND.

Your Honor, let the record show that the word *husband* was uttered and clearly heard by yours truly.

"Really? That's fantastic," I exclaim, smiling at the woman.

"Absolutely. He was very helpful in an extremely difficult period," says Barbara fondly. "By the way, how is Flash?"

"He is great. He seems happy in his new home."

This talk of Flash leaves a funny taste in my mouth, as if I should remember something that escapes me right now. It's not just a question of memory, but also of distraction, because the crew is flocking toward the house, clamoring to reach the cars and vans and finally go on lunch break.

Alejandro gives me a look full of resentment as he drops a little bag of sandwiches on the seat of the car that he will drive to the office to search for the missing lighting bag. From a distance, Mara shoots me a knowing glance, calling Alejandro's attention to the afternoon work.

Reluctantly, I move away from Davide. As much as it bothers me to abandon my turf, I have a job to do.

When I sneak between the parked cars, I see Cristina wandering around like a tormented soul, massaging her stomach. "Everything OK?" I ask when she reaches me close to Alejandro's car.

"I think I'm going to throw up!"

Oh, crap! I hurriedly open the car door, grab the bag of sandwiches from the seat, and place it in front of her mouth just in time for her to lose her breakfast into it.

"I'm so sorry!" she says.

"Don't worry about it," I answer. Come to think of it . . . "Actually, thank you."

As she walks away to rinse her hands and mouth in the fountain, I close the bag and throw it back on the seat. I try to undo the helmet, but all I manage to do is break a fingernail.

"Is there something wrong?" Carlo asks.

"You should ask her," I reply, pointing to Cristina, who is sitting on the edge of the fountain and dipping her hands in up to her wrists. "She's very tired."

"She should have stayed home."

"She wanted to be near you."

Carlo bites his lip and looks at the time. "We are at a good point with work, but we can't let ourselves get distracted."

"Take this thing off me," I say, referring to the helmet.

Carlo tries to unfasten the strap under my chin.

"You're right about one thing," I add thoughtfully, moving my eyes toward Cristina. "We can't let ourselves get distracted."

He understands that I'm not referring to work and abandons his effort to try and free me.

"Come on, undo it!"

"I can't, and you don't deserve a favor from me anyway. Instead of rubbing salt in my wounds, why don't you focus on your Golden Boy and go fetch him from wherever he's ended up?"

"Tio?" I won't tell him that I'm arguing with Tio, too; although it's basically his fault.

Carlo looks at me and then shifts his gaze to Davide and Barbara with the hint of a smile. "We can't let ourselves get distracted . . ."

I don't bother telling him to go to hell; Carlo can find the way on his own. I walk away with a dismissive wave of my hand and head directly for Andrea Magni.

When he notices me, he straightens his back and attempts a smile. Something's bothering him, and he is unable to hide it.

"Excuse me, Andrea, do you know where I can find Tio?" I ask, still trying to unfasten the helmet strap and only succeeding in tightening it even more.

Magni has lost his affable look and gives me a frown. "We were in the vicinity of the filming site when he announced his need to be alone."

"Ah, I see . . ." I say, and I head off into the woods, thinking about how to broach the conversation with Tio without hurting him any more than necessary or any more than I already have. But damn, it's not going to be easy. When Alejandro dumped me, there were times when I felt like I wanted to die.

Oh god. I stop to collect my thoughts when I see that the set that we are preparing overlooks a ravine of at least fifty feet.

OK, let's not be melodramatic. I mean, whatever I'm imagining, Tio would never dream of doing something like that. To get the thought out of my mind, I lean over the ravine a little to see what's below.

"I wouldn't do that if I were you. Even with the helmet, I mean," warns a voice behind me, and then someone grabs my arm.

"You're alive!" I turn around and fly at him, bumping against his chest like a rugby player.

He doesn't hug me back, and after a couple of seconds of bewildered stiffness, he walks away. "Why are you here?"

"We need to talk."

"I really don't think so."

"But you have to let me explain. I understand how you feel . . . but it's wrong. I'm here because I care about you, and I want us to think through things together."

"Alice, really, just drop it . . . so that neither of us gets hurt. I thought I wanted to talk to you about it, but maybe it's always been difficult because I felt that you wouldn't understand me." He kicks a few pebbles that roll down into the ravine. "The problem is that I really care about you, but I didn't want to have to lie anymore in order to be close to you. Paola told me more than once to tell you but . . ."

"Paola?"

Tio nods. "She knew immediately, but I begged her to keep it to herself."

"I'm sorry," I say in a low voice. "I wish that things could stay as they were."

"I wanted that, too, but there comes a point when it's impossible to keep hiding the truth. And, believe me, it's very difficult for me. I've never told anyone before ... But with you, Alice ... With you it's different. Well, it was different."

"Tio, please try to understand. It's not easy for me either. I never suspected anything. I know this is hurting you, but I just can't ... I can't accept it."

"Andrea told me that I couldn't trust you! Hell, are we in the twenty-first century or not?"

I blink; dumbfounded. Andrea was also in on the secret? Why don't we add someone else? My parents? The cleaning lady? "And what does Andrea have to do with it? Anyway, some things never change. It's not like things are so different today from the Middle Ages ..."

"Honey, wake up!" he exclaims, passing a hand through his hair. "I have news for you: society has evolved. You're the one thinking like an old bigot."

I stare at him with my mouth wide open. "Me, a bigot? I'm just a person with morals!"

I may be old, but I'm still agile enough to give him a good kick in the shin. Things are evidently deteriorating.

"This is the way you resolve things, is it? Like the good cave-woman that you are! But what can I expect from someone who defines her friend's feelings as promiscuous and threatens to tell others about him so that he is ostracized?"

"So you don't think that I am right to defend a pregnant woman?" I yell angrily. "And I have no reason to be angry if Carlo wants to cheat and mess up the wedding? But of course, take his side. After all, you're a man, too. Clearly, I don't have an open mind, but for me Cristina is in need of a friend now more than ever, and I don't know if telling her the truth would really improve the situation. That's why I came to talk to you; I wanted your advice, but I'm sorry that you misunderstood. And I'm sorry I hurt your feelings . . . but I know what mine are, Tio, and I can't . . . I can't love you. For me you are a very special friend, but I can't offer you anything else. I am afraid of losing you, too. Believe me, I am terrified of that possibility, but what can I do?"

I am out of breath, the words flowing from my lips mingling with the tears from my eyes.

"Stop! Enough, Alice! Enough!" he said raising his hands in surrender. I close my eyes, deflated.

When I open them again, Tio is in front of me, his face a few inches from my nose. His fingers fumble with the evil buckle, and after a few attempts, he is able to open it. I'm free at last. As soon as he lifts the helmet off, I feel like I can breathe again.

Tio takes my face in his hands, and I see the hint of a smile. He looks into my eyes, and they are blue, as clear and honest as ever.

"Alice, I'm gay."

"Excuse me?"

"I'm gay. That's what I've been trying to tell you for the past half hour. I've been trying to tell you for a while, even when you came to me before. But then you started all this talk about promiscuity, saying that you couldn't accept me . . ."

"I was talking about Carlo."

"I know. I know that now." He sighs and looks up at the sky. "I don't know how you feel about it, but you don't have to worry about the fact that you're not in love with me. I don't love you either . . . not in that sense, at least. But I love you like a sister, stubborn little mule that you are."

"Oh, Tio!" I exclaim through tears. "I don't love you either."

We give each other a massive hug, because no one is in love with anyone.

Tio goes to change and then head to lunch, and in the parking lot, all that's left is Mara's small car. She is waiting for me, leaning against the hood with her arms crossed over her chest.

When she sees me, she stands up straight and slips a hand into her pocket.

"Here. Nardi asked me to give this to you because he had to leave." I frown and take the note.

I'll be back Tuesday. I'll pick you up at eight. Alice, this isn't a request.

"Everything OK?" Mara asks.

Over the past couple of weeks, Mara and I have discovered that we actually have a lot in common. In addition to our dead and buried flings with Alejandro, we are both Libras, which made her like a zodiac sister to me.

"Yes," I murmur, lost in thought.

She stretches out her arms behind her back, walking around to the trunk of the car. "Did you throw out *his* lunch?" she asks.

I fold the paper and slip it into my pocket. "I did even better," I reply.

Then I smile, thinking about the moment when Alejandro will shove his hand into the bag of sandwiches and find the filling that Cristina so kindly added to them.

Mara opens the trunk. "What should we do with this?"

And there it is, bag number four, the one with the spotlights that Ferruccio was looking for. I sigh, looking at my watch. "In ten minutes, we'll call him, tell him that we've found it, and that he should come back."

As soon as we close the door, we see Tio coming toward us and we both smile, as innocently as Thelma and Louise.

23

A Story of Streets, Libras, and Crime

Even gurus have their shortcomings, and Paola, my personal guru, subjects me to shopping.

The result is that on my day off I have spent forty-five minutes in a jewelry shop looking at earrings . . . *all* the earrings in the shop.

"Paola . . ." I try to call her to order by drumming my fingers on the counter.

It doesn't work, and she goes back to rummaging through the shelves. I turn to examine the bracelets. I really have to make it stop. There must be a way to sedate her, even at the price of having to carry her home myself.

It's not that I don't like to shop. It's just that today my hours are limited. But Paola doesn't know that.

"Excuse me . . ."

The saleswoman ambushes me behind the mirror.

"I'm just looking, thank you."

"Of course. But a man came in before ... It's a bit strange, but he left fifty euros for you to spend however you wish."

She pulls out the banknote and shows it to me. On it is written: *Meet me, I'm at the café opposite.*

I squint in the direction of the café, but the window is tinted, and only shadows are visible. At the tables outside, there is just one couple being accosted by a flower vendor.

Roses ...

"What was he like? Could you describe him for me?" I ask, feeling the blood drain from my face.

"Hmm ... Let's see ... Not too tall; average, I'd say," begins the saleswoman. "Average length hair, average build, eyes ..."

"Average," I finish her sentence.

"Who?" Paola asks, approaching us with her hands full of trinkets.

"Some guy that left us fifty euros to spend here," I explain, giving her a hard stare, because I don't want to speak about my personal stalker in the store.

"And what sign do you think he was?" asks Paola ironically while I drag her away, muttering, "Idiot. Move it."

I enter the café impulsively, bursting through the door like a gunman in a saloon, but there's not a damn soul inside.

"We've lost him," I announce bitterly.

Meanwhile, there are a lot of people in the street and my psychotic benefactor could be any one of them.

"Well," says Paola, stopping to lean against the wall and rub her foot. "Why don't you take a chill pill? You can't chase—this time literally chase—after every man who shows the slightest bit of interest in you. Come on!"

"Don't you get it, Paola?" I explain that our mysterious banker is most likely not Prince Charming or Superman, but more simply the Riddler of the yellow roses.

"Oh, fuck!"

And for her to come out with a bad word is a sign of an epiphany indicative of an inner volcanic eruption.

Since we are both terribly upset, we see no other solution than to immerse ourselves in lingerie.

"Thong or Brazilian?"

I truly believe that a new outfit is just what I need to get me in the mood for an evening with Davide. Not that I want to go that far, really! I would never . . . Well, I mean, there's always a chance it could happen . . .

"Didn't you say after Alejandro that you wouldn't buy anything sexy again until the next *committed* boyfriend? Are you hiding something from me?"

I head for the dressing room at full speed. "Like how my best guy friend is gay and my supposed best girlfriend knew all about it and didn't tell me, causing me to make a complete ass of myself?"

I give the curtain a dramatic yank, hiding in the dressing room.

The truth is that I haven't told a soul about my date tonight with Davide. Neither Paola nor Tio.

I don't know why. Maybe it's because I don't want to hear words, judgments, advice . . . I want it to be just the two of us, me and Davide.

Outside, I hear Paola snort. "I already told you I was sorry, but I still think that it's his business, and if he wanted to tell you, as ended up happening, he should be the one to do it."

I open the curtain to show off the first lingerie set I've tried on.

She looks at me from head to toe. "Did you just get a wax?" she asks, squinting.

I roll my eyes. "Sometimes even I have to do it, Paola."

"Mhmm . . ." I hear Paola again outside the dressing room.

I show her the second version of the outfit.

"Very sexy. It looks good on you. Now tell me, Miss Fifty Shades of Clutching at Straws, who are you going out with tonight?"

I pretend not to hear. As I'm putting my clothes back on, I try to come up with a plausible lie that I can spin for her. "Why does someone getting a wax necessarily mean she has a date? I love myself and take care of my body for myself."

"Sure, and tomorrow I'm going to dinner with Brad Pitt."

I wrinkle my nose while I pass her to go pay. "Giacomo and Angelina won't be too happy about that."

"Alice, I'm not prying into your business for no good reason . . ."

"Hmm . . . and knowing a name would put you at ease?" I take her hands. "Listen, I want to do this thing alone. He is too important for me, and I don't want to spoil everything by filling my head with other people's thoughts. I want to enjoy the evening and . . . really see how it goes; to stand on my own two feet for once."

After a few seconds of looking at me puzzled, Paola hugs me. "Oh, honey. I'm so proud of you. Just promise me you'll be careful."

I smile at the clerk and swipe my credit card with nonchalance, under the sweet, proud gaze of my friend.

"Just a moment."

The clerk stops us when we are at the doorway.

"When you were upstairs, a gentleman came in and asked me to give you these," says the girl, reaching under the counter and taking out three magnificent yellow roses.

24

Torture Me, But Kill Me with Leo

If I thought that things would be simple this time and that the evening would run smoothly, I couldn't have been more wrong.

Davide's note said eight, but I've been here, sitting on the edge of my sofa with my purse on my knees for over twenty minutes.

I glance at the phone, but there are no calls or messages. I give myself yet another once-over in the bedroom mirror, contemplating the possibility of calling him, or rather combating the possibility of calling him. But no, it's better to play the busy, emotionally independent woman who has forgotten all about the date.

When I go out on the balcony, my eyes dart toward the street, and I see him. He's double-parked across the street and is pacing from the car to the entrance of my building. The first time, I think that he's forgotten something because he opens the car door again and is about to get in. The second time, I think maybe he hasn't locked the door because he just goes up to the handle. The third time, he stops halfway, and I have to ask myself what the hell he is up to.

Between the leaves, I see him pull out his cell phone, and when mine rings, I crawl like a marine through the French doors to grab it from the coffee table.

"Hello?"

"Hello . . . Alice?"

I don't recognize the voice on the other end of the phone. I was expecting Davide, for heaven's sake.

"Who is this?"

"I am . . . My name is Daniele. I'm a friend of Karin's. I am a Pisces with Virgo Ascendant."

"What? Oh, good."

From the window, I see Davide still pacing, his phone pressed to his ear.

"And you?" says Daniele, Pisces with Virgo Ascendant.

"Daniele, you'll have to excuse me. This isn't a great time for me."

After a quick goodbye, I'm able to hang up. Now what do I do?

I run to the intercom as soon as I hear it ring.

"Alice are you home?"

Where else does he think I would be, given that I answered?

"Are you here?" Since we seem to be competing for the world's stupidest question, I might as well catch up.

. . .

We park near the Porta Venezia gardens. It's one of the first really warm evenings here in the city, and strolling between ponds and flower beds, you don't even feel like you're in Milan. Luckily, I'm wearing a comfortable pair of boots, but my feet are the least of my problems, given that just being beside him makes me feel like I'm walking on air. The thing that really makes me suspect that this is a dream is that for the first time, he is speaking freely.

"I realize that I have always been a bit aloof, but I prefer to really reflect on situations and understand what the consequences of my actions could be."

In fact, that's one of the things that I like about him, that he seems like a real strong and protective man.

I steal a glance at him and secretly ask myself what sign he might be and what his astrological chart is . . .

The question is on the tip of my tongue, but I swallow it.

Just like I didn't want to say anything to Paola, I've made up my mind that I don't want to know anything about his zodiac sign and the various possible planets.

A bicycle whizzes by inches away and Davide instinctively moves me out of harm's way, sliding his arm around my waist. The heat of his fingers burns through my clothing to my skin, spreading throughout my body. I want those hands everywhere on me, and for a second, I'm afraid that I've spoken that wish out loud, because he looks at me with wide eyes, embarrassed.

His hand starts sliding away, and I stop him.

I keep my eyes firmly focused on his as our fingers come together.

"Don't do that . . ." I hear him whisper. It's almost imperceptible, but we are very close.

"Do what?" I ask, trying to provoke him, pushing myself a step forward.

The tip of his tongue moistens his lips, then Davide steps back.

"What is that?" he asks, abruptly diverting our conversation.

I whirl around. "The Planetarium."

"Really! We could . . . Do you want to go there? It might help with the show."

The show. OK. But he hasn't let go of my hand.

We sit on the benches in the back while the lights fade and the audience hushes at the sound of the opening music.

"Davide, I just don't understand you . . ." I whisper as the presentation begins.

His hand squeezes mine even tighter. "It's beautiful," he murmurs. I see his profile rise toward the dome where a sky is slowly illuminated with an infinite expanse of planets and then filled with falling stars.

". . . and these so-called falling stars are not really stars at all. They are called Perseids, and they are only dust that burns because of the speed, like when we light a match," says the lecturer. "It never hurts to make a wish, and here at the Planetarium there are tons of falling stars."

I turn toward Davide, longing to tell him that my only wish is to have him, but I am tongue-tied.

"Zodiac signs and astrology don't really make much sense either," continues the lecturer. "Constellations are drawn by man two-dimensionally, but if we look at the sky from another perspective, we see how the figures change geometrically; how stars that are a great distance away from one another are part of the same constellation."

Davide chuckles next to me. "Andrea hasn't used these arguments on Tio yet."

"Mmm . . . I think he's brought out plenty of others."

"What?"

"Oh, nothing . . . I mean there are so many things that you can say against astrology . . . on closer examination, we shouldn't rely on it too heavily."

"Are you changing sides? And to think that even I am starting to trust it a little bit. For example, I'm a Leo."

Oh god. No. This can't be happening. He's not actually telling me.

Cover your ears, I tell myself. *Blablabla. I don't want to hear. I don't want to know.*

"August twenty-second, 1978, at eleven twenty in the morning. And I have to say, ever since we started working on your show, I've found some accuracies, at least in terms of my character."

He said it. As much as I try to forget it, my interior voice keeps obsessively repeating his birth date.

"This is all bullshit," I say drily, more to myself than to him, and out loud, to try to quiet that interior voice still obsessively repeating the date.

August 22, 1978. 11:20 a.m.

I try to distract myself by looking at the sky of the Planetarium.

"It would be nice to really be able to look at the sky like this," I say. "Perhaps in the mountains, where there is true darkness."

"It would be nice . . ." he repeats, and I hear him sigh.

I gather my strength and with the excuse of getting a better look at the stars, I lie down, resting my head on his knees.

His hand removes a lock of hair from my lips with a caress. "It would be really nice," I hear him repeat. "If only it were possible."

Like all dreams, the magic of the Planetarium won't last forever. Unfortunately, and at the most beautiful moment, the lights come back on, transforming the magic into sheer awkwardness.

When we go out, he turns on his phone again and walks away to the corner of the foyer to make a phone call.

"Sorry. There was no reception . . ." I hear him say. I smile at him but he turns his back. "I'm out . . ."

I look at him and then stare at my own phone, which is switched off.
August 22, 1978. 11:20 a.m.

What if Paola is trying to reach me? She was really worried this afternoon, so you never know. I should turn it back on. Definitely. It's not an excuse, I swear.

As my phone loads everything, I see that I've received a message, not from Paola, but from Tio.

Everything OK?

There. Maybe it's a sign.

Yes, I know I said that I wouldn't do it ... but right now Davide is in the corner, muttering into his phone. And I am here alone, puzzling over my destiny.

I lift my gaze back to Davide. "... with friends," I hear him say.

I might feel more comfortable if I knew that I had some hope, right? I would be able to enjoy the evening a little more.

I hurriedly type into the display.

August 22, 1978. 11:20 a.m.

Send. Without a note or even a name, but I know that Tio will understand in an instant.

"How about we go eat something?" says Davide, putting away his cell.

Well, it must be said; it is a perfect evening.

Walking through the alleyways, we end up at a small bistro, ordering wine and *salumi* plates. Davide smiles at me, looking into my eyes, and asking me questions about my life.

When the waiter comes up and lights a candle on the table for "A touch of romance ..." I smile at him, thinking they really know how to pander to their customers, while Davide leans back, crossing his arms over his chest.

"Um, thank you ..." he says. Then, when the waiter walks away and we are alone again, he peers at me, almost with suspicion. "I feel like this isn't real," he murmurs.

"You think so?" The fact that he also feels that this is a moment of pure magic is really more than I could hope for.

I close my eyes, trying to hear some inner bell, a consciousness, a change, a shift of the Earth, in short, a signal that I am living a historic moment.

My stomach grumbles.

Davide bites his lip, and he, too, has a somewhat lost expression when he takes my hand.

"Alice, listen ..."

There, now I know what it's like when *Mr. Right* is about to make his declaration of love. It's not a volcano or an earthquake, it's much simpler than that: it's a song. I hear it start to play in the background, the first luscious notes, as Davide's gaze sends a shiver down my spine.

Now I've had the time of my life.

Patrick Swayze was so hot in that movie.

No, I never felt this way before.

In front of me, Davide is frozen with his lips parted, evidently too overcome with emotion to speak.

Yes, I swear. It's the truth, and I owe it all to you.

I ask myself if he, too, is hearing a song, to seal this moment, and what it might be.

"Alice ..."

"Tell me ..."

"I think ... I think ... isn't that your cell phone?"

I turn toward my purse. Of course I'm hearing the song from *Dirty Dancing,* because I recently made it Tio's ringtone. His name and picture are flashing across my screen now. I grab the phone and end the call. Sorry, Tio, but now is not the time.

"You're not going to answer?" asks Davide, perplexed.

"Oh, no. No ... it's nothing important. You were saying?"

Now I've had the time of my life.

"It could be important," Davide says, releasing my hand and leaning back in his chair to drink from his wineglass.

No, no, no! Tio, didn't you clearly see written in my horoscope for today: Do Not Disturb.

I sincerely hope that this is a matter of the utmost importance.

I try to smile at Davide without losing my composure. "Hello . . . ?"

"Leave. Immediately. Get. Out. Of. There."

"What?"

"Didn't you hear me? Alice, find an excuse. Goodbye. Thank you. And leave."

"But . . ." I lift my eyes to Davide. He's fiddling with the glass of Nebbiolo that we ordered, with an absent gaze. "I can't."

"Alice, now listen to me. That man, whoever he is, has charm to spare. OK. But he is terribly dangerous for you. Do you understand? *Terribly.*"

"No. I understand, but no," I reply stubbornly.

"Honey, listen up. First of all, Leo is the most self-centered sign of the Zodiac. Virgo, which this guy is on the cusp with, squares him, enhancing his charm and making him even more determined. So, if he's made up his mind to conquer you, he will."

"Exactly. Subject closed."

"No, listen! He has Mercury in Leo and Venus in Libra, and this makes it difficult for him to be constant in his affections."

"Have you finished?"

"You wish! He has Uranus in Scorpio squaring his sun, which makes him virtually indecipherable."

This time I blink, focusing again on Davide. *Touché*, I think to myself, because I've always considered this man as decipherable as the third secret of Fatima.

"And then he has Venus in his twelfth house. Do you know what that means? I'll tell you what it means . . . He is extremely independent and doesn't want any stable bonds. Go on, ask him if he wants kids, I'm curious."

"Listen, I'm having dinner and it's rude of me to be on the phone."

I end the call and discreetly put the telephone back in my bag, apologizing to Davide for the interruption.

"Don't worry," he tells me kindly, and then narrows his eyes. "It seemed important."

"Oh, well ... yes ... a friend!" Why did he narrow his eyes? It's as if he is trying to read me more deeply. Oh, shit. "Um, a friend who's having problems with her ... boyfriend ... she wants to have kids, but he doesn't even want to consider it ..."

"Well, he's not entirely wrong," he says. "Bringing children into the world is pretty irresponsible these days."

Do they give out antipanic bags here?

My phone rings again, and by now I'm so flustered that I answer without hesitation. "What now?"

"Look, I also checked out the affinity and it sucks!" Tio says, but his voice is increasingly interrupted by other noises.

"Enough, Tiziano! This is overkill," and I recognize the other voice as Andrea's.

"Wait, just one more thing: between your two birth charts, there is a Midheaven moon opposition!" Tio nearly chokes on his last words.

"Tiziano, good Lord, I've never heard such a load of nonsense!"

"You don't understand, Andrea. This union is not only impossible ... the Moon-Pluto Opposition predicts violence and aggression!"

"For pity's sake, say goodbye to Alice and hang up. Alice, please, have a good evening."

"Oh Lord ..."

"Is something wrong?" Davide asks, worried, and when he leans forward to take my hand, I snap back like a spring.

This is a nightmare. I knew I shouldn't have sent him the birth date. Dammit, Alice!

"Are you all right?" Davide doesn't wait for my answer and nods to the waiter, asking him for fresh water. "You look pale." When he puts his hand on my cheek, I feel all his warmth, like a current that runs through me and goes straight to my heart.

Tio must have made a mistake this time.

I want this man; I want him with every fiber of my body, and I read the same thing in his eyes. Even now, as he raises my hand and brings it to his lips.

To hell with Tio and his astrology!

"I wanted to say . . ." resumes Davide. "In reality, I wanted to say that I'm sorry for how this evening is going. I wanted to talk to you. To tell you . . . To tell you something important. But it's very difficult for me because . . . because I'm selfish and I'm afraid of ruining everything. Forgive . . ."

I place my finger on his lips. "There is nothing to forgive."

He looks around. "What do you say we get out of here? I'm suffocating."

Outside, a light drizzle forces us to take shelter in a doorway.

"When I told you before that this evening seemed like it wasn't real, I wasn't lying, Alice. I feel good with you. And that's trouble, real trouble."

I smile at him defiantly, raising my face toward him, my lashes getting wet from the rain. "Can't we set aside logic, just this once?"

He closes his eyes and sighs, lifting his face toward the sky.

His hand rests on the back of my neck, pulling me forward against his chest.

I feel his heart beating, thudding against my forehead. He lays a kiss on top of my head.

"You don't know what you're asking," he murmurs.

I try to lift my face toward him, making my way between the buttons of his shirt, the fabric of his collar, the soft leather of his jacket. I find his chin first, and my lips barely touch it, too afraid to give him a true kiss.

His fingers plunge into my hair, moving my head away. Then, all of a sudden, his lips are on mine, his mouth seeking me with sweet ferocity, eager to open me, taste me, as our breaths mingle with the patter of the rain.

I love him.

Oh, yes, I love him.

Tio can say whatever he wants. Let him present me with Davide's natal chart signed in wax by the pope himself. I love him. Davide's lips detach from mine for the space of a breath. "Alice, this is all wrong. You can't want this . . ."

My head is spinning like crazy; my legs are weak. "This is the *only* thing I want."

"No . . . no . . . no . . ." Yet he keeps kissing me, his lips seeking mine, his tongue desperately caressing mine. "But you don't know . . ." He pants against my skin, his hand pushing aside the fabric of my blouse, the heat of his words warming my neck. "You don't know because you've never asked me one question."

I detach myself from him, but only those few centimeters that allow us to talk, maintaining the contact between our foreheads, his eyes closed, because it seems like our skin might rip if we were suddenly to part. "Davide, Houdini has nothing on you and your ability to evade questions. I've always asked you questions. I've always wanted to know everything about you."

His lips part close to mine. "You never asked me if I was free."

His words are a shot too close to my heart. I'm confused. I must have misunderstood.

"Wha . . ." My voice is hoarse, as if I were clambering over rocks to try and escape. "You aren't?"

And now he tears his face from mine, and I feel the cold as he moves away, leaning back against the wall of the building.

"No, I'm not," he admits and rubs his face, keeping his hand over his mouth as he watches me, perhaps in embarrassment for what he just said, perhaps to hold back kisses that he would have kept giving me.

I know exactly what I should do now. I know that I should turn around and cross the street. I know that I should leave.

"I really like you, Alice." He reaches out a hand, without leaving the safety of the wall, and caresses my face.

My head is screaming at me to move away, telling me that Tio was right after all, and that this is a punishment. It is too much to have arrived at such happiness to then discover that there were—that there are—so many lies between us.

But instead of escaping, I bend my face toward him, rubbing my cheek on his palm.

"What do you suggest I do?" he asks me, pleading.

I raise my head and look into his eyes, those eyes that I thought I knew so well, that I thought must be hiding a man wounded by life, by a woman and a betrayal, for him to keep such a distance from me. Now I seem to read them more clearly, and the big question he once asked me takes on a whole new meaning: *Have you ever cheated on someone?* He didn't ask me to see if I was faithful or if I could have hurt him the way someone else had, but to know if I would have ever consented to be the "other."

"Leave her; be with me." I am direct, sharp, and perhaps even unjust toward this other woman, who is guiltless as I am.

His eyes slowly lower. "It's not possible. Not now . . . Even though things aren't good between us. Barbara is vulnerable, especially since her husband died."

"*Barbara?*"

"You met her at the castle," he confirms. "When I asked her to let us film on her property, I thought it would be simple to present it to you as a fait accompli. I would avoid speaking to you about it and just introduce her to you as my partner. But then . . . when I saw you come in, I knew that I would hurt you and you didn't deserve that; that I was a selfish egomaniac who wasn't taking responsibility."

That's why he wanted to take me away. That's why, when that plan failed because I had to work, he ended up taking her away and asking to see me tonight.

Barbara Buchneim-Wessler Ricci Pastori. How can I compete with perfection?

"I'm an asshole, Alice."

I close my eyes and force myself to breathe. "Yes. You are."

"I'll take you home."

I raise my arm, making him stop. "I'd rather take a taxi."

25

Don't Bother to Knock for the Libra

By now, I've gotten the hang of being rejected; I know how to deal with the situation. It's entirely a matter of drawers. Mentally putting things in drawers, that is. I take the things that I don't want to see, the situations that I can't face, and I seal them all in a watertight compartment, a drawer that is not to be opened for quite some time ... if at all.

Tonight, for example, I am lost amid the crush of bodies crammed into a nightclub, having an evening with friends that makes me feel young and full of energy. And full of alcohol. I really enjoyed myself. I danced, I sang ...

This damn taxi seems to be taking forever, and the old jazz tune playing on the radio is ripping through my defenses.

I am tired: tired of believing, tired of being disappointed, and tired of suffering. I'm tired of putting myself back together, every time. I'm tired of being "strong" and being told that I am strong as if it were an excuse to treat me badly. I can't take it anymore; I don't believe in it anymore.

I pay the taxi driver quickly, my house keys already in my hand.

The staircase light is still on the fritz and the neon light keeps flickering in and out without ever lighting up completely. This sucks.

I try the elevator, but some inconsiderate neighbor must have left the doors open because when I push the button, it fails to move. I start going up on foot, and climb over the yellow rose that someone has dropped. Distractedly, I stroke the handrail. I categorically refuse to cry. Then it hits me.

Why are there rose petals on my stairs?

I frantically search for my cell phone in my purse, but I am too nervous. I stop, flattening myself against the wall, trying not to breathe so I can listen for any noises. Then I hear something: footsteps. One more flight and I'll have made it.

I see my front door illuminated intermittently by neon, but there are roses, the same yellow roses that someone keeps sending me. So I run. I fly up the stairs, gripping the key, ready to stick it into the lock at full speed. I can see a shadow peel away from the other flight of stairs, a second before the light goes out again.

"Here you are, finally!"

I turn around, ready to unleash my best Tarzan impression, but a hand strikes my mouth before I can yell.

"SHHH! Do you want to wake up the whole building?"

I try to wriggle free but the man isn't letting go.

"Calm down, Alice. *Muffin*, calm down."

I flatten myself against the door as my eyes bring him into focus, in spite of the terror and the flickering light.

"I'm back," he gloats, almost singing. "*Honey*, aren't you happy to see me? Didn't you get my flowers?"

I can hardly believe my eyes. I blink a few times, because after an evening like this, perhaps I have more than one screw loose.

Then, I take a deep breath and I ask him: "What are you doing here, Giorgio?"

26

Full Metal Gemini

So, finally the mystery is revealed. Behind every yellow rose, behind every petal, and especially behind every thorn, was always Giorgio, the man who broke my heart. OK, one of the men who have broken my heart, but he was the one who started the ball rolling on the all-too-long string of men. At the time, however, Paola had qualified Giorgio's departure by saying, "You should thank your lucky stars he's gone . . . and change your locks."

"What are you doing here, Giorgio?"

The irony of it is that, out of all the people who have ever come in and out of my life, Giorgio is not only the one person I never expected to see again, but also the one person I never wanted to see again.

"I've come to see you, Honey Bunch."

"At two in the morning? What time zone are you on, Shanghai?" I'm not being the least bit nice, I know, and for a minute I even believe I'm being unfairly bitchy to him. It only lasts a minute, because if I think back on just some of the things that he did, tripping him and knocking him down the stairs would be an act of mercy.

194

"Ha-ha, you and your sense of humor . . ." he replies, scratching his head. "I just *had* to talk to you."

"You couldn't call?"

"I tried, but I think you changed your number."

I clap my hand to my forehead. "Oh, that's right. I blocked your number."

"You've always been hotheaded," he replies cockily. "My beautiful, fiery Muffin."

Um, no. "I'm really tired, Giorgio. Can we do this another time?" Better yet, another lifetime—or two? "Give me your address; I'll get in touch."

"Well . . . that's the thing. I don't actually have an address at the moment. Ambra kicked me out. That freeloading, ungrateful bitch wants a divorce . . . and she wants my children. *My* children. Do you get the picture?"

"I guess." Even when we first met, it was the same story.

Giorgio shakes his head. "This time she really means it. She wants all of my money. The damn woman has frozen all our accounts and . . ."

In the meantime, I open the door. I'm definitely not in the mood to spend the rest of the night on the landing being a Kleenex for my ex as he cries about being dumped by the woman he dumped me for.

". . . and so I have no place to go."

"Excuse me?"

"Come on, Alice. I know that in your heart you've forgiven me. It's your nature. I'm just asking for a few nights."

"No."

"Just one night! Just to give me a break. Last night I slept in the park . . ."

I sigh. "Giorgio, listen, this is not a science-fiction novel. I can't take a person back into my home who treated me like dirt, who cheated on me, who used me to make his wife jealous . . ." Ex-wife, he had told me! "Who do you think I am, the Virgin Mary?"

He squints and stares intently at my forehead for a couple of seconds.

God, give me the strength.

"I . . . I really don't know what to do . . ." he mumbles softly, his voice cracking. I enter the apartment and immediately close the door behind me. My heart is drumming a thousand beats per minute with guilt.

I decide to fix myself some herbal tea because this encounter has rattled me so much that I am sure it will take forever to fall asleep.

Meanwhile, Giorgio is still on the stairs. He's leaned his head against the wall and thrown his jacket over his shoulders as a sort of blanket. I know, because I check through the peephole on my way between the kitchen and the hallway.

If he stays there, the superintendent will have a heart attack tomorrow morning.

How can I send him away?

I still don't know, but this is a question that will torment me more and more over the next few weeks.

27

Libra Fever

I have a pounding headache, one of the symptoms of the cold that is destroying me. I am like the *Titanic* upon sighting the iceberg: a shipwreck waiting to happen.

It would have been the perfect excuse to curl up in bed and watch all the movies in my survival kit, but instead I went to work as usual.

"Alice? Alice, are you in there? Answer me, please! Alice!"

Cristina's voice makes me jump, and my phone narrowly escapes falling in the toilet.

Yes, "we are friends" now. Or so she has decreed. However, her concept of friendship, at the moment, is based on her need, brilliantly expressed, to find an ally for support and reassurance.

"Yes, I aB here."

"Um, am I disturbing you? Are you sick?"

"I just haB a bad cold. I caBe for toilet paper." I sigh. "I 'ad to get a cold in Bay . . ." I comment, repeatedly blowing my nose.

"Yes. May . . ." Cristina repeats, and I look at her through the bathroom mirror. She has her eyes lowered and her fists clenched at her sides.

"You ready?" I ask her, trying to shake off my lethargy. We have a meeting soon, and I have to try to get a grip on myself.

"What do you mean, am I ready? Have you seen me? The wedding is coming up. I have the dress fitting on Saturday, and I am horribly fat. I look like a puffer fish, a sea lion, a whale, a hot air balloon . . . a blimp . . ."

"CristiDa: you're pregDaDt."

"I am incredibly ugly and disgusting. Even my face has expanded. It's no wonder that Carlo doesn't look at me anymore. And I have to put on that thing . . . that ridiculous white thing covered in sequins. I will look like an enormous snowball . . ."

I try to console her, and I want to say that the fact that Carlo no longer looks at her has nothing to do with her pounds.

Great friend I am. Yes, but sometimes saying nothing is better than using words as a bulldozer. For instance, I cannot be eaten up by guilt for not returning the six calls I've missed from Paola in the last two weeks.

I finally rest my head on the desk; all I want is to melt into the chipboard, to disappear like a *hot air balloon* on the horizon.

. . .

"Hello? Earth to Alice. Commence landing maneuvers. Houston . . ."

Tio looks at me, shaking his head.

"I've thought about it over and over again. Just tell me: old or new? Old or new?"

"What, Tio? Who?"

"The Mystery Leo. Come on."

"AgaiD? EDOUGH." I have absolutely no desire to talk about the Leo. "How Bany days have you beeD torBenting Be about Dis?"

"Exactly fifteen days, seven hours, and twenty-three minutes."

"I already said it's Dot iBportant. Dot iBportant because it fiDished before it begaD. And you should be happy."

"Yes, but I'm curious."

"You are a gossip."

"I am a gossip. I am a curious gossip, and I'm worried about you. I think this guy is the reason you're on edge."

"What guy? There is DO guy!"

Tio rolls his eyes. "Hello, I was looking for Alice. . . . Ah, she's still in Wonderland? Right. I'm talking about the Leo!"

"EDough!" I wave my hand to dismiss the conversation, although I know I'm on dangerous ground. "You are getting worse thaD Paola. How BaDy tiBes Bust I tell you that there is Do woD. I aB aloDe. I *live* aloDe," I caw.

But I am lying.

I mean, it's not actually a lie, because legally I am the only occupant of my apartment, but I do have a guest. And it's been more than the customary three days—Giorgio has pitched his tent at my house for the past two weeks. To be honest, he is even making himself useful around the house. It's nice to have a sort of servant/friend that brings you breakfast in bed and to come home to a clean house and dinner on the stove.

Being a quintessential, unpredictable Gemini, as luck would have it, Giorgio's multiple personalities even include the perfect "geisho," and I was in need of some helpful company.

In front of me, Tio puts a hand on my forehead and shakes his head. "Be careful, Alice. Your horoscope has nothing good to say right now. You are in a critical phase, like the caterpillar when he closes himself into his chrysalis to become a butterfly. I wish you would open up to me like you used to. If not, then how can I open up to you? To tell you the truth, I'm very worried. Andrea and I are going to lunch at his mother's this weekend. I have no idea what to wear."

"Tio, does Andrea's Bother Dow that you are a couple?"

"Well, of course not."

I give him a gentle pat on the hand. "I would work on that probleB first."

"Work! What a big word for someone lying on their desk." Raffaella appears behind him.

"Acid yellow was so last year," I say through closed teeth, because I might have a stuffy nose and a head amid clouds of Vicks VapoRub, but that doesn't blunt my memory of everything else. "I've just goD a cold."

"Ah! At least some of my prayers are being answered," says Raffaella. "Are you happy now that Alejandro abandoned me, Alice? Is this enough for you?"

"Ow!" Tio gives a glint of a smile and hums, "The Sagittarius strikes again ..."

When she leaves us, presumably to join Cristina in the bathroom and found the "Virgo" Suicides Club, Tio cries, "Ah, men!" and casts me the sideways glance of someone who is still seeking a glimmer of a conversation—about my imaginary Leo, I suppose.

I roll my eyes. "Well, ADdrea is different," I say, changing the subject.

"And I'm happy. I'm happy that he's not one of those guys who promises the Moon and then gives you such a beating that all you can see are stars. *Lions in sheep's clothing . . .* "

"Haha. FuDDy."

"I'm serious, perhaps because I'm a man too ... Call it a sixth astrological sense or whatever you wish, but I know how to recognize an idiot at first glance. The one who just came in, for example. He is a moron, one hundred percent, guaranteed. Look how he goes strutting around with that smile like a door-to-door salesman, and then turns around. . . . There he is, punctual as a pimple for a first date, anxious to look at anything that vaguely resembles a pair of tits. I'd be curious to see the face of the chick who snags him. Poor fool."

"Oh, shit . . ."

"Did you see him?"

From the other end of the loft, the "idiot" who just wandered in yells: "Muffin!"

28

Lions for Geminis

I remain motionless as Tio turns toward me. To call his expression severe would be like saying that Nero made quite a mess of Rome.

"Oh, Giorgio . . . Hi. What are you doing here?!"

I imagine the screeching strings from *Psycho* playing in the background.

"I came because I knew you needed me, babe." He empties a bag from the pharmacy onto a nearby table. "Handkerchiefs, sprays, thermometers, cough drops, and . . . Oh! Pads. *Always protects like nothing else,* Muffie."

"How thoughtful . . ." Tio comments, arms crossed.

To confirm that my astrological chart must look like a Picasso painting, the glass door opens and Nardi bursts onto the scene (I decided that from now on I will exclusively call him "Nardi"), aiming directly for me, without looking at anything or anyone else.

"How are you?" he says, after having taken me by the arm and led me away from the others.

I look around, worried, and note that in my absence, Giorgio has clung to Tio. "I have a cold," I respond rather vaguely.

"Alice, I'm sorry."

"I'll get over it."

"I don't mean the cold."

"Deither do I. I'll get over it." I wonder what this man still wants from me, because this conversation should not be happening.

"I thank you for wanting to Bake Be relive all the Bagnificent discoBfort of the last tiBe, but I assure you that there's Do Deed. I reBeBber it perfectly without a suBBary of the Bost paiDful Bo-Bents."

"I just wanted to tell you that, if I didn't care about you at all, if I didn't hold you in such high regard . . . I think I would have taken advantage of what you feel."

This really makes me lose my temper. It hurts my pride to hear him speak of emotions (only *my* emotions?) that seem not to concern him at all.

"There was odly wod kiss. As far as I'B codcerded, it's water udder the bridge. I'B here to work, and I thidk you are, too."

I walk away and my heart drops into my stomach as I see Giorgio run toward Mr. President with an outstretched hand and the sycophantic smile of the most consummate actors.

"Giorgio, for the love of God!" I summon him, grabbing him by the shirt. "I Bust work. You caD't be here."

"You're so beautiful when you play the career woman, Muffin. Ah, I should have married you, not that bitch!"

Oh, no . . . when Giorgio starts in with "that bitch of my ex," he can go on for hours.

". . . If I'm bankrupt, it's all her fault . . ."

And he's not totally lying, because his ex-wife is exactly like him. His kindred spirit is now trying to strip him of every asset down to his last sock to make him pay for his extramarital adventures, on-line poker, and the strip club, where a private investigator's camera filmed him during an evening of joie de vivre that makes *Fear and Loathing in Las Vegas* look like a home movie.

To make matters worse, Davide passes by me, trying yet again to extend one of his magnetic glances.

"Muffin, at least take the medicines," exclaims Giorgio, piercing me with a decongestant stick as if I were a skewer. "Otherwise, you'll just toss and turn in bed and snore like last night."

Unfortunately, Davide is still looking at me. He is speaking with Mr. President, but I see him shoot glances in my direction. I feel so helpless, I want to die.

After giving Giorgio a dirty look, Tio glances in the direction of Davide and the president, and then at me.

"Now I get it," he says. "You thought that I wouldn't put two and two together, knowing the sign and everything else?"

This time I hesitate.

"Alice, I don't enjoy telling you that people's astrological charts are incompatible; believe me. But here it is crystal clear. Seeing you together can't help but convince me that your Leo could be your undoing."

My eyes fill with tears, and my throat closes completely.

"Tio, I aB iD love. It's terrible, I Dow."

He stares at me, wide-eyed, for a moment and then puts a hand on my forehead. "It must be the fever. Don't worry, I'm not going to let you drown this way! I will save you!"

29

Catch Leo If You Can

We're finally in the meeting room, and the atmosphere has turned as serious as if we had suddenly changed the set and were working in a bank instead of a television network.

There are no more faces, discussions about scripts, jokes, or creativity around that oval table. My show is dissected algebraically, transformed into segments of equations that correspond to time slots, advertising, and shares.

While Mr. President speaks, explaining the wondrous world of television with the aid of a pointer, Davide's eyes—I mean Nardi's—don't leave mine.

I try with all my might to stop myself from reading something into it. Regret. Lust. Tenderness. Pain.

I'm telling myself that they are just mirrors for what I feel—for what only I feel.

He didn't want to *take advantage of my feelings.*

I can't trust anyone but myself. Perhaps not even myself, since I've always made the wrong choices and the wrong character judgments about the men that I've met.

Written on the sheet in front of me is the name of the program that I have created, *An Astrological Guide for Broken Hearts.*

Why do I always choose the wrong men? Maybe the right one is out there somewhere, perhaps closer than I think, but all I'm doing is pushing him away, not giving him a chance to come any closer.

Mr. President is still speaking. "Since everyone who deals with *Astrological Guide* is present, I think we can make a short digression to talk about the final episode."

Davide lowers his eyes for a second, as if searching for something on the sheets in front of him, but doesn't take long enough for it to be plausible.

"Yes, so we thought that the final episode of *Astrological Guide* deserved a special event . . . A truly exceptional guest."

"Professor Klauzen," interrupts Mr. President impatiently. "From the Klauzen clinics, is now world-famous for his method of programming births."

"Gee, it won't be easy to get him in the studio for an interview," says Tio.

"Klauzen is a very particular person, as well as an extremely busy doctor. He won't come to us, so we will have to go to him. We will record an interview, and Marlin and Nardi will be the ones to go to Paris and do it."

"Why not me?" exclaims Tio, quite resentful.

"Because you will have other things to prepare for the show here and because with Marlin, we will be able to avail ourselves of a women's clothing sponsor and shoot videos of her and the product around the city."

I watch my friend glower with envy, but he takes the blow with style. Dating Andrea seems to have its merits.

"Since Nardi knows the professor personally, he will accompany Marlin to Paris." Mr. President smiles, satisfied. "And you can view it as a reward, Davide, since much of the network's success is the result of you and your vision."

Davide nods without smiling. "Thank you, Mr. President."

"You have done an excellent job, Nardi. We will miss you."

Immediately, I feel the blood leave my body. It tucks itself away, compressing itself god knows where, before starting to scream through my veins again all at once.

Davide is leaving.

I knew that his assignment was temporary, but I had no idea how or when it would end. And just now I realize that, in all probability, after he goes to Paris, I will never see him again. An icy chill runs through me, and I know it is because of the hole in the center of my soul.

I make an effort to get up, but something happens. It seems that my feet sink into the floor and the plasterboard walls fold in on top of me. The table lurches toward me, and suddenly I am surrounded by nothingness.

30

Crouching Leo, Hidden Gemini

The room is dark around me. It is my own room. My dear little room with the desk, the storage units over the bed, and the display cabinet with all my toys. A slow sigh escapes my lips, and I feel relieved.

"You have a face like ..."

From the other side of the house, I start to hear voices.

"Paola, calm down. I understand that, like a good Cancer, you feel like a mother hen, but Alice will be fine. It's just a fever."

"No, she doesn't *just* have a fever! First, this stupid thing with zodiac signs and now him!"

"Please, let's not drag astrology into this, OK! Let's distinguish between friends and enemies. If you put me on the same level as this ... this Leo guy, I swear I will kill someone."

"Tio, you've just come into Alice's life now; you have no idea what this idiot has done."

"Hey, I am right here! The idiot has a name, which is Giorgio. And also a zodiac sign, which is Gemini."

"Tio, this pathetic excuse for a man is a Gemini. For what it's

208

worth, I still remember his mega-birthday pool party, and it was at the beginning of June."

"So, you remember that, huh?"

"Oh yes, I remember it. Just like I remember those two women that I found you with in the Turkish bath."

"Can I offer you coffee? Or perhaps chamomile is better," asks my mother.

I start to regain consciousness when I hear my parents' voices.

Now I remember. I passed out because I was sick, and the meeting room was hot; because Giorgio has come back into my life with a vengeance; because Carlo is marrying Cristina, even though he's in love with someone else; because Tio gives me advice on which zodiac signs to date, but he himself doesn't understand the man of his life; because I shouldn't have fallen in love with a Leo with such a disastrous astrological chart . . . And because Davide is leaving.

"Muffin! Are you awake?"

"Stupid idiot, you woke her up!" cries Paola at the door.

Instinctively, I pull the blanket up to my nose, because while I no longer fear a telling off from my mother, Paola is much more dangerous. Only when she grabs him by the arm do I notice that Giorgio has a swollen and reddened eye.

"When someone has a concussion, you shouldn't let them sleep, don't you know that, Paolie dear?"

"You're the one who's had a concussion since the day you were born. And don't you dare call me Paolie, *Muffin*, unless you want a stiletto to the jugular!"

"It's just a touch of the flu," intervenes Tio. "Part of the Negative Transit—"

"Enough of this nonsense! There's no wonder that she's lost her mind with all the crap you've been feeding her for months!" cries Paola.

"I was only trying to help her, since her radar for men works about as well as a Chinese kitchen robot. Let me remind you that you made her go out with that Aries colleague of yours, Luca, who dumped her not even halfway through the first date."

"And you did excellent work with Alejandro. Bravo."

"I told her that it was a bad idea to go out with that underdeveloped tango dancer. Never trust a Sagittarius, not without checking his astrological chart."

"I'm sick of you two!" blurts out my ex-boyfriend. "I'm here with Alice now. My dear gypsy with the crystal ball, I recall that you didn't know what to do when Alice practically had a heart attack a little while ago; you were crying like a little girl. Miss Praying Mantis here wasn't even there; she only showed up later to make trouble."

"Whereas you, my dear Gemini-ex-Leo, you arrived just in time to take a punch from Nardi. My only regret is that I wasn't the one to give it to you."

I reemerge from the duvet, putting out my antennae like a timid snail. Did I hear right? Why would Davide ever punch Giorgio?

"Um . . . Excuse me for interrupting, but . . . Does someone want to tell me what happened?"

And then, they begin.

Paola's version: Florence Nightingale's Call to Arms

I was at my mother's house helping her to make lasagna, when I received Tio's call.

I tried to calm him down on the telephone. "Tio, Tio, what's going on? I can't understand you if you cry. Take deep breaths. Good boy. Breathe!"

"It's Alice! I . . . I don't know what to do anymore. Help me, Paola! Only you can save her."

And when I arrived . . . God, I wondered if my strength

would be enough to save everyone. I pushed my way through the screaming crowd until I found you, in Tio's arms.

He was in such a state of shock that I had to slap him. "Now listen here, you have to let go of her. I'm here. I'll handle it. OK?"

Ah, men, they can't hold up at all when someone is ill.

"Then, once they called the ambulance," my best friend continues, "I saw him. I saw that imbecile ex of yours bashing people all over the hall. A shameful spectacle."

"Shameful, indeed!" interrupts Giorgio. "There are people who don't have the slightest idea of the basic rules of hand-to-hand combat."

Giorgio's version: Rambo Apocalypse . . . Now!

Milan. Shit. I'm back in Milan.

I sniff the air, feeling in my bones that something is wrong.

There are two women, civilians, eyeballing me, but I spy something at nine o'clock. It's a brute well over six feet tall carrying you away.

I yell, "God forgives, I do not!" in Chinese, of course. Then, I'm on top of him.

Once I've torn you from his grasp, I desperately try to revive you, giving you mouth-to-mouth resuscitation and cardiac massage.

"And he was likely to break your ribs, if Nardi—who was trying to carry you to the bench by the window—hadn't punched him."

"And I punched him back!" says Giorgio. " 'In town, you're the law,' I told him. 'Out here, it's me.' It's a quote from *Rambo*. I know it by heart. And obviously I shout it in Chinese, Muffin. You know when I'm angry, I always speak Chinese."

Of course, Giorgio speaks Chinese . . . and Lithuanian. It's true that at first glance he may seem like an idiot, and he really is. But like a cross between Rain Man and the Six Million Dollar Man, he has acquired abilities that, however exceptional they might be, are completely useless in someone like him.

Paola believes his brain should be donated to science, but as soon as possible, to do the world a favor.

There was a time when these quirks made him exceptional in my eyes; more than my white knight, he was my knight in shining multicolor. It took months of Paola therapy to bring me to my senses.

"But I mean, how? How could you take someone like this back?" Tio jumps in, pointing to Giorgio. "After everything I taught you."

Tio's version: Space, The Final Frontier . . .

Julian Date: 2,456,402.92. Latitude: 45.28, Longitude: -9.12. Planet: Earth.

The behavior of the Libra had already begun to worry me in recent weeks. Especially because she herself had confessed to having gone out with a Leo with Libra Ascendant, a man with an astrological chart that, in dynamic combination with hers, could have potentially disastrous results.

So, this morning, after having carefully checked her horoscope, I decided to face her head-on, with the intention of easing the Negative Transit and letting her feel my support.

I'm not one to dramatically mistake someone's zodiac sign, but the Libra had been busy muddying the waters, giving me the wrong date on purpose, and my Mercury in Taurus must have done the rest, making me obstinately blind.

Angry with her, I hadn't given too much weight to the excessive load of the Square of the Sun in Negative Transit with her Birth Moon that actually made her faint.

Unfortunately, I have Neptune in Sagittarius, which pre-
vents me from intervening promptly in certain situations, but
when the other Gemini engaged in a relentless struggle with . . .

Tio stares at me, speechless. "With . . . Nardi," he says. Then he
shakes his head in my direction and whispers, "The Leo. The Leo
tried to protect you."

I bite my lip and lower my eyes. "Go on . . ."

He doesn't have time, however, because my parents burst into
my room, brimming with excitement. "You're on television!"

One of the video journalists tells the camera that they were just
leaving after an interview with a soccer player, but he and the camera
operator were drawn back by the screams coming from the loft of
the production offices. Behind him, you can glimpse my feet.

"Oh my god." I look at Tio angrily, since he's the one holding me
in his arms. "I have hair in my face. And you didn't even close my
mouth!"

"I'm sorry!" he says and bursts into tears. "I was so scared!"

Then, quick as a fox, Paola appears on the TV, with her first aid
kit in hand.

Soon after, we glimpse Giorgio standing out from an indis-
tinct group of people. He must have climbed onto a desk and then
thrown himself into the fray, screaming.

I can only mutter "Oh my god" like a mantra.

"Go away," I say. "Everyone out of here."

We need a solution here.

All I can think about is the fool I just made of myself on TVs
worldwide . . . and of Davide, who threw himself on Giorgio to defend me.

Nonsense; I should focus on more important things, like my
work, if I still have one.

How could this have happened?

Paola is right when she says that I have to learn to love myself. On the other hand, Tio is also right when he says that generosity is inherent in my natal chart.

On second thought, it's all very clear, obvious, even. When I looked at Giorgio's astrological chart a couple days ago, I found correlations that made my hair stand on end: specifically, his sixth house in Leo speaks of his love of luxury goods. And Davide? With Jupiter in his ninth house, it's obvious that he would live a life of constant travel, while Venus in his twelfth house clearly implies that he is allergic to close bonds. As for Alejandro, there's not much to say. The eighth house in Cancer, combined with the Moon in the third and Mercury and Venus in the first clearly underlined the fact that he has a desperate need to be liked, hence his proclivity to move from one woman to the next.

Do you need any other proof, Your Honor?

Henceforth, zodiac or death.

31

Leoless

I wrinkle my nose, disoriented by the smell of fried food. I try to curl up under the covers, clinging to the dream that I was having, but this time when I look at Davide, at the seashore, I see him with a Tyrolean hat complete with a feather.

Since I'm dreaming, the situation doesn't disturb me in the least, and if he were to start singing "Edelweiss," I would be more than happy to join him in a Julie Andrews–style chorus. But he takes my hand, brings it to his lips, and looking into my eyes, he says . . .

"Cuckoo, Muffin," and kisses me.

His lips are hot and fiery, and taste like . . . sausage and mustard?

"Good morning!" Giorgio is straddling me in his underwear, trying to kill me with a fork pointed at my face.

I grimace. "Sausages at . . ." I check my telephone, charging on my nightstand. "At six twenty-five on Sunday morning?"

"English breakfast," he says.

"Italian fuck you," I respond, taking refuge like a cat under the sheets.

Unfortunately, I only get to doze for another half an hour, since

215

the continuous banging and clanging of pots and pans in the kitchen is hardly conducive to sleep.

"What the hell are you doing?" I ask Giorgio as he stands in the kitchen in his underwear and a Kiss the Cook apron with his arm shoved up the backside of a gigantic bird.

"Stuffed turkey for Thanksgiving," he answers, as if it were the most natural thing in the world—except that we're in Italy, and it's the end of May.

"Isn't Thanksgiving in November?"

"But I want to thank you now. I'm making stuffed turkey."

"Giorgio, I have plans for lunch today ..."

"What? You're going out? And what about me?"

Should I try to explain to him that I still want to have a social life?

"I've already made the stuffing, peeled the potatoes, and dressed the salad.... And who are you going out with?"

"I'm having brunch with Tio and Andrea; it's been planned for days."

"So you're abandoning me here to go frolic with your fan club," he says resentfully.

"What fan club? It's brunch with friends, Giorgio."

"*Male* friends; that means that they will spend the whole time thinking about sex."

That may well be true, but knowing Tio and Andrea, their sexy thoughts will definitely not involve me; but far be it from me to share this with Giorgio.

And before continuing this conversation I need an intravenous dose of coffee and my computer to check the ephemeris and planetary conjunctions today. I know that Tio does not agree, but I want to take astrology seriously from now on. So I've started to check my stars every day by myself.

I have several Positive Transits that are hard to believe, and it's almost a shame that it's not a workday. With Saturn Positive with my birth planet Uranus, it would be worthwhile to take advantage of the situation. The most interesting aspect is the Transit of Jupiter with Pluto that predicts imminent creative changes in my life and could help me to earn the favor of someone influential.

"So, Muffin, you just couldn't care less? What am I supposed to do?"

"Well, for starters, you might consider looking for a job."

At the word *job*, I see him pale. "I'll do that next week. I had the perfect afternoon planned; just the two of us here at home with board games: Connect Four, a few hands of gin rummy . . ."

Wow. As I slip into the shower, I can't imagine how I could possibly pass on such a wonderful offer.

While I finish getting dressed, I hear him pacing back and forth in the hall on phone call after phone call. When I go to say goodbye to him at the door, he does something even stranger.

He turns and stares at me seriously. "Has someone called you lately asking about me?"

. . .

"You've gotten it into your head that you can do it on your own but it doesn't work that way, dear." Tio wags his finger theatrically.

"Aren't you the one always saying that I have to believe in myself and my own abilities more?" I mumble with my mouth still full of chocolate cheesecake.

"For heaven's sake, that is Paola!" he immediately shoots back. "I am absolutely convinced of your inability to be proactive."

I raise my eyes to the ceiling. "God! You have to admit that I've gotten better. And more careful. I don't trust anyone anymore without first checking their astrological chart."

This time it's Andrea who intervenes after clearing his throat. "Um, my dear, Tio is worried about your association with that individual, one Giorgio, who persists in staying overnight on your sofa. He believes he is manipulating you."

"Giorgio is not manipulating me. At least, not anymore. He has no one else to help him, Andrea."

"On the other hand, facing the harsh realities of homelessness may inspire him to make a more concerted effort to look for a job, Alice."

I stare at the remaining four thousand five hundred calories of cheesecake still on my plate. "He swore that next week he would roll up his sleeves and look for work."

"Oh, don't tell me that you're taking a Gemini seriously!" mutters Tio sarcastically.

"You're a Gemini, too!" I retort.

"Our astrological charts are very different. He has Mars in Cancer! And it shows; he is narcissistic, dictatorial, and inconclusive."

"Things that are totally alien to you, of course."

"Since you're such an expert now, you should realize that it's your Moon in Pisces that reveals your Achilles' heel with that creature; otherwise you would have already thrown him out."

Now that he's hitting below the belt and I am offended, I naturally want to give him a taste of his own medicine. "And you're sure that's not your Venus in Leo talking? It seems that if someone is not bowing and scraping at your feet over and over again, you hold it against them as if you had suffered high treason."

I think I've hurt him because he gasps, unable to say anything for ten seconds. "Look who's talking about need for recognition and affection!" he exclaims when he's recovered. "You're the one with Saturn in Libra!"

"At least I don't have Pluto in the first house," I shoot back.

"But you have Scorpio in the eleventh!"

"And you have a Negative aspect between the Moon and Midheaven, Mr. Fickle!"

"Saturn in Libra!" yells Tio angrily.

"Doesn't it occur to either one of you, even for a second, that you're insane?" interrupts Andrea.

"But she told me that I have Pluto . . . implying that I always want to be the center of attention."

"And him?" I grumble, swallowing a third of the cake without even tasting it. "It's not my fault that I have Saturn in Libra! Andrea, Saturn in Libra delays marriage and perhaps means that you'll marry an old man. What do you think was crueler: me telling him that he is self-centered or him telling me I'm destined to be an old maid?"

"But it's not Tiziano's fault if you have Saturn in Libra . . ." There was a moment of silence. "Oh geez, what are you making me say, Alice?! Do you realize the nonsense that you have been spouting?"

"It's not nonsense!" Tio and I answer in chorus.

"There, not even my boyfriend supports me," exclaims Tio.

"Oh no, honey. Don't say that," I say. "I'm here!"

And him: "Gotcha! Moon in Pisces!"

"That's not fair!" He always gets me, but I'm actually not angry; I'm laughing.

Tio gives me a pat on the back and laughs along with me. "Now then, speaking of serious things, you know that it's time to get busy, right?"

"Do you mean Jupiter's Transit with Pluto?"

Andrea raises his eyes to the ceiling. For him we are probably "rather strange creatures," but he loves us anyway.

"Exactly. Don't you feel electrified?"

Electrified is definitely the right word at the right time, because I jump up in my chair as I feel my cell phone vibrate in the pocket of my jeans. "Excuse me," I say pulling it out. "Gotta take a call."

Tio snorts and then must become aware of the expression on my face. "Don't tell me: the Leo? Hang up."

"No, but . . . what if it's important?"

"Important like getting chicken pox? Hang up!"

"Hello?" I get up to stop Tio, who is flailing his arms at me the entire time, from taking the phone out of my hand.

On the other end: "Alice?"

Why does his voice always have the power to melt my knees? "Davide."

"Where are you?"

I look around, as if for a moment I had completely forgotten. "I'm . . . I'm at California Bakery. Why?"

"Great. I'm coming."

I know that Tio is angry. His face is grim, and he won't look me in the eye.

I bite my lip before I tell him: "He's coming."

"He's already here," says my friend.

Andrea turns around, making a noise with his chair.

I am about to turn around as well when *his* voice stops me, blocking everything inside of me: my brain, yes, but also my heart, liver, and kidneys. "Can I sit down?"

Davide looks at the menu and then asks the waiter for a coffee. He does everything with such calm that it makes Tio even more irritable. "I was in the neighborhood," he says by way of explanation. "Does anyone know how the tarte tatin is here?"

Even for Tio, although he's accustomed to theatrical improvisation, this unexpected appearance out of context is disconcerting. And again, I have to feign an ounce of superiority in attempting to explain Davide's behavior: "Look who's good at obfuscation. He has Mercury in the tenth house."

Tio looks at Davide, who still seems intent on consulting the menu. "Yes, and an Opposition between his Moon and the Ascendant. Not to mention Venus in the twelfth house," he says grimly, for my benefit alone.

I know what he's telling me. That aspect, in Davide's astrological chart, signifies that he has difficulty in relationships and seeks out solitude more than anything else. What's more, there's Venus in his twelfth house, which translates to "instability in love"; in other words, 2–0, game over.

"Can you cut it out?" Davide frowns.

"But of course," Tio says. "We will stop immediately. Let's talk about serious things. By the way, how is Barbara?"

With every ounce of audacity he possesses, Davide takes my fork and digs it into Tio's plate, into the chocolate cake that he still hasn't finished. "Excellent," Davide says, chewing under my friend's murderous gaze.

"What brings you here, Mr. Nardi?" Andrea asks. "We can well imagine that it must be an issue that requires immediate assistance."

"Yes," Davide mutters. I raise my eyebrow while he glares at Tio. "I had to see Alice to speak about our trip."

"Trip?" all three of us say together.

"The trip to Paris."

"But weren't you supposed to go with Marlin?"

"She was called for an audition, so you will have to come with me," answers Davide peremptorily.

"But why not take me?" says Tio. "I am the host of the show."

Davide stares at him with an ice-cold expression for a seemingly interminable moment, and I see Tio's Adam's apple go up and down in discomfort. "Because I want Alice."

32

The Day the Pisces Came Out

My train for Paris leaves tomorrow at 6:00 a.m. sharp, so I really should be spending tonight focusing on work and on packing, but in less than an hour, I am supposed to go out and meet Daniele, Karin's friend, at an exhibition. I could have explained that it would be better to rearrange, but after blowing him off a million times, I couldn't bring myself to do it. Actually, I forced myself to accept his invitation for tonight in hopes of distracting myself from the thought of the days ahead where Davide and I will be alone in the world capital of romance.

If my internal hell wasn't enough, I'm also dealing with an external pain in the ass. Giorgio is currently on a suicide mission to stop me from doing whatever I need to do in the little time I have left to do it.

A whole other problem is the incessant voices in my head. Clearly it's the first sign of my decent into madness, but I have the excuse of being a double sign and of having significant planets in diametrically opposed constellations. At the idea of being cheek to cheek with Davide for three days, my Neptune in Sagittarius has already put on Swarovski crystal, while Mercury in Scorpio is telling me that I'm a total idiot.

"Why don't you wear the yellow sweater for the interview?" Giorgio hops around me, playing three-card monte with my clothes scattered on the bed.

"I want the blue dress. Stop bouncing around me like a pinball. I am running late as it is."

"You could have skipped going out tonight. You would have had more time and more rest. Not to mention, you don't even know this guy. He could be dangerous!"

More dangerous than spending the evening at home with him? I don't think so. If he keeps on like this, I'm in danger of being handed a life sentence for involuntary manslaughter.

Although, I must admit, I'm not jumping for joy at the prospect of going out. I would much rather take a bath, listen to some music, have a glass of wine, and indulge in dreams about Davide and me, without thinking about the pathetic figure that I will cut if I continue down this slippery slope.

I try to put Neptune and Mercury in their kennel as I slip into the bathroom to put on my makeup, but one of the two (probably the forked tongue of Mercury) hisses that rather than indulge in silly excitement, I should be angry with Davide for torpedoing into my life. Don't I want to smash him in the face?

Wouldn't I rather that he take me in his arms and kiss me again?

Shut up, Neptune, shut up. For goodness' sake. It's best to go leave the apartment, and fast!

Once in the taxi, I focus my thoughts on this guy, Daniele. He has really been very understanding, considering my propensity to hang up on him and constantly reschedule our first date. Not to mention that I'm curious, since he is a Pisces with Virgo rising, and he has a very interesting birth chart. He deserves at least one evening. Although this is really not the evening for either one of us, because when I called him to reschedule our dinner tomorrow, he invited me out tonight, saying he had a previous commitment but wanted me to join him.

After a few minutes, the taxi stops at a sidewalk crowded with people and umbrellas. Damn, I was so lost in thought that I didn't realize that it had started to rain. Why can I never meet a man in a state of grace? There always has to be something, an atmospheric agent or an Astral Conjunction that intervenes, even when I don't have great expectations for the evening. Of course, I don't expect to find the perfect man this way, on a blind date, while I'm an emotional mess and my ex is growing roots on my couch, but I would be grateful if at least the hair gods would be on my side tonight.

"You must be Alice."

The first thing I see when I open the cab door is a reassuring umbrella covering my head. Only then do I notice the face of the man who is holding it and staring at me with a big smile and a pair of honest, green eyes.

"Daniele," he says, offering me his free hand.

I stammer something like: "GnaaaaAliceuaaa . . ." while trying to regain the use of my jaw and roll the kilometer of tongue back into my mouth. He is gorgeous.

Just gorgeous? Neptune screams indignantly. *You should run to the nearest church and light a candle.*

He accompanies me to the entrance. Then he helps me take off my coat and, without any hesitation, entrusts it to the cloakroom clerk together with the umbrella.

While he performs all these maneuvers, I have the opportunity to study him. He's tall and has long, coppery brown hair that he keeps tied in a bun. His glasses give him an intellectual air, enhanced by his faded jeans and his untucked shirt.

Would a guy like this really want to date you? Mercury questions, pragmatic but also decidedly sour.

Why not? Why can't you, yes you, be the protagonist of a wonderful story? replies Neptune, batting his lashes and pursing his lips.

Daniele accompanies me to the corridor leading to the exhibition and thanks me for having accepted such a last-minute invitation.

He is a very affable, hands-on type. While we speak, looking casually at the photos on display on the gallery walls, he makes me feel lighter, as if we have known each other forever and this was not our first date.

"Hey, Daniele!"

He turns, smiling, and introduces me to someone called Franco, accompanied by a brunette with a cocked beret.

"This is wonderful, you know? And, I wanted to thank you."

"What for, Franco? There's no need."

While Franco takes him aside, the girl in the beret explains, "Daniele is one of the few who stayed close to Franco at a very difficult time. He's incredibly sensitive, as you can see from his photos."

I look around, as if the walls were suddenly illuminated, revealing the photos for the first time. He took these?

But of course. This is not just an exhibition. This is *his* exhibition.

When he returns and Franco and the girl say goodbye, Daniele apologizes for leaving me alone.

"You never told me that I was going out with the artist himself. They are beautiful. Congratulations."

"Oh." He shrugs. "The photographs are just a testimony, a way to bring attention to the stories behind them."

He seems slightly embarrassed.

Neptune: *Maybe the Prince Charming factory has reopened its doors.*

Mercury: *Well, it's clear that it's simply a clever tactic to impress and maybe . . . take you to bed tonight. Bimbo.*

"I would like to know what you think," he says while I cast the nagging voices out of my head.

We are in front of one of his photographs. The image shows a group of people crowding into a square. They are dancing, and on their faces is a joy that makes even the oldest appear young.

"It seems . . ." I hesitate. "It's as if you waited to shoot until everything was perfect—not only the framing, but also the emotion—until the moment when you were feeling what they were feeling. You can feel people. You love people . . ." I clear my throat; this time I'm the one who's a bit embarrassed.

"I'm very impressed, Alice. This is the first time someone has told me my pictures make them feel like that." He looks deep into my eyes. "And you are a Libra with Sagittarius Ascendant," he adds. "Spirit and matter. A nice combination."

Wait a second. I can't have heard right. "Are you talking about my . . ."

"About your astrological chart . . . I know that in our culture it's considered nonsense, but in others it's held in high esteem. In India, for example, the parents would never give consent to the marriage of their children if the couple's astrological charts were not in harmony."

"You've been to India?"

"I like to discover the world. And, more than anything else, try to understand the people I come into contact with. Each of us is a treasure trove of loneliness, desires, fears, and hope. But you know this. You are a person of rare sensitivity."

I swallow. "Well . . . I do have the Moon in Pisces . . ."

He nods mysteriously, as if this revelation had thrown a new and wonderful light on me, as if I had just said that I was the last descendant of Mahatma Gandhi, or Buddha, or Elvis Presley.

We move away, and I feel and see myself differently; as if beside

Daniele, I'm not Alice, but a better, more beautiful, and confident woman.

Then, while sipping a glass of something nonalcoholic (all proceeds from the exhibition will be donated to a charity fighting alcoholism), I feel a sudden chill that brings me back to reality and back to Alice, with all her bad moods and frustrations. I guess you really can't escape yourself.

A few steps away from me stands the woman whose last name is shorter only than the amount of zeros in her bank account: Barbara Buchneim-Wessler Ricci Pastori. The very same woman who, unfortunately, also happens to be dating the man who I cannot get out of my head or my life.

Daniele, attentive, immediately asks me if there is something wrong. "Is it the mocktail? Is it too cold?"

I stick to the topic of the sad photograph that is near us.

"You are a very empathetic woman."

And I, in all my empathy, look at Barbara Buchneim etcetera, etcetera out of the corner of my eye and wonder if Davide will make an appearance, too. Meanwhile, Mercury reminds me that I am a very, very terrible person.

"Good evening, Daniele."

I activate my sweet, affable yet detached smile, but she doesn't seem to notice me.

"As always, compliments from the Wessler Foundation. You have such an *exotic* vision. Are you considering the possibility of publishing a catalog?"

"For fund-raising, sure. But don't ask me to write the text. I don't see myself in a writer's shoes . . ." Then he turns toward me. "But maybe Alice could help me. I haven't even introduced you, I'm sorry. Alice Bassi, Barbara Buchneim-Wessler Ricci Pastori. Barbara is the patron of the foundation I am collaborating with."

I notice that her eyes narrow for an instant and then widen in surprise. "I believe we've already met," she says without offering me her hand. "I think you work with my boyfriend. Am I right?"

Am I wrong, or did she pause for a second on the word *my*?

I don't move a muscle, for fear of stepping on the bed of nails suddenly in front of me. "Um, yes, he is the supervisor of our programs," I explain, more for the benefit of Daniele than for Barbara, who surely is aware of her boyfriend's job.

"Not for much longer," she says with a feline grin. "In two weeks, he's going to be working on the start-up for my estate in Brittany, which I am planning to transform into a wellness center. It will take time, at least a year or a year and a half, but that place holds a lot of memories for us, and it won't bother us in the least if we need to hide away there for a while. All alone."

Great. Where were we again? Ah, right. I was looking for a rope to attach to the ceiling.

I make an attempt to smile, hoping that my teeth don't shatter with all the ice in the air, but luckily the splendid man beside me intervenes.

"We'll need to schedule the portrait session you asked me for soon, then. Tomorrow perhaps?"

"Unfortunately, Davide won't be here tomorrow. He's leaving for Paris on business," replies Barbara.

Daniele briefly shifts his glance toward me, then smiles and shrugs. "Over the weekend, then."

Fortunately, the torture doesn't last long. When Barbara finally walks away, Daniele tells me that he is a little tired of being stuck indoors and asks if I would like to take a walk with him.

Outside, the still-wet sidewalk sparkles under the streetlights, and our reflections chase each other in the shadows.

"Are you OK?" he asks, taking off his jacket to put it on my shoulders, just like in the movies.

"Yes . . ." I take a generous mouthful of air and realize that it is true. I really am OK. The mere presence of Daniele gives me a certain heartwarming tranquility.

"I got the impression," he begins, sitting down on a bench, "that there was something wrong. Alice, I know that someone like me can't enter your life like this—impertinently, shall we say—and not expect that you might still have other things going on."

I don't know what to say. Luckily, he doesn't seem to expect me to say anything, because he continues.

"I really like you. And I would like to go out with you, if you'll let me." This perfect and beautiful man takes my hand and brings it to his lips. "So, know that, when you get back from your trip with Davide, I will be here."

33

A Leo Named Desire

It's embarrassing that my subconscious is at such an elementary level that it can't even produce a respectable nightmare. I was chasing a man with a lion's head, but when I turned the corner where I thought I had seen him hide, I am met instead by a man with a fish tail trying to grab me. How terribly didactic. It doesn't take Freud to explain it. My love life *and* my dreams are second-rate.

Lack of imagination aside, it's quite obvious that my sleep was restless, dominated by Daniele-I-Am-the-Man-for-You versus Davide-Anyone-Who-Understands-Me-Is-Brilliant.

As if the dream weren't enough, now that I've finally managed to fall asleep again, the bed is a problem; it has never felt so uncomfortable. I must have contorted myself into such impossible positions that now I seem to have a pole in my kidneys, and I am probably sleeping with my mouth wide open. I end up waking myself by snoring too loudly only to plunge from one unimaginative nightmare into the next, very much in line with my karma. It's only then I realize that I am not in my own bed. I'm not even in Daniele's, which could have been interesting.

As the memories of the last few hours of my life come back to me, I despairingly realize that I have fallen asleep on the train, and am consequently sprawled out all over the seat like a contortionist. Not only that, but my head is resting on Davide's shoulder.

I want to die. Right here. Right now. Thank you.

"Sleep well?"

I sit up immediately, feigning a dignity that I don't have. "How much farther?"

"No more than an hour," he responds. "I was flipping through a biography of Klauzen."

"Klauzen . . ." I repeat, catching my reflection in the glass and paying more attention to my squashed hair than anything else. "We were lucky. He doesn't grant many interviews."

I look at the photo of the professor in the press kit and glance over a biography filled with accolades. Obviously, I've already ascertained that he is a Capricorn with Scorpio Ascendant and the Moon in Aquarius. Everything in this man's natal chart suggests he has the determination of a tank. How else could he have come by a private jet, or a villa in Brittany?

In Brittany.

"He's a friend of Barbara's, right?" I ask him, discouraged.

Davide stares at the papers in front of him. "He was a good friend of her husband's. They used to hunt together."

I don't know why, but for a moment I imagine the two of them at a colonial estate, with his boot planted on the head of some poor animal while she floats ethereally behind, preparing cups of tea at 110 degrees in the shade.

"Well! Someone certainly has a finger in every pie," I comment.

"I'm not her puppet, if that's what you mean." Davide looks at me grimly, but his cell phone starts ringing cheerfully, causing him to snap to attention. He stumbles into the table in front of us as he tries to climb over me.

"Hey, wait!" I get up, too, causing Davide and me to remain wedged between the seats and the table, our bodies stuck together, our hearts beating together, and our eyes . . . Those eyes . . . damn him and his magnetic stare! And damn the attraction generated by the Venus-Pluto Conjunctions!

"Hi, Barbara . . . Yes, I'm still on the train."

At the mention of her name, bile starts to rise in my throat.

I repeat like a mantra that Daniele could be the man of my dreams, that continuing to chase someone like Davide makes no sense, unless I'm hell-bent on skipping merrily to my own funeral.

I watch him move a couple of seats away from me.

God, I'm out of breath just looking at him. Is there not an ounce of justice in this world?

"Excuse me. Do you *do it* often?"

I turn around, startled after hearing such an inappropriate question. I widen my eyes even more when I find myself in front of a little woman with gray hair.

"Excuse me?"

The woman snorts. "I asked if you do that often, miss," she replies, pointing at my shoes. "Do you always take your shoes off on the train? Because I can assure you, it's not very hygienic . . ."

Ah. I must have taken them off during my contortionist's nap. And that is obviously why I misunderstood her question.

I let her pass by and I sit back down, checking my cell phone. I have a message from Daniele. How sweet!

"Tea, coffee, *sex*, or snacks?"

Next to me is the guy with the catering cart, and he just offered me sex. I feel the roots of my hair burning with embarrassment.

"What?" I stammer.

"Tea, coffee, *espresso*, snacks?" he repeats innocently.

I know what I heard, loud and clear. He said the word *sex*! I can't be wrong this time!

Davide is back and he's looking at me with concern.

"Sex," someone else whispers.

I look around, but everyone has their eyes transfixed on a cell phone, iPad, newspaper, or book, minding their own business. I get up and race to the other side of the car where I ask myself what kind of Trine, Quadrature, or god-knows-what Astral Conjunction is creating this unidentified hormonal storm in me.

I look back at Davide again.

Breathe, Alice. Send oxygen to your neurons.

This is exactly what I wanted to avoid, what I feared about having to spend three days alone with him on a trip.

"Are you all right?"

"Of course. Why wouldn't I be?"

(SEX). Shut up, possessed neuron!

"I didn't get much sleep last night," I say, trying to pass by him to return to my seat, where perhaps I can find another yoga pose to try. (SEX!) To sleep. SLEEP.

"Maybe it wasn't so wise to go out last night," he comments harshly.

I spin around.

"Since you had a train at six and a long journey ahead."

So, Lady B told him that she ran into me at the exhibit . . . with Daniele. Great!

"I think I'm capable of deciding what is best for me and my life. In fact, I've recently fine-tuned my intuition . . . It's much better."

"Do you really think so?"

I can't believe that he is being so arrogant.

Then his Sun-Moon Trine comes out, causing his attitude to completely change. He takes my hand and I read deep melancholy in his eyes.

"Alice . . ."

Damn him.

"I'm very worried about you." He bites his lip and looks around, then lowers his voice. "I don't understand what you're up to. Last night you were at that exhibit . . . and you're living with that other man . . . I mean, if you're doing all this to make me jealous, you should know that you're only hurting yourself."

"What?!" OK, no more nonviolent protests. "You really have some nerve talking to me like this. Typical self-centered Leo with Mercury in Leo!"

"Are you talking about my horoscope?"

"I'm taking about your *birth chart.* After twelve episodes, you haven't even learned the difference?"

"Eleven . . . I think we still need to discuss the last one."

Oh, right. We haven't even written the last episode yet."

"Anyway, that man is no good for you."

"When I need your help to decide who I sleep with, I'll call you, OK?"

"So you're sleeping with him?"

I bite my lip and call on all the powers of my Pluto and Mercury conjunction, which among other things says that I should keep my personal life private.

"What's it to you? You're sleeping with Barbara, and I can't say anything about it."

He then says, "Technically . . ."

Here comes the moment in which I play Glenn Close in *Fatal Attraction* and try to press the panic button on his heart. What kind of an answer is "technically"? And it wasn't even a question. What do I care if he does or doesn't have sex with Barbara? The important thing is that he doesn't want to have it with me.

But what the hell does he mean by "technically"? Technically yes? Technically no? *Technically* this man is driving me crazy.

34

No Sex Please, We're Libras

Knowing that Paris is a magical, romantic city makes my torment all the more intense. Our taxi crosses town like a bat out of hell, but it's as if the two of us aren't really there, sitting on opposite sides of the backseat, shielding ourselves from each other with the press pack. I would have liked to go to the hotel first and freshen up, but Klauzen, in line with his tenth house in Virgo, has a very strict schedule and will unquestionably be waiting for us for lunch.

However, we are the ones left waiting, providing ample time for my gaze to shift from Davide to the baguettes elaborately arranged as a centerpiece. I don't know which of the two I would eat first.

Alice, repeat after me: "Out with the Leo and on to the Pisces." Unfortunately, ousting a person from your heart is not as simple as opening a door and telling him to wait outside.

Three-quarters of an hour pass before Klauzen arrives with his entourage, pointing a pair of glacial gray eyes at us.

"Without further ado. Point one: We will do the interview tomorrow morning at ten in the living room of my loft. The lighting is perfect there. Point two: I will grant you an hour. Given that the whole thing will last three minutes, this is a more than suitable amount of time for television. Point three: You will be allowed four questions. You will find them enclosed in the file that my assistant will give you."

Prompt and silent like a robot, the platinum-blond girl at his side hands me an envelope.

"You will also find the B roll material to be incorporated. No more than seventy seconds, to be distributed throughout the course of the piece. She will explain where and what to use after the interview. Now, you two can leave." He moves his chair to sit down at the table, and Davide pulls back his and motions for me to do the same.

"Point four," I say, addressing Davide through clenched teeth. "I'd rather have Edward Scissorhands as a gynecologist than him."

I realize that it is only two o'clock, which means we have all the time in the world before tomorrow morning and the interview. For the next twenty hours, Davide and I are alone.

. . .

My survival instinct, or rather my Sextile aspect between Saturn and my Ascendant, tells me that I should steer clear of Davide as much as possible to avoid problems.

I take out the city guide that I remembered to stuff in my bag at the last second. There, the Eiffel Tower could be the perfect solution. Looking at Paris alone from the top of the Eiffel Tower will give me a sense of infinity and control, I am sure of it.

I dog-ear the page and close the little book, and my stomach howls like a werewolf. Damn Klauzen and the pyramid of baguettes I left untouched out of politeness.

"If you like, I know a really nice bistro where we could go after we drop off our bags in the room."

Between hunger and anxiety, I cannot help but look back at him, eyes widening.

Room?! He can't have meant that there is just *one* room, but why do I have this obsession? Damn, as soon as I'm looking at him I can't help but think of anything but sex.

"Oh, I thought I would take a walk around the city. I don't want to sit down to eat just yet."

Excellent. Let him do what he likes. It's not like we're joined at the hip.

But when the taxi stops at the hotel, tachycardia hits me. What if there really is only one room? I am gasping for air by the time we reach the reception desk.

"*Bonjour, mademoiselle. Nous avons réservé deux chambres pour le compte de Rete Mi-A-Mi,*" says Davide, laying his passport on the counter.

The young woman types quickly into her computer keyboard.

"*Oui, monsieur . . .*" she says. Then she lifts her eyes and frowns. "*Je suis désolée, mais il y a un petit problème avec votre chambres.*"

Even with my limited French, this seems to sound like: I'm sorry, but there's been a problem with your rooms.

Oh, damn. I knew it! There is a whole romantic filmography of accidents like this!

I wonder where the blood goes when I feel it all drain out of my body like it does now.

While Davide asks: "*Quel genre de problème?*" I mentally review that (a) I did get waxed; (b) the lingerie that I brought is not overly sexy, but not from the supermarket either; and (c) I brought penguin pajamas. Damn!

And so on, practically until I reach z, which is nonsense, because I really don't want anything to happen between Davide and me.

"*Vous avez demandé deux chambres sur le même étage, mais ce n'est pas possible. Donc je dois vous donner une au troisième étage et l'autre au cinquième. Je suis désolée . . .*"

My French stops more or less at *Oui, je suis Catherine Deneuve,* so I don't really know what's happening. Then the receptionist puts two keys on the counter.

"*Pas de problème,*" says Davide.

No problem.

"What?" I ask quietly. Inside me, John Travolta is still dancing in *Saturday Night Fever.*

"They don't have two rooms on the same floor. Yours is on the fifth and mine is on the third. Not a huge problem, right?"

My interior John Travolta stops dancing, turns on the buzzing neon lights, and begins to sadly tidy up the confetti from the party. "No, not at all . . . Not a problem."

I take refuge in my room and consider the possibility of taking a cold shower, but then I go to the bathroom and see a magnificent double Jacuzzi, perfect for a romantic encounter, and I close the door with a crash. Best avoided.

Actually . . . That gives me an idea.

In the elevator, when Davide said, "Half an hour . . . ?" I didn't answer, so . . .

I pee quickly and then check my purse before grabbing the keys and leaving in a hurry. If I go downstairs immediately, he will still be in his room. Then I can immerse myself in the streets of Paris, alone and undisturbed. I will send him a message when I am safely in the Metro, just to get rid of my guilt, although I have no idea what I will say. I practically throw the keys onto the reception desk as I dash toward the revolving door like a hundred-meter runner in the final rush.

"You're already ready. Great!" Davide closes his newspaper and leaves it on the table, getting up to join me. "What would you like to eat?"

"Actually . . ." No need to invent anything. "I wanted to walk around a bit on my own," I admit. I am sure that he understands. He must understand.

"But you have to at least stop to eat something. Keep me company at the kiosk next door. I love galettes, but I hate eating alone."

I blink a few more times, in a continuous attempt to avoid direct contact with those eyes, capable of transforming me into jelly.

"OK, OK . . ." I give in. After all, we're just going to eat. It seems a modest price to pay for the freedom that I will enjoy afterward.

We devour the first *galette* in silence.

On the second, we start to emit a caveman-like grunt of appreciation.

On the third, he says, "You sure are high-maintenance . . . What an appetite, ha!"

I stop with a mouthful of food halfway down my throat, then gulp it down with a sip of Coca-Cola.

"Look who's talking!? We've eaten the same amount."

"But I'm a man."

"So?"

"Aren't women supposed to eat like birds?"

"I've read that birds eat eight times their bodyweight."

"Know-it-all."

"Sexist."

We both bite our lips to hold back the laughter; Davide, because he doesn't want to be first, I imagine, and me, because I don't want to give in—and also because I'm worried I have food in my teeth. Then those little wrinkles that accentuate his sharp eyes get the best of me, and I can't help myself.

"Must be the Paris air . . ." he says, smiling and shrugging. "Everything's magical, isn't it?"

"Do you like it?"

"I lived here for a couple of years."

"Paris, too?"

Davide shrugs and starts telling me about when he moved here to do a master's at the Sorbonne, right after college.

Oh god, I feel so small and stupid. He has lived in the world, and other than as a tourist. I haven't even moved away from the neighborhood where I was born.

"It's best if I go," I say out of the blue, pretending to look at the time. "Since you know Paris so well, I don't want to force you to be a tourist." I take out my wallet and fish out twenty euros that I place on the table for the bill.

Davide puts his hand on mine. "No, I'll get this . . ."

"I can put it on production expenses," I reply, resolute, laying down my wallet to grab the bill.

"You're still mad at me, Alice."

It's not a question, but I'm forced to look up.

And I must not trust his Mercury in Leo, because it would be capable of selling ice to Eskimos. "We are only here together for work, Davide."

He sighs. "We're not friends anymore, then?"

I'm seething with anger. "When have we ever been friends?" I say, without expecting an answer. Then I shake my head at the hurt in his eyes. "I'm just trying to live my life, Davide."

"And you don't want me to be part of it."

I bite my lip, as if something in me wanted to eat those words, too, but then I say, "No. I don't want you to be part of it."

35

You Will Meet a Tall, Dark Leo

Paris is a seriously overrated city.

It's like walking barefoot on glass. At every glance, it whittles you down, pushing its thorns deeper into your flesh with its colorful bistros, tree-lined streets, and postcard corners—where there is always a couple kissing or asking you to take a photo of them. They should write it in the brochure: if you have a broken heart, you should not come to Paris. Admission reserved for happy couples only.

"Fuck Paris."

My cell phone rings. "Whatever you are thinking, stop, right now. And remember to buy me a present. An Hermès scarf, if you're on the Champs-Elysées . . ."

"I'm not on the Champs-Elysées."

"What a shame."

"Not for my credit card. What's up, Tio?"

"Your horoscope is a disaster today."

"Not just my horoscope."

"Exactly."

It turns out that these days are "a bit tense," astrologically speaking, because I have seven Negative Transits out of ten. I would say that is almost a record. My Birth Moon must withstand an attack on all fronts from the Sun, Mars, and Neptune, who offer me unforgettable moments of irritability, depression, lack of objectivity, and mood swings. In short, it will be as if I have constant PMS.

"I can't take it," I say. "Paris, Davide . . . Doesn't it seem like too much? Why are the stars so cruel? Why don't they leave me alone and let me have a calm, classic, bump-free relationship, at least for a while? I'm tired."

"Because this is the time to open yourself up to change, sweetie," says Tio. "To be able to give up, even on what you set out to achieve. Alice, you also have a Positive Transit—between Mercury and Uranus—which means awareness and adaptation to new situations. You are a Libra, which isn't easy, because you'd like to build your castles in the sky out of steel. But you have to let it go. Hon, that's what the stars are trying to tell you right now. Don't keep on beating a dead horse and simply . . . let things be."

"Bye, Tio," I say, with a lump in my throat the size of a turkey.

"Wait, Alice!"

But I don't want to hear any more and quickly end the phone call. I find a bench and sit down, tucking my legs against my chest and leaning my chin on my knees, like I did as a child.

A couple passes by me, and I watch as they tenderly embrace each other. If I had gasoline and a lighter, I would set them on fire.

With an angry gesture, I take the guidebook and toss it in the trash. To hell with this romantic city and its romantic monuments; to hell with all my plans and everything I've set my sights on.

I start wandering, slipping through side streets, going up and down stairs, popping into small or large, more or less crowded squares. I want Paris to absorb me and show me who she is, if she has the strength.

Paris is resting on my shoulders with the weight of many hours of lost sleep, an endless journey, and a heart that has been shattered into more pieces than I ever could have imagined.

The problem is that now I don't have the slightest idea where I am, and, what's more, because I was stupid enough to throw away the guidebook with the map and all the other information I need, I have to go and buy another one if I want to have any chance of figuring out where I am.

"Bravo, Alice," I tell myself, ducking into a bookstore to grab a map only to realize, when I get to the checkout line, that my wallet is no longer in my purse.

Panic.

How the hell do I get back to the hotel?

Shit. My passport!

The only thing left for me to do is to prepare myself to swallow down all of my bile and call Davide to come and get me.

While fiddling with my phone, I prepare to cross the street.

I wait diligently for the light to change and, as soon as it clicks, I stare straight in front of me and take a couple of steps into the crosswalk, but I stop, right in the center.

Davide is in front of me, on the other side.

"Are you following me?" he says.

"You followed me!" I reply.

I press hard on the screen of the smartphone to cancel the call that I was about to make. Too late. He rummages in his pocket and pulls out his phone, which evidently is only on vibrate mode, and he looks at me, lifting a corner of his mouth. I shift my eyes away, and he doesn't say anything.

"Where were you going?" he asks me when we are safe and sound on the sidewalk.

"Nowhere," I admit, pretending to be interested in a pair of shoes in a store window. "I'm lost."

"You could have just used the navigation on your phone."

Technology and Me, chapter one: "The Basics."

"Anyway, it's running out of battery, and I was robbed. That's the worst of it. My wallet is gone and that means that I'm in trouble. What do you do in situations like this? Do you go to the embassy? The police? The *gendarmerie?*"

Davide smiles again and shakes his head. "No police. And no *gendarmerie.*"

"So a life in *clandestinité* awaits me."

"No, you just have to say, 'Thank you, Davide.'"

I turn toward him as, like a magician, he pulls something out of the inside pocket of his jacket.

Mon salvateur! It's my wallet. How the hell . . . ?

"You left it on the table at the café, when you slipped away, and it gave me the perfect excuse to follow you."

"You were following me?"

"I *followed* you. I wasn't *following* you. If you say following, it makes me sound like some sort of stalker."

"OK. Followed."

"Yes. But then I lost you. And you reemerged right in front of me at that intersection."

"Why didn't you come up to me?"

Davide shrugs. "I thought that you might rip me to pieces, in spite of the *galettes.* You looked . . ."

I shrug, trying to steer the conversation to a safer topic, to anything other than *us.*

"I wanted to see if Paris would amaze me . . . outside of the usual tourist destinations."

"Well," he says, trying to offer me his arm like a gentleman from the *Belle époque*, "what better guide than a slightly nostalgic ex-Parisian?"

At this point, I don't even have the strength to say no. "What's in your Guide to Paris for Skeptical Women?"

36

The Leo on the Bridge

Et voilà, la Promendade Plantée," says Davide.

We are on an old redbrick bridge, a former railway track that has been transformed into a walkway with a garden.

"It doesn't even feel like we're in a city."

"I used to come here a lot when I lived here, on beautiful days like this."

I imagine that he came here to read or perhaps to study; this place certainly lends itself to it.

"I bet you came here on walks with some beautiful French girl . . ." I say, specifically seeking a detached tone, like that of an old friend nudging him. I give him a sideways glance, and once again I see the image of a man seeking solitude. I ask myself what that could mean in his life and also for his future.

"No . . ." He hesitates. We sit on a bench.

"What?"

Davide shakes his head and smiles enigmatically, as only someone with Pluto in their twelfth house can, then stares at something in front of him.

Just behind the trees, we can make out the windows from the upper levels of the houses. A woman appears in one of the windows, carrying an evening dress on a hanger. I watch her open the closet door to put it away.

"I've never brought anyone here," he says then, without turning toward me.

"I'm the first?" The thought hits me as soon as I've uttered the words. I gulp trying to drive my heart back to its place.

"So many years have passed."

"Does it seem different?"

"I am . . . different. But I still find it fascinating." He carries on staring ahead. "What do you think that woman will do tonight?"

"I don't know. Probably have dinner, I imagine. Do you know her?"

"No, but I've always loved peeking into houses and wondering what kind of life the people inside them lead."

This is very odd. I never would have imagined him doing something like this.

"Maybe she needs to go out to dinner," I say.

Davide looks at me skeptically. "With a man? Perhaps a man who is secretly in love with her . . ."

I bite my lip without saying anything else. Sometimes, it's so easy to be with him.

After crossing the strip of garden for about a mile, we go down the stairs and immerse ourselves in the colorful galleries under the arches.

"This is Viaduc des Arts, the Viaduct of the Arts. For the most part, the spaces were converted into ateliers for artists."

There are paintings, textiles, and souvenir shops that would make Paola's eyes gleam, and I can't deny that they have the same effect on me. For a couple of minutes, I lose myself among the stalls, trying to decide what to bring home.

"I buy a magnet from every place that I visit, to stick on my refrigerator. I know it's not a very original souvenir, but I like it," I say.

"I never buy anything," he replies.

"Too bad! Your fridge would be a masterpiece!" I reply, laughing.

He shrugs. "When you know that every object you buy means another box for the next move, you really consider whether you want it or not."

"Practical!"

"You would learn to be practical if ever since you were seven years old you knew that all you could take from place to place was one backpack and one suitcase."

The sun is setting as we emerge from the subway at Havre-Caumartin, and Davide crosses the threshold of the big Printemps stores where he decided that we should eat dinner. While we sip champagne on this beautiful panoramic terrace, the city lights up and shines with the colors of evening, and the tower sparkles more than anything else as if it were studded with diamonds.

"Thank you, my cicerone," I tell him, clinking my glass against his.

I look around and sigh. I don't feel any knots in my stomach, and I don't feel anxiety, tremors, or discomfort. "Thanks to you, I am seeing beautiful places, and for once in my life, just once, I really feel at peace with myself. You know, work aside, I want to enjoy these two days as if they are a vacation from myself, and I promise you that I will try not to think about all my problems." I look at him and admit, "Even between us."

I really mean it. *Peace and love,* I think. And if there can't be love . . . I sigh. Well, let there at least be peace.

"Sorry, I interrupted you," Alice said.

Davide looks at me, the fine lines around his eyes slightly more pronounced. He is tired. After a second, he smiles.

"I forgot."

"So it was a lie," I reply chuckling.

"I don't tell lies . . ."

I do my best to glower at him. "I said that I feel at peace with myself, not that I've suddenly become a complete idiot."

He laughs. "As you wish. Let's say it was a lie."

We turn toward the rooftops of Paris, the tower, Montmartre, the lights, and I start to think that everything about this moment could be defined like that: a lie.

Even our hands, our pinkies brushing against one another, intertwining for barely a second as we remain silent, staring at the city in front of us.

It's a beautiful, sparkling lie.

37

A Night Full of Rain and Horoscopes

Under a heavy downpour, we run, laughing like children, to the entrance of the hotel.

"I hope there is a hairdresser near the hotel. Otherwise, in tomorrow morning's interview, the cameraman will have a hard time shooting Klauzen from underneath my bushy hair."

"Always self-deprecating."

I shrug. "It's because of Mercury in Scorpio."

The elevator doors open and we enter, in silence. Davide looks at me without saying anything, pushing the button for his floor.

"Listen, Alice. The fact that we are here in Paris together . . . I wanted to apologize to you for having organized everything so last-minute. I know that you had other plans for the week, but it was very important that—"

The elevator stops and the doors open onto the hallway.

"I know," I tell him, cutting him off. "It's OK."

This is goodbye, and deep down I've always known. By now, the

251

hours separating us from the rest of our lives can be counted on our fingers.

"Today was a dream, Davide. Let's keep it that way. Reality can wait until tomorrow. Good night." I lean toward him and my lips touch his cheek.

His hand rests on my arm, but just for an instant. "Good night, Alice."

When the elevator doors close again and I start to go up, I feel like I'm sinking into an abyss. The truth is I won't be brought back to reality tomorrow; I can already perceive it in all its bitterness. In one of my films, a vacuum like this would be a mistake in the script. Unfortunately, life is not made up only of significant scenes, but also of moments like these; dead times in which the senselessness of everything hits you like a speeding bullet.

The elevator stops gently and the number five lights up above the door. When the doors open, I stand there, frozen.

Davide is leaning with his elbow against the doorpost, red-faced and bent slightly forward as he tries to catch his breath.

I raise my head to check the floor number, in case the elevator hasn't moved, but it is my floor.

"What are you doing here?"

"A . . . A . . . Alice . . ." Behind him, the door to the back stairs is still swinging.

After a few seconds, the elevator starts to close again, but he extends his arm toward me and grabs me.

"Forgive me. I'm sorry . . . but I can't let you go like this," he manages to say, still out of breath.

Then he kisses me.

I wish I could remain frozen and unresponsive, or push him away, but instead I return his kisses, immediately, completely surrendering to the feelings that overwhelm me, to the sweetness and the heat.

He whispers something as he continues to kiss my face and neck, something unintelligible, but it's as if I understood all the same. There is no need for words.

When the elevator doors hint at closing again, he pulls me out of the car and keeps kissing me in the hallway, pressing me against the wall.

"Davide . . ."

"Forgive me," he murmurs against my lips. "I couldn't let you go. I should be in my room . . . But as soon as the elevator doors closed, I felt like an idiot. I couldn't just go to my room and pretend like nothing had happened. So I ran up the stairs. Actually, I'm still out of breath. But I couldn't let you go. You said that today was a dream, that it's not real, but you're wrong. It is real, Alice, and more than ever. Right now, it seems to me that there is nothing more real than this: you and me. Now."

Then, I kiss him. I can hardly believe it, having the freedom to do this, to touch him. To kiss him. God, every fiber of my body wants to break into song.

My hands shake, and the room key card almost drops to the ground. We're on the bed in an instant, and he's unbuttoning my blouse.

I don't even know how long I've waited, how long I've *dreamed* about this moment. Davide presses his body against mine and kisses me as if his whole life depended on it. He tries to pull his shirt over his head, awkwardly, and it gets caught while I lunge at him to at least undo the top buttons.

I laugh, but he shuts me up with another kiss. "You won't get away from me anymore," he whispers, leaning on my chest and traveling down my abdomen with his tongue.

"You won't get away from me anymore . . ." More than anything else in the world, I long for his embrace, to feel his weight and his scent on me.

What I feel making love to him is a volcano; hot lava running through my system. It's not just a physical sensation; my mind is as involved as my body. I can't stop staring at him. I want to keep on kissing him, even though it takes my breath away. It's the end of the world, here in this bed, where nothing exists but Paris, the two of us, and the rain.

In life, there are moments that forever remain imprinted on your brain, and I know that this will be one of them. I will never be able to forget Davide's face resting on my shoulder, the sensation of his forehead against my lips, and his strong, open hands around my waist.

"What are you thinking about?"

He sighs, closing his eyes for a moment. "You know, how we ran into each other today in the middle of the street. Some couples are never able to do that their whole lives."

I stay silent for a little while. "And . . . are we a couple?"

"Alice."

I snort. "And now? What are you thinking about?"

I feel him move under the comforter. "Alice, look, this thing . . . This idea of telling each other every little thing that goes through our minds . . . I'm not an advocate of it. In fact, I don't think any guy is."

He kisses me again and makes love to me again, before we fall asleep embracing each other.

. . .

When I open my eyes, my legs are entwined with his and his nose is buried in my hair.

As soon as I remember what happened, I find it hard to breathe

again and even to move because I am afraid that everything is going
to disappear.

Then the alarm sounds.

But I didn't set any alarm.

In fact, it's a phone, and Davide lifts his head instantly, stretching out from the mattress in search of his pants. He gives me a look
before getting up. "Hello? Yes. No. I'm not in my room, exactly."

I sit up, leaning against the headboard of the bed, hugging the
pillow, while he puts his pants on and reaches for the door.

"It's . . . shit, nine?" He opens the door but then turns toward me
with an urgent look and, balancing the phone between his chin and
his shoulder, indicates his wrist where he's not wearing any watch.
He steps out of the room, barefoot and wearing only his pants, and
half closes the door. "Barbara, no, look, I woke up early and I went
down to read newspapers in the lobby," I hear him say when I approach.

His words strike through me like an arctic chill.

I'm not only stunned by the readiness with which he is able to
concoct a lie barely three minutes after waking up, but more so by
the misery of his entire pantomime: the exit from the room while
he buttons his pants, the voice that he tries to disguise against the
receiver, and above all the pathetic cliché of a roll in the hay with a
colleague on a business trip.

Suddenly, I can no longer see the Davide I fell madly in love
with. All I see is a petty user, a slick seducer who, in the end, was
able to get exactly what he wanted. Now I am nothing more than
something to hide behind a half-closed door.

I rest my hand on the door handle while I hear him say goodbye
to her and tell her that he will see her tomorrow. I swallow my anger
until I feel him push the door to come back inside. And that's when
I show my strength, closing it on his face.

38

Sex, Lies, and Leos

Luckily, I was able to change my train reservation with my smartphone. After the interview, I will be heading directly to the station.

Hell, let Barbara keep him for herself. She certainly deserves him. If he tries to get close to me with his gentle manners and his beautiful words, I'll bite his hand off.

Naturally, I don't give a damn about Klauzen; I just can't wait until this whole thing is over and I can turn my back on that monster (Davide, not Klauzen) and go home.

"*Mademoiselle, pardonnez-moi.*"

At first, I don't even turn around, but then someone taps me on the shoulder, and I find a girl in a blue hotel uniform standing in front of me, holding out an envelope.

"*C'est pour vous . . . par Monsieur Nardi.*"

She hands me a letter . . . from Davide.

Alice,
   You have every reason to be angry, and think badly of me.

Whatever I could say to try to excuse myself, it wouldn't be fair to write it in a hurried note.

Unfortunately, I have to leave, and it is very urgent. But there's something that I absolutely must tell you, which coincides with the real reason why you and I are in Paris right now.

I couldn't tell you before, unfortunately.

No, I mustn't lie . . . I could have told you yesterday, but I didn't want to ruin the moment between us. I am a jerk . . . I know.

I was the one who arranged for Marlin to have an audition during these days so that she wouldn't be able to come to Paris.

I wanted you to come with me, because I had to take you away from Milan.

Giorgio, the man you have allowed to stay in your home, is a criminal. There is a warrant out for his arrest for insurance fraud. After he visited you at the studios, he was recognized and the network was approached by the police.

For now, I've been able to keep the president out of this matter, but I needed to get you away from your house so that you wouldn't obstruct the investigation and above all end up in the middle of everything.

There are other things that I need to tell you. Very important things, but they need to be said face-to-face, and right now, I don't have time.

I can't explain, but I have to run. It concerns Barbara, but not in the way you think.

I beg you, please trust me just this once. Just me, without looking at horoscopes or making a thousand guesses about my zodiac chart.

For the interview, I trust you. Give it your all!

I want to give you a kiss, but you probably wouldn't let me.

Davide

I don't even know how I manage to reach the taxi, and hand over the paper with Klauzen's address. My legs are so weak that it seems like I have rubber knees, and my head is spinning.

Aside from Davide and that fact that he chose Barbara after all, now there's Giorgio and whatever mess he's gotten me into.

For a moment, I toy with the idea of changing my ticket again and flying to Timbuktu.

The room that I am ushered into is completely white and has a sterility about it that reminds me of a hospital or the final scene of *2001: A Space Odyssey*.

Klauzen is seated on an armchair in front of the window letting in the morning light and doesn't bother to turn around as I approach.

It seems I won't be fighting for the attention of this presumptuous Capricorn, who will not even deign to look at me, so I decide not to make the slightest attempt to curry favor with him.

The Viking who serves as his assistant explains how to conduct the interview, where to sit, and what questions to ask. I could have tried to impose my will in some way, but I used it all up when I forced myself to come all the way here on my own. Instead, I am as quiet as a mouse and I just nod at her instructions.

I can't wait to be home . . . but god knows what will be waiting for me when I get there.

Oh my god, the police! Who knows if I'll even still have an apartment when I get back to Milan . . .

It is only when I sit down in front of Klauzen and the assistant leans into his ear to whisper respectfully that we are ready that he closes the newspaper and points his icy eyes at me.

"Let's get the ball rolling," he says without a preamble, snapping his fingers as if I were a circus poodle, while the assistant puts his silver hair into place with maniacal zeal.

"Pardon?"

He raises his eyes to the ceiling, impatiently. Inga stares at me without betraying any expression. "Professor speaks. No qvestions."

With that, I motion to Pierre, Klauzen's cameraman, to start recording, and I muster all the good grace that I possess.

Klauzen smugly begins to talk about his favorite subject: himself. The Klauzen Foundation, the Klauzen Laboratories, the Klauzen Clinics, the Klauzen Method . . .

It is so Klauzen-centric that my head starts to spin.

"In your *lovely* show," he says, suddenly ironic, "you speak about horoscopes . . . and well, as you well know, my dear, this has nothing to do with science. However, recent studies would seem to strengthen the hypothesis that there is a link between the time of an individual's birth and his specific qualities. For example, children conceived in May are more likely to be born prematurely, resulting in fragile health. Similarly, it seems that those born in October are able to achieve excellent academic results, which is more difficult for those who come into the world in July, but who, on the other hand, might enjoy other characteristics, such as a more resistant physical form. And it's precisely this vision that puts the Klauzen Method at the cutting edge, providing a parent with the necessary information to make the most appropriate decision and deal with these unpleasant problems that parents, the unborn child himself, and society might regret."

"I'm sorry, but isn't this a sort of discrimination?"

Klauzen stops his monologue and stares at me grimly. "Evidently, you missed the fact that you were supposed to remain silent."

Yes, I am a serious professional and I need this interview for the program, but I can't seem to care as I let the next words escape my mouth.

"You know what? You can go to hell. You and the Klauzen Foundation. Are you aware of the fact that eugenics has been banned for decades? What you are proposing is disgraceful. You want to churn out perfect children custom-ordered by their parents; kids who will be privileged because of the way in which they were conceived and born. Above all, rich kids; children of rich parents who can afford your care. What about everyone else? Will we be slaves to these privileged individuals? Don't we all have the right to be able to dream about changing our lives?"

Inga has so much electricity running through her that she is about to short out as she stands in front of the doctor, shielding him with her body.

"Let's recall the army of clones," I say, pointing at her. "I'm proud of my imperfections! The world as you would like it to be would be deathly boring. And with that, I bid you farewell."

39

It's a Mad, Mad, Mad, Mad Gemini

When I set foot on the station platform, I feel like I'm emerging from a bubble, with all the strangeness that it entails.

I'm really back. I'm home, in Milan, alone. Now I have to deal with what remains of my life and put everything back into place; to once more make order out of chaos and rebuild myself.

This sucks.

At the top of my to-do list is a "Davide . . . who?" mental cleanse.

For the moment, however, as I leave the station and try to find a taxi, I have much more practical concerns.

Although the pains of young Alice are still my greatest worry, they are closely followed by anxiety about the Giorgio situation and the police, increasing with every step I take toward my apartment.

The queue of people waiting for taxis is disproportionate, even more so because there aren't any taxis, which is rather strange for Garibaldi station at seven thirty in the evening.

"They say that there's hellish traffic and that the taxis are all caught in it," someone explains impatiently.

"Police cars came by before," says someone else. "Something must have happened."

Fortunately, I don't live that far away. I opt for the subway, where I make a voyage of hope, stuffed like a sardine into the cloud of afternoon underarm odors.

When I finally emerge onto the street I, too, see police cars passing by. Above me, a helicopter flies noisily and close to the ground.

Suddenly, a hundred action movie scenes explode in my head of police hunting down criminals by blowing up cars under bypasses and opening fire, while Giorgio, wearing a leather jacket and dark glasses, plays at dodging bullets in slow motion as if he were Neo in *The Matrix*.

I cling to my suitcase like a crutch, a single thought reverberating through my mind: *I. MUST. GET. HOME. IMMEDIATELY.*

In front of my house everything seems to be okay. Perplexed, I stare at the intercom, trying to decide what to do. In theory, I am supposed to be an innocent party. Therefore, it's only right that I go up and see what's going on. The police might become suspicious if I changed my habits all of the sudden.

I put the key in the lock, feeling a bit like Judas.

Most likely, both of our phones are being monitored, but I didn't think to warn Giorgio, especially out of fear that he would get the crazy idea for us to run away together. I would prefer a life sentence in isolation to spending the rest of my life with him doing a *Bonnie and Clyde*.

The apartment seems strangely quiet, except that . . .

I hear moans; a kind of lament in the background, like the cry of a wounded animal.

For a moment, I think they must have actually shot him and left him to bleed to death in my apartment.

Although I'm terrified, I force myself to move and find out

what's going on. One cautious step at a time, I reach the kitchen, where the noise seems to be coming from.

I stand at the door, petrified, with a hand over my mouth to keep from screaming.

Giorgio is completely naked except for my oven mitt, which is being used to spank a perfect stranger, who is on all fours on top of my kitchen table.

I shield my eyes with my hand to spare myself the embarrassment of all this nakedness.

"What the fuck are you doing?"

"And who is this?" asks the stranger.

"My sister!" exclaims my ex-boyfriend.

Of course, coming back home, I would have expected anything other than finding two people having sex between the oven and the dishwasher. What about the police? Where the hell are the police?

"Your sister?" I repeat.

"Muffie, I can explain everything," he says quietly, winking. "Let me work," he whispers.

Let him work?

"Get dressed," I say drily. "And then tell me what this woman is doing in my house. In fact, I can see exactly what she is doing . . . so get dressed!"

What happened to the police? Outside, I still hear sirens.

Did they get the wrong address? Should I call them?

What comes to mind, however, is that at this point, since I came home a day early, I will be here when they come to arrest him. In short, in one reckless move, I've blown the cover for my trip to Paris.

"Giorgio, listen . . ." The only thing that comes to mind is that, if I want to stay out of this, he should not be captured in my house. Nor anywhere near me. "Listen, you need to leave immediately."

"OK, but you listen to me," he says, pulling on his boxers. "I'm getting on a plane in less than three hours."

"What?" Well, at least we agree on the fact that he needs to be through that door in no time flat.

"I'm afraid that the police are looking for me. A misunderstanding. Bureaucratic stuff. Insurance and so on. Just before you left, my lawyer called to warn me. And . . ." He gestures toward the hallway and, consequently, the kitchen. "I needed a lot of money for the flight. You didn't have it . . ." I don't know how he has the nerve, but he looks at me resentfully. "That's why she's here."

"You fucked someone from the bank to get a loan?"

He shrugs, then lifts up the upper part of my bed to reveal the big drawer. His suitcase is in there, already packed.

I don't realize right away, but after he has removed it and is about to close my bed again, I exclaim: "Where is all my stuff? Where . . . where are my videotapes?"

The drawer under my bed is empty. My survival kit has disappeared, along with the rest of my things.

Giorgio looks at me bewildered. "All that old stuff? I took it to the dump," he says, as if it were the most natural thing in the world.

I have to lean against the cabinet to prevent myself from fainting.

"But, Muffie, they were only some old VHS tapes. I got you a Blu-ray. You'll see how much better it is with Dolby Surround."

I'm not even listening to him anymore. "You threw out . . ." I can hardly breathe. "You threw out . . ." Oh god, I'm dying. My number one, the first videotape that I bought at thirteen years old. And *Ghost, Pretty Woman, Dirty Dancing* . . . "How dare you!" I cry, pushing him toward the door.

"But, Muff, why are you acting like this?"

"Why am I acting like this? Because I can't stand you anymore!

You've been washed up on my couch for two months with the excuse that you don't have a job and have to pay alimony to your ex-wife."

"Ex . . . ?" I hear screaming from the kitchen.

"Wife! And two children!" I add.

I hear the sound of heels down the hall and the front door slamming.

Giorgio makes a pouty face, as if I had ruined his fun. "Are you jealous, little Pandora?"

"Yes, I am jealous! I'm jealous of my life, of my house, my things, and my time! Ah, but what good is it to try and explain this to a . . . a . . . an idiot for whom a fun evening is seeing how many vodka shots he can handle before spewing his guts out all over the carpet?"

I grab him by the neck and push him, just as he is, toward the hallway. I don't give a damn that he is shirtless. I open the door and am about to throw him out, but out there are two frowning men staring at us.

"Hello . . . We're looking for Mr. Giorgio Pifferetti."

I breathe a sigh of relief. "Are you the police?"

They look at each other, perplexed. "Well, yes."

"You're late!"

I push Giorgio into their arms, slamming the door without waiting for an answer.

40

What Ever Happened to Baby Libra?

What I was left with, apart from the tears of rage and despair, was a house turned upside down, an empty and broken heart, and not even the possibility of drowning myself in the oblivion of *Pretty Woman*.

In the absence of my usual cinematic support, I tried to anesthetize myself to the sound of Lysol spray, tidying and cleaning up my house down to the most forgotten corner. And now that I'm done and have a beautiful "single woman" apartment, I allow myself to sit down and cry.

I cry out of relief.

I feel strangely free and light. I have a good feeling that, from here on out, I'm really going to be able to start over, without Giorgio, without Davide . . . And yes, of course, even without my precious survival kit.

Every new beginning starts with the end of something, right?

No more tears, Alice. From now on, you are growing up, and that's that.

I am dabbing my eyes with cold water when I hear the doorbell ringing.

Oh no, I think, disheartened. I didn't answer Paola's last telephone call and she must have rushed over here again. But it's not the face of my friend that I find in the doorway.

"I need your help!"

Cristina is staring at me with sparkling eyes and trembling lips.

As if it were the most natural thing in the world, she throws herself into my arms, sobbing, and says, "Carlo is looking for me . . . You have to hide me!"

. . .

"Her problem is the Moon in the twelfth house. When you have a Moon in the twelfth house, you always have trouble in love. And emotional instability," I say, blowing on a cup of tea.

"Her problem is that your ex-boyfriend, her future husband, is a total bastard. That's her problem," replies Paola.

The problem is that Cristina found out what she was not supposed to: that Carlo, the Aquarius and tireless lover of freedom, has gotten a crush on another woman the moment he's about to become a father. So Cristina, upset even though she is a Virgo with Mercury in Libra, has turned up at my house seeking asylum, indefinitely.

"Yes, but it is also *my* problem," I hiss softly, moving Paola away from the couch where Cristina is dozing.

Maybe I'm a bad person, but I've never been a big fan of movies about female friendships and helping your sisters in need. My life is already messed up enough as it is.

"We have to understand how we can fix the situation, not immediately think of the worst."

And that's exactly why I called her: Paola is the friend that everyone would like to have. She is a Cancer with Cancer Ascendant, which explains her deep humanity, and with Pluto in the third house it's obvious that she is able to feel empathy for people.

Not knowing which way to turn when Cristina landed in my house in tears, I did what anyone who knew Paola would have done: I picked up the phone and called her.

In keeping with her astrological chart, in just five minutes, she was able to obtain three things from Cristina: she made her stop crying, tell us word for word what had happened, and sleep.

We will be getting a patent on this technique immediately so we can sell it to the world.

Then Paola raises an eyebrow, bringing the cup of tea to her lips. "And Davide?" she says, throwing down the gauntlet a moment later. Well, yes, it's only natural that I told her about Davide and what happened between us in Paris.

"Davide is . . . the exception that proves the rule," I answer, getting up to pretend to look for something in the closet as an excuse not to make eye contact. "That is, even if you know that your chart is completely incompatible with his . . . you bang your head against the brick wall anyway and go against the stars."

"It's called attraction," replies Paola calmly. "And I would do a statistical survey to see how many successful marriages are based on a pair of winning astrological combinations. Shall we try?"

"Um . . ." I am about to respond when the noise of the vacuum cleaner kills the conversation and sends us running into the living room. I must have infected Cristina with the cleansing bug, because now she is the one who wants to do a big spring cleaning.

After a moment of bewilderment, Paola and I register that there is a woman who is more than six months pregnant standing on tip-toe on my couch, with the rod of the vacuum cleaner raised over her head like a javelin, hell-bent on removing the stubborn dirt particles from the top of my bookcases.

"Cris, stop!" I cry.

Again, Paola proves herself useful in disarming the pregnant woman. However, in doing so, she ended up bumping into the box that has been sitting on my bookcase for months, the one that my parents foisted on me when they were repainting the house and that still needs to be sorted through.

"Careful!" I make the heroic gesture of sticking out my wrist to save both of them from being hit by a shower of books, papers, and various trinkets.

"Damn . . . is anything broken?" asks Paola, immediately coming to my aid.

"I have no idea," I tell her, going over to Cristina who, in the meantime, has returned to crying on the couch. "Calm down, please. Come on."

On the floor are my university notebooks and even one of the dolls I was really fond of as a child, pens, and papers. Mom must have emptied some old drawer directly into the box.

"And this?" exclaims Paola, lifting something from the floor as if she had found treasure. "What is a spoon doing in the midst of all these papers and notebooks?"

I snort and take it from her. "This is not just any spoon. This is a lucky spoon—a gift from my uncle when I was born," I explain with considerable pride. "Don't you see? There's my date of birth, time of birth, the length . . ."

I start to get up from the couch.

I sit back down on the couch.

I stare directly in front of me for a couple of seconds.

Paola gets up from the ground. "Is everything OK?"

I continue staring in front of me. "I don't know."

"What do you mean? Do you feel sick?" She runs up to me to put a hand on my forehead.

In response, I lift up the spoon, as if exhibiting a piece of evidence.

She, obviously, doesn't understand.

"The time . . ." I mutter. "Look at the time."

"Alice Bassi, born at 11:45 p.m. OK? And?"

"My mother always told me that I was born at eleven."

Paola raises an eyebrow and looks at me as if she were deciding whether to call 9-1-1. "So? You were born at 11:45."

"Yes, but at night!" I exclaim. And this time I tear myself from the couch to run to the telephone and call my parents.

"Sweetie, how are you?" asks my father at the other end of the line.

"Dad, when was I born?" I exclaim, skipping the formalities, my voice trembling in my throat.

"What happened, little one?" asks Dad.

"Daddy, I need to know what time I was born. The exact time."

"Adalgisa, what time was Alice born?"

I can almost see my mother sticking her head out of the kitchen and looking at him with a frown. I hear her mutter something, but I can't make out what.

"Your mother says eleven o'clock," he says.

"Yes, but eleven in the morning or at night?" And then, can we specify that it was eleven forty-five? Is time such a relative concept?

"At night." I hear my mother's voice, and I sink to my knees.

"Alice? Alice, hello?"

When I turn around, Cristina has stopped crying and offers me a glass of water that I gulp down without a moment's hesitation.

"So?" Paola presses, with her arms crossed over her chest.

I ignore her, and I drag myself toward the computer, where I open the astrology program and enter my information for the new calculation.

Some things haven't changed. The position of the planets is almost the same, but the planets in the houses, and the houses in relation to the sign as well as the aspects of the planets, and even the Ascendant, are not what they were before.

They never were what they were before.

Oh Lord, I have to sit down.

I'm already sitting down.

I barely manage to open my mouth, and only a wisp of a voice comes out: "Who am I? Who am I?"

41

Lost in Astrology

There are too many people. That's the first thing that comes to mind when I open the door to the loft and the hustle and bustle assaults me. Someone turns toward me and greets me, "Hi, Alice!"

"Good morning, Alice."

"Hey, Alice."

"Alice . . ."

Alice. Alice. Alice.

All they do is repeat a name, which has never before felt so removed from my person.

"Good morning," says my boss, with a smile as wide as an interstate highway. "I brought brioches for everyone, don't you want some?"

I open my mouth, but I am unable to say anything. How would Alice behave? The Alice who is a Libra with Leo Ascendant with the Sun in the fourth house, Mars in the second, the sixth house in Capricorn, and so on and so forth with all the planets, Trines, Conjunctions, and Oppositions?

After contemplating my muteness for a second, he shrugs, turns around, and walks away. "If you change your mind soon, there could still be one left. But in a half hour, I can't guarantee anything."

I take advantage of a moment of quiet to reread my new birth chart. My stomach churns.

How can I be me—with my longing for a real love story, a family, and stability—when the Square between the Moon and Neptune says that I'm unable to put down roots? Elsewhere, I am even described as an individualist . . . Apparently, I'm also energetic, authoritarian, and egocentric. But what if I don't even know where I'm most at home? In terms of the energies, I definitely need someone to shake me up.

And I know exactly who.

Tio still hasn't replied to my messages, which is strange, because he is usually so quick to come to my aid.

Suddenly, something comes to mind, and I skim through the five-page printout.

Eleventh house in Taurus: your friends might get close to you for their personal economic benefit.

Oh my god. What if I've been conned?

How stupid; what would Tio have gotten out of it?

Well, he became a television star. Hmm . . .

Then I spot him. He's made it through the unruly line for Enrico the Brioche Man, and with his Jamaican pirate hairstyle and his arms lifted above his head to protect his trophies—a brioche and a cannolo—it is practically impossible to miss him.

"Alice, my little one!" he exclaims as he lunges toward me.

If he thinks he can placate me with an IV of saturated fats, he really has no idea what I am made of.

"Tio!" I yell. I am frustrated, yes, but I can't help but throw my arms around his neck.

"Hey, calm down . . ." he says, winking. "You could have come and celebrated with Enrico. It seems like his wife has come back home, at last."

I look up and catch Enrico laughing heartily. And I am happy for him. We needed some good news, a little happy ending—at least for someone.

But how can Tio think about food when the entire planet is in danger?!

Maybe I'm exaggerating, but try to understand, it's as if at almost forty years old you are told that you were switched at birth, adopted, or stolen as a child by your parents. Well, more or less.

"Did you read the e-mail? And the attachment?"

Tio, however, does not seem to have grasped the seriousness of the situation and brings his hand to his mouth to hide a yawn.

"I had a look. I was out late with Andrea. I need another coffee."

OK, if this is the price for paying attention to me, I'll go to Brazil and gather and toast the beans myself.

"So?" I ask him, ten minutes and one coffee from the café later.

"Alice, this is wonderful."

"What do you mean 'wonderful'? Tio, do you realize what you are saying? Do you know what this means for me?"

For him, it's "wonderful." I didn't sleep a wink all night. I kept getting up to look in the mirror, convinced that my face would start crumbling, like in the *Invasion of the Body Snatchers*.

"Of course, sweetie. First of all, it's wonderful that you can become this type of strong and resolute woman. And besides, did you check the compatibility with . . . Well, you know who? Perhaps it's not so bad now."

Obviously, that's the first thing that I did. Well, the second, if you count slamming my head against the wall. The third thing I did was go back to slamming my head against the wall. Mine and Davide's astrological charts are even more at odds than before.

"It doesn't matter," I cut him off. "This is not me!" I exclaim, tapping my index finger against the new astrological chart that has thrown me into an abyss of uncertainty, ripped apart my identity, and sent me into paranoia. "Here it says that I have Leo rising, no less. And that, therefore, I should have the personality of a leader. And then, here . . . I have Mars in the second house, which means I have an innate ability to make money. As if!"

"Oh, come on, Alice," Tio says, dismissing my panic with a regal wave. "Frankly, after all these months, I thought that you would understand a little bit more." He pulls the papers out of my hand. "Here. Your Ascendant. It's true that Leo is usually a sign of leadership, but look here: 'is endowed with enormous creativity, but has the tendency to dramatize every little thing, probably because of inner insecurity,'" he proclaims, with a certain satisfaction. "This *is* you."

I snatch the papers out of his hands and find what he just read. It's a line and a half in the middle of at least fifteen others that speak about how much I love to stand out, take charge, and lead groups of people and even, why not, to be a source of inspiration for them. Source of inspiration! At best, I have been able to inspire men . . . to leave me.

"And all this?" I ask him, showing him the rest of the astrological epitaph.

Tio shrugs his shoulders. "In reality, you could well be like this, but you haven't yet found the strength to come out of your shell. But listen, this is right: 'You have a big heart, and you are so kind and generous that you feel hurt when you have to deal with cruelty and selfishness in others.'"

I snort and take back my birth chart, beckoning for Luciano to come over. "Listen," I say to my colleague, "if someone reading your horoscope were to say to you: 'You have a big heart and you are so kind and generous that you feel hurt when you have to deal with cruelty and selfishness in others . . .'"

Luciano nods. "Well said, Alice. Couldn't be more accurate. There aren't many who understand it, I can assure you. I have a very sensitive soul."

After he walks away, sighing, Tio claps his hands and says. "Excellent! And?"

"Anyone would tell you they recognize themselves in this description."

He squints and then crosses his arms over his chest, on the defensive. "But not you . . ."

"Of course I recognize myself in it. But, if anyone can, what value does it have? Tio, why don't you understand? If, for all these months, I was able to live my life believing that I was the woman from the other birth chart, seeing myself in every word, following the movements of the stars every day as if they were talking to me, I can't simply say: 'Oops . . . let's cross this out and start a new chapter, with an entirely different Alice.' Because that's what this birth chart is telling me, Tio, that I am a different person."

"You are you, regardless, honey . . ."

I sigh. "Exactly. That's the thing, Tio. Exactly that. I am me, *regardless*." I shake my head. "It would be best if you went into the studio now."

. . .

A couple minutes later, I am at the door of the recording studio. I poke my head inside, just in time to see a neon sign saying "An Astrological Guide for" swaying toward the floor on steel cables.

Ferruccio oversees the dismantling operation as the sets from my television program are stacked on the cart, ready to be stored in the warehouse where they will be repainted and transformed into something else. The second part of the sign, "Broken Hearts," is still hanging and glowing boldly in the emptiness. Sitting just below it, I notice Carlo. The description couldn't be more striking if there were an arrow pointing at him.

"So?" I ask him, trying to swallow my sense of guilt. It was only a little while ago that Cristina made me sign an oath in blood not to reveal where she was.

"Uh ..." he responds with a dejected sigh.

It's not very Aquarian to be lost for words, and even less like Carlo, but I understand that this isn't a particularly happy time for him either. I clear my throat.

"On the one hand, isn't this what you wanted? How could you have spent your life with a woman who you didn't love, when you wanted to be with someone else?"

"But how do I know what I want? How do any of us know, Alice? Are you sure about what you want? Is it always so black and white?"

No, it never is. Not anymore. Maybe once upon a time it was, but with age, your view is clouded, and you have to keep forcing yourself to see all the nuances. Carlo's words are strangely illuminating. We are all scared; no one really knows where to go.

I offer him my hand, and when he gets up, I hug him.

"It will all work out. You'll see," I whisper. I will speak to Cristina and try to convince her to talk to him again. In this moment, I feel very Zen and at peace with the world.

When Carlo steps away from me, his eyes are so full of tears that the words "Cristina is at my house!" almost roll off the tip of my tongue.

But he speaks first. "I almost forgot ... I bumped into the president before, and he told me that he wanted to speak with you."

Ah. Well, clearly you can't be Zen and at peace with the world for more than thirty seconds.

As I leave the studio and go upstairs, I am still trying to reconcile myself to my new astrological chart, because in moments like these, I would really love to know what to expect.

Tio would say that it is typical of a Libra not to love surprises and to want everything to be under control. At this point, I would say that it is typical of me, who happens to be a Libra, but who knows. If I were born in March, perhaps I wouldn't even be that different.

Instinctively, I call Paola, because I am sure that two words from her will steer my thoughts back on track.

"First, find out what he wants. Then call me back and we'll talk about it."

That's Pragmatic Paola, the most practical woman in the universe. And she's not wrong. Why don't I think about things the way she does? They don't seem like such complicated solutions.

"You won't know what he wants until you speak to him," stresses my friend, and I feel a little calmer. "After all, apart from that little incident with Giorgio that caused him a bit of trouble with the law—plus a black eye and topsy-turvy offices—why should he be mad at you?"

I stop in front of the president's door with my knuckles poised, about to knock. I knock.

"Come in."

"Mr. President."

"Alice, take a seat."

When I close the door behind me twenty minutes later, I seem to have entered one of those science-fiction films where all you have to do is walk through a doorway and you are living in a parallel reality.

Mr. President asked me to leave the Mi-A-Mi Network.

Not because I've been fired. At least, not in the real sense of the word.

In the past months, *Astrological Guide for Broken Hearts* has drawn audiences away from the main channels, and many people noticed it. In addition to an offer for a merger that will save it from ruin, the network received a proposal to take over the format of the show, and a production company asked for me. They want to interview me. In Rome. If I'm interested.

Am I interested?

Without even realizing it, I stop in front of a closed door. If I'm looking for a place to meditate, there's nowhere better than an empty office.

Maybe it will do me good, seeing it without Davide and all his belongings. It will help me to clear his image from my mind, to create a turning point after which he will no longer be part of my life—after which, if I were to accept that offer, many of the people I know now would no longer be part of my life. I don't know if I have the strength.

On the one hand, the idea galvanizes me; on the other hand, I am terrified.

I push the door handle.

The room is suffused with light and silence. On the desk, there is a large box and not much else. The marks on the white walls scarcely betray a past of posters and frames. By the window, there is a can of paint that will erase all traces of Davide's presence here.

I sigh quietly and turn around to leave, but the door that I left open is now closed, and although I can hardly believe it, Davide is in front of me.

"What are you doing here?" I ask him in a shrill voice.

"Well, it's my office. At least, for today." He points to the box on the table.

I wish that my heart wouldn't beat so strongly in my ears, so hard that I can't think straight while the memory of our kisses tears me away from reality for a second.

"So..."

"Alice..."

We speak at the same time, one over the other. Even our words long to embrace one another.

I am such a hopeless romantic. This man can say whatever he likes, but the truth is that he has used me in the worst way.

"I'll let you finish sorting out your things," I tell him, detaching my gaze from his and taking a step toward the door. It's a risky move, since he's in front of it, but I have to give him a clear signal that he can't keep playing games. "Excuse me," I say, making him understand that I need him to move.

Davide does step aside, but he keeps his hand on the door.

"Please, Alice. We haven't been able to talk after . . . Paris."

My emotions knot in my stomach. "There is nothing to say, Davide. We got caught up in the situation, by the attraction that we've felt for each other over the past few months. We got carried away. Let's leave it at that and go back to our normal lives."

He stares at me, frowning, then finally removes his hand from the door, but only to take mine. "You're not wrong in saying that in all these months we were drawn to each other like magnets." I feel his thumb caressing the back of my hand. "Alice . . . it's not easy for me. I am . . . Ugh. I'm not able to trust people. My life has never been very stable, ever since I was a kid. I told you. So, I have real problems with . . . letting myself get attached, and I end up hurting myself and hurting those who want to be close to me. Look at Barbara . . ."

Oh no, please. Not the beatification of Barbara. I can't take this.

"Listen, Davide. You don't need to explain yourself." With an enormous amount of willpower, I successfully remove my hand from his. "I've thought about it, too, and it really wouldn't work out between us anyway. Our astrological charts are completely incompatible, for starters. And, to tell the truth, you aren't what I want in life. I want a man who is really there. I want a man who makes me feel like a queen every time he looks at me. I don't want to be anxious every time we say goodbye because I don't know when I'll see him again, if he's hiding something from me, or what kind of mood he is in." I sigh. "I don't want to joke around anymore. I want a man I can build something with. Or at least, believe that I can." Davide opens his mouth again to speak, but I stop him, saying, "And maybe Daniele can be that man."

My heart leaps into my throat when I say it. It seems that an ax has fallen heavily between a before and after, and now the two pieces of what my life has been up to this point can never be sewn back together.

Davide looks at me. Then he walks past me to reach the desk and his box.

"I'm happy that you are so clear-minded," he says, keeping his back to me. "You are a beautiful person, Alice." He turns to face me for a second, and his crooked smile, sweet and slightly melancholic, still makes me weak at the knees. "If the only good thing to come out of all this is that you understand that, and you found your determination . . . I can only be happy."

42

The Unbearable Lightness of Virgo

"I brought you this," Daniele says, lifting up a paper bag. He is waiting for me just outside the Mi-A-Mi gate, leaning against his car.

"What's this? A gift?" I'm a little embarrassed as I take the bag and look inside.

"It's just a poncho. I saw it in a store window and thought it would look great with your hair."

I sigh, barely holding back a smile as I pull out the poncho from the package and try it on. It's a little out of style, but he is the cutest person on the planet. I get up on my tiptoes and graze his lips with a kiss.

We have been dating for three weeks. Religiously. In other words, ever since we got together, hardly a day has gone by that we haven't seen each other, so it seems like we've been dating for much longer. Maybe it's because my life with Daniele is far more interesting than it was without him.

In addition to being a ruggedly handsome, Joe Manganiello type, he is also one of those socially responsible people who gives the impression of being in total harmony with the universe. Like last Sunday, when we went to clean up the waters of that stream . . . the what-was-it-called?

"Tonight, we are going out. I want to give you a treat, so I am bringing you to a place that you are going to love."

I clap my hands with excitement and give him another kiss on the cheek. It's nice to have a boyfriend with initiative, and his ideas are always exceptional.

In the car, I turn on my phone and it immediately starts to blow up with messages and missed calls.

Two are from Tio, and I instantly feel my throat tighten in anxiety. I delete the notifications right away, deciding to ignore them. I haven't spoken to him in more than two weeks.

It's not that I'm mad at him. I've just made the conscious decision to avoid falling down the tunnel of astrological temptation; a tunnel that he dropped me into. And no, I don't feel guilty. I decided that I shouldn't feel guilty for making a mature choice to release someone from my life. It's part of my growth plan to acquire the awareness of an adult woman.

Picking up the phone and returning that notorious call from the production company in Rome should be part of the same plan, but I haven't been able to do it yet.

I also have a missed call and a text from Paola.

Call me as soon as possible.

OK, *her* I better call, I think. After all, she's always been there when I've needed her, and it's only right that she feels she can count on me as I do her. Maybe after dinner, though. It's not polite to be on the phone when you have company.

And I have thirty-two missed calls from Cristina.

I start viciously scratching my neck.

Daniele smiles at me patiently and stretches his hand to caress my neck. "You need some of that green tea ointment that I used in Kenya for rashes. Don't keep scratching yourself; you're only making it worse."

But I can't help it. I can't take her anymore—Cristina, I mean. Just hearing her voice or, in this case, seeing her name on my phone causes me to break out in hives.

"Hello, Cristina? Is everything OK?" My voice is casual, but my insides are spitting fire like a dragon with slow digestion.

"I'm done with all of them," she yells, blowing out my eardrum.

"What happened?"

"My mother refuses to let me cancel the ceremony. She took over the planning of my wedding and has called everyone saying that 'obviously' it will still take place. Obviously, my ass! I'm not going to marry Carlo, not even under pain of torture!"

When your belly is the size of a gigantic watermelon and you have the psychological stability of Alex DeLarge in *A Clockwork Orange* because your boyfriend has admitted to you that he's fallen for someone else, it's hardly surprising that you're not sprinting down the aisle to say "I do."

Although, marrying Carlo just to spend the rest of your life tormenting him doesn't seem like such a bad idea to me.

"Cris, don't you at least want to talk—"

"Really?! You've gone over to their side? You're not my friend anymore! If you're not my friend, you can just say so. I know you've always hated me. I know you've never been able to accept—"

"Please, Cristina, calm down. Look, I'm out to dinner tonight . . . No, I won't be late. Yes, I'll call your mother and tell her to go fuck herself . . . Definitely. OK . . . But try to stay calm. Bye. Of course, I love you . . . No, I don't hate you because you are a fat, crazy, pregnant woman. Bye . . . Uh, sure . . . I'll bring you some pickles and tuna sauce? I'll ask the restaurant . . . Bye. Bye. Yes, bye." I end the call and collapse onto the seat, staring into space.

Daniele touches my arm, and when I look at him, he leans toward me to give me a passionate kiss on the lips. "Better not say all those nasty things to her mother. She might be offended, and I'm sure your friend doesn't really feel that way," he adds, before getting out of the car.

When I get out, I'm not prepared for the muddy track that greets me, and my foot slides forward.

"Careful!" Daniele grabs me, putting his arm around my waist, holding me until we reach the door. "Can you make it?"

Can I make it through the door? Hmm, let's see . . . I look at him and sigh, squeezing my lips into a smile. "It'll be tough, but I'll try."

"Hold on, then." He steps in front of me and holds the door open for me.

OK, he didn't get my joke. Never mind. I mumble a "thank you" and walk inside.

The first thing I notice is that we are in a farmhouse with granite flooring, like what my parents had when I was little, i.e., three restructurings ago. The lights are cool white neon, and one of them, in the back corner of the large room, flashes continuously, as if it's about to burn out at any moment.

"Isn't this a fantastic place?" says Daniele.

Oh god, that's not exactly the word I would use to describe it. As I take my seat, I tell myself that, for now, I should be satisfied that I'm not having a seizure, and that we have our backs to the flashing neon lights.

I don't intend to be mean, it's just that as a Libra with Venus in Libra and the Moon in Pisces—someone who is naturally predisposed to appreciate beauty and luxury—I immediately notice when there are improvements to be made in an environment. It's genetic.

Oh no. I did it again. I give myself a slap as punishment for this astrological failing.

"You don't like it?" Daniele asks, worried.

"Oh no, it's not that. It's just . . . I forgot something. This is great!" I reach out my hand and intertwine my fingers with his. "It's very rustic . . ." I say, looking at the peeling paint.

Daniele smiles and puts the menu in front of me. Now my jaw drops.

From a place like this, I would have expected anything but this elegant book bound in silk, and definitely not the dishes that are listed inside . . .

Shrimp in chocolate with tomatoes, almonds, and pistachios; risotto with scallops and coral cream, thyme, lemon, and saffron . . . I didn't even know that you could eat coral. I smile at him.

"I knew you'd like this place, and you haven't even seen it all yet. The entire farm is part of a project to restore the area."

He's about to start telling me about it when my cell phone starts ringing again. It's Paola, and I don't have the heart to let it go to voice mail.

"Excuse me for a second," I say to Daniele. "Hello, Paola . . ."

"Alice, you have to do something!" My best friend's voice has none of the usual Zen calm that, frankly, I sometimes find irritating. "I can't take it anymore. Giacomo can't take it anymore. And Sandrino is getting hives."

"What's going on?"

"*Your* friend Cristina calls me all the time. I've heard about her entire relationship *with* Carlo, everything *about* Carlo, and her whole life *without* Carlo. I want to have a life of my own, too. You have to call Carlo!" she finishes in an exasperated and final tone.

"Paola, I can't call him. I promised. And you said yourself that she had to be the one to deal with Carlo."

"That's what I thought, before I gave her my phone number. Honestly, Alice, I'm risking divorce here. Giacomo and I were just about to . . . you know . . . the baby's with my mother, you know how it is . . . we want to . . ."

"OK, I get it, I get it. I'll call her right now. Calm down."

"Call Carlo. They can sort it out between themselves."

"OK. I'll handle it." I sigh, exasperated, and it takes me a couple of seconds to get my bearings and remember what I was talking about with Daniele. "You were saying?"

But my phone starts to ring again, and this time it's Cristina.

"Oh, no!"

In front of me, Daniele presses his hand to his face.

I'm about to put it down. But what if she's sick? I cast a glance at the phone. It's not ringing anymore.

I try to relax and enjoy the wonderful meal that has just been put in front of me, forgetting Cristina, Paola, and any other outside interference.

This man is perfect, I think. Maybe it was worth going through all those disappointments if they were just preparation for this man with whom I can exist in perfect harmony.

"The poncho, the flowers, this special restaurant . . . it almost seems like we are celebrating something. Have I forgotten our anniversary?" I say, joking, although I am genuinely a bit confused.

Daniele dries his lips and looks at me puzzled. "Well, an anniversary is celebrated after a year, Alice. We've only been dating for a couple of weeks."

Maybe I should explain I was just joking around. I mean, we are *almost* totally compatible. After all, what couple doesn't have to do a little bit of work?

"I want to talk to you about something . . ." I tell him, swallowing fearfully.

I still haven't responded to the job offer in Rome. To tell the truth, I've been avoiding the topic for three weeks, but my future is at stake, so we have to talk about it.

"Actually, we do have something to celebrate," he says, interrupting me and giving me an intense look. "Alice, like I said before, we haven't been dating for very long, but I feel like you are becoming someone important in my life."

I frown. "Yes, well, it has only been three weeks. Not much time at all."

"Yes, but I don't want to lose you, Alice."

He turns to the waiter and nods, then gets up and asks me to follow him. We go through a different door than the one we came in, which opens onto the courtyard of the farm. I cross it, focusing on the warmth of Daniele's hand on my side.

"I've just been offered an incredible project, one of those things that you dream about your whole life," he says.

We reach what at first seems like a wooden panel, but he grabs one end and slides it across; it's a door.

"This place is never what it seems," I reply, with a hint of nervousness as I begin to glimpse figures moving in the shadows, other people.

"The Wessler Foundation believes strongly in this and is willing to sponsor me for two years, the entire duration of the project."

"Two years?" I turn around. "OK . . ." I don't know what to say. "Where?"

"Around the world. I won't be in the same place for more than two months."

Man, and to think I've been afraid to talk to him about Rome.

"Alice . . ." He looks me in the eye and holds my hands, bringing them to his lips. "I want you to come with me."

"What?"

I ask myself why it's suddenly so hot in here and why I have the feeling that this sculpture, which looks like an enormous curved beehive, is about to fall on me.

I breathe and think of how much the mere idea of changing cities freaks me out, not to mention traveling the world for two years.

"Daniele, I don't know . . ."

All of a sudden, I miss Tio: his reassuring, fraternal hugs, his nonsense that helps me overcome my problems, his lightness. Getting away from Daniele makes me feel lighter, and I start wandering around the place, as if I were floating.

Of course, as he says, I could see the world. It would be a rare and unique opportunity to check almost everything off my list that I've ever wanted to see. But then what? What do you wish for when you have nothing more to wish for?

Oh god. I feel dizzy.

The problem is that I feel too small to tackle all this. It's not that I don't feel up to it; it's just that it seems impossible that this woman that I am imagining could be me. Me, Alice Bassi, the minion who dreamed of making films and instead is practically drowning under the paperwork for talk shows at a small TV station. The production assistant that a production company in Rome wants to interview. Even that seems like a dream bigger than me. The problem is that it could be *my* dream. . . .

Behind me, the lights are switched on. When I turn around, I notice a small stage, just a small raised platform with a microphone. Someone starts to clap and I do the same, hoping to blend in with the crowd, but when I recognize the man climbing the platform, I get a cramp in my arms.

"Oh shit . . ." I murmur.

"It's Professor Klauzen," explains Daniele, who in the meantime has joined me. "Part of the proceeds from tonight's auction will be donated to his research. He really is a great man," Daniele whispers in my ear. "He literally fell in love with my work and wants me to do a report on his research. Complete with a portrait." He gives me a kiss on the cheek. "Having a person of his caliber on my side is fundamental."

Oh, sure. How could he not see the arrogant and conceited jerk that Klauzen actually is? And, above all, how could that same jerk not be of fundamental importance for his career?

Klauzen, meanwhile, continues to overact on the stage, while I wonder where to hide. Of course, when he finishes playing Marlon Brando, Daniele will want to go over and say hello; and I don't want to be there to ruin his career.

"I'm going to powder my nose . . ."

I feel the weight of Daniele's gaze on me. "Powder your nose? You are already quite pale."

I close my eyes and take a deep breath.

"I mean that I need to go pee," I explain, translating for him.

"Oh. The bathrooms are down there. I'll wait for you here."

Obviously, I find this very comforting.

With all the unbelievable remodeling that they've done, I have to say that the bathroom is a real disappointment. It's practically a three-by-three-foot room with a single stall, which at the moment is occupied.

While I wait, my gaze falls on the mirror. Yes, I do have the complexion of a Corpse Bride.

I'm a bitch. What am I complaining about? I have a perfect, nice, attentive man . . . Sure, he has all the wit of an ironing board, but what does that matter? Everyone is different.

Damn, if there were just one person that I never wanted to see again in my life it would be Klauzen! I sigh. Just my luck.

I hear the toilet flush in the stall. I dry my hands and straighten up, trying to assume an expression of friendly neutrality.

And I stand corrected.

Of the top ten people I never wanted to come face-to-face with in my life again, I suddenly realize that Klauzen is not number one. At the top of the list is Barbara Buchneim-Wessler Ricci Pastori, who is standing in front of me right now.

For a second, I think that it is some sort of vision. The second thought that crosses my mind is: Barbara Buchneim-Wessler Ricci Pastori pees like us mere mortals. And, furthermore, she also rearranges the elastic of the underwear pinching her behind.

It's an idiotic thought, but it is comforting.

I hope in vain to blend in with the sink, but it's useless to try and escape. Barbara looks at me with those green, catlike eyes, and her face changes from the relaxation of someone who has just found honest relief to the annoyed stiffness of someone who has just noticed an unpleasant souvenir under their shoe.

Neither of us says a word, and the sound of water running into the sink is as deafening as a waterfall.

A second later, she leaves, and I close myself in the stall. What now?

I close the toilet seat and sit on top of it, putting my head in my hands. Damn it, how is it that one way or another, I always end up crying about my life in a toilet stall?

Can things get any worse?

Well . . . I could see Davide here next to his girlfriend.

Oh, no. Please, St. Jude, patron saint of hopeless causes, at least spare me this. I call the only person who can rescue me now.

"Hello?"

"Babe! I can't believe that you finally called me back!" Tio's voice is full of emotion, and against my will, I smile.

"I'm sorry . . . it's just that . . . I'm trying to take my life into my own hands and not be dependent on horoscopes."

"No worries, hon. Now, where are you?"

"Um, in a toilet stall . . ."

"Well, that seems like an excellent way to take your life into your own hands."

"Tio, I'm at a farm just outside Milan. You know those places that are restored partly to be cool and partly for doing good works . . . They also have art exhibitions here."

"Mmm, yes. I know where you are. I went there a couple weeks ago with Andrea. Excellent food." He is silent, waiting for me to say something, and when I don't he continues. "And how is the bathroom?"

"Eh . . . disappointing."

"Ah, I see. That's where the architects always fall short."

"Tio, Klauzen is out there."

"Oh, shit."

"And I just bumped into Barbara Buchneim-Wessler, etc., etc."

"Double shit, etc., etc. There's no window you can escape out of without being seen?"

I raise my head and notice a little one with bars.

"Tio, I can't escape: I'm with Daniele."

"Well, then, fake a heart attack and have him take you home."

"Of course, and I'll especially enjoy giving Dr. Klauzen the satisfaction of feeling my tits while he plays the hero."

"Well, at least you might make friends . . . this time."

"If he recognized me, I bet he'd crack a couple ribs on purpose—or even leave me there to die," I say, fiddling with the roll of toilet paper.

"OK, then I'll come get you in the next couple of days . . . from the toilet where you now reside."

"Be serious."

"No, you be serious," he blurts out, losing his cool. "You've avoided your best friend for three weeks. Now, you've shut yourself in a restaurant bathroom. Is this how you intend to be an adult, Alice? Do you think being an adult means taking refuge in comfortable situations in order to avoid making serious decisions? To renounce amazing opportunities because you might have to finally come face-to-face with yourself?"

"What are you saying?"

"I'm saying that I know you were offered an interview in Rome, and you haven't answered yet. Shit, Alice, do you want to lose your shot at having the job of a lifetime for the latest man who you don't really love?"

I knew it was a mistake to call him. Now I have a lump in my throat that's the size of a gravestone.

"You . . . you . . . you!" is all I can say, as if I had hung up on him.

"I, nothing. Now go back out there and show them what you're made of. You are Alice Bassi. Thanks to you and your program, a television network that everyone thought was hopeless has come thundering back with an audience that all the major channels are jealous of. You are a survivor, you are tough, and you always fight your way back. Always. And even though you don't believe it, there is more strength in those skimpy little arms of yours than in the arms of a sumo wrestler. Go back in there and rip out that viper's eyes!"

I spring up, more galvanized by his pep talk than Rocky Balboa on his way to the world title.

"I'm going out there. *I must break them.*"

"Excellent. See you in hell, *gringa.*"

And so I go, but even after I fling open the bathroom door with the boldness of a bandit from the Wild West, as the hubbub gets louder and the lights get dimmer, my courage starts to waver.

Maybe I don't exactly need to *break him.* Maybe I just need to say a quick hello, pretend to faint, and get myself taken home. This also seems like an excellent plan.

As luck would have it, Daniele is at the stage and at his side are both Klauzen and Barbara. As if that weren't enough, now that the presentation is over, the lights have been switched back on and, even if I wanted to, I wouldn't have the slightest chance of hiding.

I'm heading straight into the eye of the storm.

"There you are!" Daniele exclaims euphorically.

Then, strangely, while Barbara sourly purses her lips, Klauzen wrinkles his forehead and smiles at me. Okay, let's say that he shows his repeatedly whitened teeth and offers me his hand.

"So, you're Daniele's famous steady girl, then?"

Point One: I haven't been called anyone's "steady girl" since middle school when Giampiero Guastamacchia's father caught us making out on the benches below his house.

Point Two: I don't know if this Santa Claus version of Klauzen frightens me more or less than the one in the SS costume.

Point Three: This level of friendliness can mean only one of two things, a trap or an aneurism.

"Um, girlfriend. I mean . . . Let's just say I'm a friend," I reply, distancing myself.

"Oh yes, of course," intervenes Barbara, this time she is smiling, too, but it's not in the least bit reassuring. "Nowadays the word 'friendship' means so many things."

What she is really trying to say escapes me, but it's better to play along.

"You!" Klauzen exclaims, suddenly.

I jump and prepare for the worst. Now he will tell me that I am inept, that he will have me barred from any registry I have any intention of ever enrolling in, and he will ensure that my hysterical premenstrual outburst is seen on world television.

"Your face is very familiar. Do you have relatives in Brittany, by any chance?"

"Um . . ." Seriously, he doesn't recognize me? "Actually, no."

"Perhaps . . ." intervenes Barbara with a sly grin, "in *Paris?*"

Klauzen shakes his head. "Paris? Why? I only go there for work. I hardly know anyone in Paris."

I raise an eyebrow, wondering if he is screwing with me, if this isn't a way to hang me out to dry and make me repent for all my sins.

If I'm not skating on thin ice with Klauzen, I certainly am with Barbara, so I try to quickly focus their attention on my "steady guy."

"Daniele told me about the project you proposed for him," I say.

"I've asked Alice to come with me. I think that she could be very useful to the venture," adds Daniele.

But Barbara keeps pressing, saying, in these exact words, "Oh, I don't doubt it. Miss Bassi always knows how to keep busy."

As she speaks, she gives me a pointed look and, oh god, I understand—she knows everything about what happened in Paris between Davide and me. If I didn't hate him enough for using me, now I hate him even more for wanting to wipe his conscience clean with his girlfriend, probably making me out to be worse than Mata Hari.

Klauzen stares at me dumbfounded. "Really, how so? What kind of work do you do, Miss Bassi?"

"Um, I work . . . I work in television. I am a director of production." I tell myself that now he will remember. Now, he will put two and two together and take me to his laboratory to perform dehumanizing experiments on me.

"Bah! Television. I don't hold it in high regard," he mutters. "Recently I had the worst experience in an interview. I was in Paris, actually, and there was this moron of a journalist . . ." He looks in my eyes, and I gulp. "Extremely, extremely rude."

"Weren't you in Paris recently, honey?" intervenes the guy who, if he continues like this, in a short time will be my ex-*steady guy* or ex-photographer, because I will end up biting his hand off.

"I, well . . . Not too recently. But I hardly had time to see anything."

"That's what happens when you're shut up in a hotel room," says Barbara, staring at me grimly, and then she adds, "working."

Well, I'm really beating the crap out of them like Tio suggested. "I'll let you all chat about work. I'm going to get something to drink . . ."

I've barely turned around when Barbara announces, "I'll come with you."

I make a mental note to not leave my glass unattended, so that she's not tempted to play a little Lucrezia Borgia.

Caught in god knows what strange state of momentary mental daze, I order a Sex on the Beach, leaving myself vulnerable to her comment, "Very apt."

I bite my lip as we both wait for our drinks in silence. Then, Barbara turns to me, saying, "You make me laugh, you know?"

"Really? Happy to help you finally move a muscle in your face," I reply. Now that the two of us are alone, there's no need to pretend to be polite.

She lifts a corner of her mouth. "It makes me laugh to see how hard you've worked, how much trouble you've taken to reach your goals, and yet you're still here. A poor girl, who's not even that cute, trying to ensnare the latest idiot so that she can move ahead in her career and become someone she could never have been on her own."

I put down the glass, and delicately remove the umbrella. For a second, I think of piercing it in her throat like the heroine of *Kill Bill* would do.

"I imagine that's how it worked for you. It's all about who you know."

She warbles a laugh. "I don't think you get it. I don't have to prove anything; there's nothing I need. It's everyone else that wants something from me, who needs *me*. Davide wanted me in his bed from the moment he set foot on my husband's property." She stares at me intensely, waiting for the jab to penetrate straight through my heart.

What she doesn't know, however, is that her wound is already starting to heal. "You are, undoubtedly, very beautiful. It's normal that you arouse sexual desire in men. But that's not the same as love."

She shakes her head. "Ah, love! Davide tried that line . . . No, Alice, it's not only beauty. What I have is class, and you can't buy that at Zara, I'm sorry." She clicks her tongue sharply. "You, with your tawdry clothes and your middle-class lifestyle. You think that all people are equal and should have the same opportunities. God, Davide tortured me with those speeches—amongst other things." She makes a vague gesture with her hand after setting down her glass. "But I was tired of him anyway. He's a fool if he thinks the world revolves around love." She smiles. "And besides . . . you chose the beautiful Daniele, who has a chance to become rich and famous in just a couple of years. I would say 'congratulations' if it weren't that you forgot to factor in one fundamental variable."

"And what might that be?"

"Me, honey." She sashays away, with a virtually imperceptible wiggle, and I see many men's heads turn as she walks.

My heart is pounding in my chest with everything that I wish I could say to her. Instead, I am frozen by one solitary thought.

Davide left her.

43

Aquarius of a Summer Night

I'm dizzy. I can't breathe. My hands and arms are tingling. My entire body is in the throes of a coup d'état fought to the sound of an aggressive symphony.

I decide to go outside, leaving behind the hubbub ringing in my ears.

Davide and Barbara are no longer together.

Yes, but aren't I in love with Daniele? Our relationship is beautiful, linear, and clear. I am an idiot to think that ...

Davide was right to leave her, anyway. He must have realized what a bitch she is. It doesn't mean that he did it for me. Perhaps sleeping with me cleared his mind about their relationship, made him realize that he didn't love her. Can't I at least be happy about that? Then why does it feel all wrong? Why am I wishing for him to come back to me?

I am about to step foot outside the door when I see something in the corner that I haven't seen for ten—no, realistically, for at least twenty—years.

In the rustic, luxury restaurant, there is an old-fashioned, mousy-gray telephone booth; one of those with a door that make it seem like those spaceship rides with the coin slot and perforated plastic walls inside.

I step inside and instantly feel a little better, as if I were in my grandmother's arms. I think about how I used booths like this as a girl to call my latest crush when I was on vacation. I let myself slide to the ground, where I would tuck my knees under my chin, and wrap arms around myself.

Tio is right to say that I am afraid to take my life into my own hands. *Fight* and *fail* start with the same letter after all. What if I, Alice Bassi, were to fail, by myself? What if I couldn't blame someone else, or the stars, or fate for having made a real mess of things? That would be really tragic.

Wouldn't it be worse, though, if I realized, in twenty or thirty years, that I'd never done anything on my own? That I'd never had the strength, had never made decisions without allowing others, always others, to make them for me?

Davide and Barbara broke up.

I don't know what it means.

I don't know what to do.

But I understand deep down that my horoscope doesn't matter. Or perhaps it could matter, but only if I take it as what it really is: a suggestion to understand my potential. After all, I am a Leo Ascendant, aren't I?

I jump when the cabin resounds with three thuds. When I look up, Tio's face, disheveled and smiling, is framed by the long and narrow glass of the door. I feel a tear slide down my face; just one, of relief. He grabs the handle, opens the door, and faces me.

"Are you decent or are you putting on your Superman costume?"

I apologize again, trying to explain why I'd had to stay away from him, and that I'd really missed him. Tio almost starts to cry. I do, too, but I don't give in. He drives into the night.

"OK, as you wish. No more astrology."

"Great. Excellent." I cross my arms, although my addiction to horoscopes right now seems like the least of my problems.

"So..."

"Uh..."

"Yes."

"Look at all the stars," I say, looking out the window.

"Don't start again!"

"Ugh. Look, horoscopes are not my only problem. You're right. I have to be braver. I owe it to myself." I avoid telling him about Davide and Barbara's relationship, because it would seem like falling into the vicious cycle of errors if I even considered it. They broke up. So what? It doesn't concern me. I have to focus on *my* life now.

"That interview ... It's true. I'll call them tomorrow to set up a meeting."

Tio turns toward me with a big smile. "Wonderful, my little one! And listen ..." He stops for a second. "Your energies are at an excellent level; you just have to believe in your abilities ..." He bites his lip, like someone who is not free to speak as they wish.

I warn him: "Tio ..."

"*In my opinion*, this is an excellent period for you to take some sort of initiative at work."

I sigh, exasperated. "And this is because of a *Trine?*"

"Positive aspect of Mars with the Sun," he admits, speaking rapidly.

Both of us start laughing. When the light turns red and we have to stop, I undo my seat belt and lean over to hug him.

"I love you, you lunatic!" he says.

"I love you, too."

Then we let go, and I sniffle, still somewhat emotional.

"Are you sure you're OK?" he asks me with an inquiring gaze.

"Yeah, yeah," I respond, vaguely.

Then, he adds, "I'm sorry for what I said before on the phone."

"What?"

"That you're not really in love with Daniele."

"Oh."

"And that I don't understand you . . . He certainly is a nice hunk of meat."

"Tio!"

"Come on, he is hot. But I've seen you lose your mind; I've seen you dance; I've seen you shine like . . . a star when you were in love."

"Maybe that was passion, Tio. And, as you know, everything went wrong." I shrug. "Perhaps something calmer and less hectic is better."

He sighs, and I see him shake his head. "It's not love."

I bite my lip. "I guess. But maybe it's what I need right now."

I am fastening my belt again, and Tio has his foot on the gas, ready to set off, when a fire truck passes us at full speed. Right behind it, I see an ambulance with a flashing siren turn at the next light, right into my street.

"See?" says Tio. "Stop complaining. There's always someone worse off than you."

I lean forward to turn up the radio, as they're playing a song that I love.

"Oh, for the rings of Saturn, don't tell me Giorgio is back on the loose!"

I lift my head as Tio is turning onto my street and see a roadblock and the ambulance from before parked in the driveway of my building.

"Oh my god," I exclaim, unfastening my seat belt again and jumping out of the car before it's fully stopped. "Cristina!" My heart feels like it's pounding between my temples. If something has happened to her, I will never forgive myself.

Oh god, I didn't answer her call at the restaurant. I will die of guilt!

I start to slow down when, several feet ahead, behind the ambulance, I hear the moans of someone who is racked by deep pains.

The baby is being born! I think. So, what the hell are the paramedics doing?

Suddenly, I think I can also hear the strumming of a guitar. As I move closer, the groaning gets louder and more articulate.

"Cristinaaaa, Cristinaaaa, Cristina . . . a-a-a-a-a!"

I stop and roll my eyes, then I look back and see Tio, who has followed me, slumped on the hood of a parked car, cracking up with laughter.

Someone yells from a window: "Enough! It's almost two in the morning!"

But Carlo, oblivious to the paramedics staring at him dumbfounded and the approaching firemen, continues to sing.

"What the hell?" I hear one of the guys from the ambulance say. "They called us for this guy?"

"They must have thought he was about to die. Have you heard him singing? It sounds like he's been shot in the knee," comments the other.

I look up at the facade of my building, already anticipating the complaint letter from the condominium directors to the administration.

"God, why is everyone out to ruin my life tonight?" I mutter. While I look for the keys, I stumble across my phone flashing a message from Paola.

I couldn't take it anymore. I'm sorry, but I called Carlo to get her to calm down.

And now the mystery of why Carlo came to my house at this hour, armed with a guitar and in such good spirits, is revealed.

"Let's go, man . . . be good now," says one of the firemen, touching Carlo's arm, who continues to tirelessly strum the only guitar piece he has learned, modulating his heartbreaking lament with head held high. "You can't keep yelling at this hour. Come on!"

Carlo, however, doesn't pay attention to anything or anyone, and keeps staring at my living room window. My heart is so close to breaking that I run with my keys toward the door. If Cristina doesn't come out of her own accord, I'll drag her down here myself.

Before closing the gate, I look at Tio again, who gives me a thumbs-up in approval. I skip up the stairs, two at a time, but when I get to the landing between the second and third floor, I see Cristina's name flashing on my phone.

"Hello!" I exclaim.

Through the receiver, I hear her whisper: "Alice . . . he's here! Carlo. He's downstairs."

I stop to catch my breath. "I know. I'm outside the door. Please open up."

Ten seconds later, I hear quiet steps, and then the sound of the lock turning.

"He's down there!" she hisses again, with wide eyes and flushed cheeks.

"Yes, I saw him. Actually, I *heard* him."

"He's serenading me!" she squeaks.

"More than anything else, I'd say he's risking prison time." Maybe there are rehabilitation programs where he could learn to sing—at last—but I don't think that Cristina would be interested in this. "Go to him."

"No, I'm not going down."

"Cristina, that man in the street down there is . . ." I shrug. "OK, he's a dick."

She pulls a face.

"But he loves you, and you love him."

"He's an idiot. He ruined everything," she replies, pouting.

"He's a forty-year-old baby, Cristina. And you knew that even before you got together. He was scared: to get married, to be a father, to start a family. Damn, I would probably be going crazy in the street myself!"

"I'm scared, too," she admits, grabbing hold of me. "I'm afraid of not being able to handle this life growing in my belly, of not being a good mother. I'm afraid of being a mother, period!"

"So, tell him," I whisper.

We take the elevator, in silence, with Cristina anxiously tapping her foot on the ground. I accompany her to the gate, keeping my arm around her shoulders, as excited as if I were accompanying her to the altar.

When he sees her, Carlo stops playing and puts his guitar on the ground. Applause erupts all around him—I think more for the fact that he stopped playing than in encouragement of what might happen next.

I see him extend his closed wrists to the policeman, like in movies where the bandit lets himself be handcuffed. The two agents exchange a look and the older one shakes his head.

"Go home to your girlfriend, moron," he says with a sigh.

Carlo and Cristina embrace and kiss with difficulty and none of the fluidity that you see in films, but this isn't a scene that will be reshot a hundred times until it is perfect. This is real life, and you have to get it right the first time. There are no do-overs. You either accept the outcome, or you have to be satisfied with changing course, reinventing yourself, and evolving. Which is exactly what I'm going to do.

I look at Carlo and Cristina, who have found each other again, who gave in to their love, and I think that, after all, this is an ending where love triumphs, even though it's not my ending.

I feel Tio's hand on my shoulder and I turn into his embrace. I'm feeling truly strong, happy about everything that I've learned, and I'm ready.

Yes. Now, I am truly ready.

EPILOGUE:

The Libra Who Went Up a Hill But Came Down a Mountain

Outdoors. Night. One of those dark yet reassuring nights with a sky full of stars. Every once in a while, you glimpse a shooting star. On top of the hill are two figures, a man and a woman, sitting on the grass; two dark silhouettes with their noses in the air.

"Now, make a wish."

"Doesn't it seem ridiculous that something you wish for might come true just because you saw a falling star? Doesn't it seem futile?"

"No. Not if it makes you reflect on what you really want. Getting lost in the stars is a bit like taking your soul by the hand and finding out where you want to go."

The two look at each other. She sighs. "That's beautiful. And very true."

"So? Did you make a wish?"

"Yes." She hesitates, as if embarrassed. "And you?"

He smiles and brings his face closer to hers. "I can only hope that your wish is the same as mine."

She leans toward him, ready to give him a kiss.

"And ... CUT!" yells a rough, smoke-ravaged voice.

"I'd say we're good," I comment, and then raise my voice so that the whole crew can hear me. "Lunch break!"

Lights come on and the blue screen is visible again, replacing the stars that the computer was projecting on top of it. Silvain Morel jumps down from the top of the fake grass hill, rifling through his pockets for a cigarette.

"Hey! Can somebody get me down?" shouts Nicoletta Orsini, the beautiful actress who plays the role of Alessia, the protagonist in my film.

OK, perhaps not exactly *my* film. To tell the truth, it's Lars Franchini's film, known to the public as Lanfranco Franchini, a renowned TV director with ambitions of making great cinema, hence why we call him Lars. But it is a bit my film, too. From the moment we first met, Lars and I have been as thick as thieves. In no time at all, I've become his right arm or his "always right" arm, as he tells me, winking.

It's strange, but true. It really seems that Lars loves my ideas, my stories, and my dialogues. The one that Silvain and Nicoletta have just brought to life was written by me, Alice Bassi, assistant director of the miniseries *I Loved You Under the Stars*. Of course, it's hardly Woody Allen, but I'm just getting started.

"*Alors, Alissse. C'est bien l'accent?*" asks Silvain, putting the cigarette in his mouth.

"It was good," I tell him, removing the cigarette from his lips before he lights it and creates a falling star effect for real, as we are in a closed environment with no windows that is full of electrical equipment. "But it would be better if you learned Italian, since you work here all the time. It would also save us a fortune on voice coaches."

He gives me a crooked and pleasing smile. "*Et toi*, you go out wiz me, if I learn Italian *pour toi?*" Then he lifts up his shirt, pretending to wipe the greasepaint from his forehead, but purely to let me admire the considerable deployment of abs below.

I bite my lip to keep from laughing. I know his muscular apparatus well. I was the one who made the selection from the portfolios of the actors. In Silvain's portfolio, there is maybe only one photo where he is wearing something that covers his chest. But ever since Alejandro, I have come to realize that the muscle that interests me the most in a man is the one hidden in his skull. Perhaps that's why I'm still single, although I think a million and a half Italian women would give anything to be in my place right now, as Silvain's popularity rating is inversely proportional to his IQ.

"Hmm," I say, pretending to think about it. "What star sign are you?"

"Taurus, *ma chérie*."

I sigh. "I'm so sorry. Ah, Libra with Taurus . . ." I pull a face and snap my fingers, as if to imply that it's a real shame. "No, it would never work," I add, walking away. "Enjoy your lunch."

I go to retrieve my bag because, although I called a break, I will be remaining on set to go over some notes with Lars.

When I bend down to pick it up, I hear barking outside, and I frown, wondering if perhaps I accidentally forgot that there is a dog in one of the scenes we have to film this afternoon. I don't go through the trouble of checking the agenda. I know perfectly well that there are no scenes with dogs, other than those with Caspar Belli, which alas have been imposed on us by Production. So, I just poke my head out of the studio and blink under the strong midday sun. I don't see any dogs, though I think I glimpse a flicker of movement down the road, but that thing is tall enough to be a pony. It's probably for the new *Spartacus* series that they are shooting next door.

I go back inside to retrieve my sandwich, and I greet the script supervisor, the live recording engineer, and the costume designer. Mario, the camera assistant, approaches me, scratching his nose.

"Sorry to disturb you, Alice, but could you clarify something here?" He indicates the script where Lars has marked his notes regarding their work.

"Lanfranco was thinking of a dolly," I explain, interpreting the hieroglyphics marked in pencil. "But to keep within the budget, I suggested a cart."

"Ah, great! That makes my job easier, thank you. And I think that also works very well in terms of storytelling, because I think that here Silvain—"

"So?" we hear someone thunder from the door. The director, a big man of about fifty, tall and imposing like Orson Welles, approaches us, taking off his glasses and scratching his beard. "Can you leave my girl in peace? Go on, Marietto, away with you!"

Mario bites his lip. "Sorry, Lars . . . um, Lanfranco." Then he says to me, "Aren't you going to eat?"

I lift up my bag with my lunch. "I brought a *schiscetta.*"

Mario frowns and I start to laugh, because sometimes I forget that I'm not in Milan but in Rome, and they don't understand our expressions here.

"It means a packed lunch," I explain. "In *Milanese,*" I add, playing up my nasal accent and giving them a wink.

"Bauuuuscia!" Mario yells from the door, trying to imitate my pronunciation. Then he laughs and disappears into the sunlight. I laugh, too, although I'm tired. We're less than a week away from the end of shooting, and I'm practically sleeping on the set.

"Tell me everything, Lars."

He grimaces as soon as he hears his nickname, but then claps me on the shoulder, winking. I am the only one here who can get away with teasing him and calling him Lars, without risking being hung from the dolly and publicly flogged in the style of that scene from *I, Claudius*.

"I'll get the script with the notes. How about we go sit up there?" he proposes, pointing to the top of the fake hill where we just finished wrapping up the shooting-star scene. I raise an eyebrow.

"Are you sure?" I know him well enough to know that he usually prefers the comfort of his director's chair, and I guess offhand that, although pretty much anyone would be able to climb to the top of that small hill, it would take a lot of effort for Lars, with the extra pounds he's gained from years of pasta consumption.

"Yes, yes. Actually, take these." He passes me the headphones and radio link that we use to communicate when we have to be at different points on the set. "Give me a hand to fix up the set—you and I understand each other straightaway. If I have to explain myself to Omar, it won't be long before I get an ulcer."

As he says this, I notice his eyes shining, and I see the tip of his tongue run across his lips, as if he were impatient about something.

"Are you sure you're OK? You're not going to have a stroke, are you?"

I've already pointed out to him, more than once, that with the pace we are working at, he should lose weight. But how do you sell that to someone who greets an oxtail stew with the face of a kid on Christmas morning?

"Hey!" he replies, giving me the evil eye. "Now someone is on the verge of a stroke because they're happy about something?"

I frown. "What happened? News about the Delfino film?" I ask him hopefully. I know that he presented his project a few weeks ago. If it were approved, it could mean only one thing: movies! Finally.

"Uh, no. I mean, yes . . . Almost." He is suddenly serious. "Alice!" he exclaims, in his gruffest tone, the one that he uses to avoid getting lost in too many pleasantries and explanations with the crew, who in fact think that he's some kind of ogre, a heartless asshole. "Let's not waste energy, OK?! You know that my triglycerides are getting high. Now, put on those headphones and do as you're told."

"OK, don't get stressed out."

"OK, OK," he says, recovering with a smile and pinching my cheek. "If we don't finish, how are you going to get to Milan for your special day?"

I snort. "My Sacred Day, Lars. My Sacred Day. I'm going to get my nails done, it's not like I'm getting married."

"Ugh. Whatever," he replies, turning around and making a vague gesture with his hands. "You're the only person who goes all the way to Milan to get her nails done. They do give manicures in Rome, you know."

Of course, but Karin is in Milan. And most importantly, Paola is in Milan. And as much as I can't complain about my life in the capital, I would never give up my Sacred Day with my best friend, even if I went to work in Hollywood.

Seven months ago, after Cristina embraced Carlo, after the paramedics gave up and realized that no one needed to be hospitalized, I went back to being the sole owner and tenant of my apartment, and I finally made that famous phone call.

Not even two weeks later, I was in Rome, with mother Adalgisa and father Guido in tow. Because even if your daughter is past thirty, you'd better make sure—in person—that the place that hired her is not full of sexual predators and hopeless drug addicts.

"People in television are like that," says my father with a certain complacency.

"Dad, I've been working in television for ten years."

"Yes, yes, but I mean people in serious television."

"Ah, I see. Very different."

I started out managing several different entertainment broadcasts until I met Lars at a production party, and it was love at first sight. Oh, please! I don't mean that kind of love, but rather a sort of elective affinity. Lars is definitely a bit like me: he's been divorced three times and no longer believes in love, but he vents his emotions by churning out the most saccharine nighttime soap operas that TV has ever seen, to the delight of every housewife in central Italy.

It hasn't taken me three marriages or, thank God, having to sign three alimony checks every month, to understand that love is not everything in life. In fact, I can say that I've discovered how nice it is to live in the present, as a protagonist, without waiting for someone to choose me and then dump me as soon as I start to get used to him.

And, if I'm not like Lars—who vents with food and by writing dramas where, if he fights with one of the actresses, he can give her a heart attack or a car accident or, if he's feeling generous, a sudden vocation to be a missionary in some pleasant land—it's just because I am able to see love in many things. I like observing it when I walk through Rome. I see it on the benches, in the colors of the sky, and in glimpses of historic streets.

Tio repeatedly assures me that I just have to wait, that it will come . . . but I keep telling myself that we aren't all lucky in the same way. It's not written anywhere, let alone among the stars, that love will come to everyone. Nor that, like him, I will find my own Andrea, willing to follow me to Rome and to the end of the earth if they offer me a job as a TV host, as happened to him. But even if my story doesn't feature the words "and they lived happily ever after," it doesn't mean that it is sad.

Now that it's spring, when I'm able to make it home before the sun sets, I go out onto the balcony of my apartment and watch Rome fading into so many precious colors, and I tell myself that, finally, this is happiness: a house, a dream job, a purring cat, and pots filled with geraniums. When you've learned to love yourself, it's much easier to care for others, without ever losing yourself in the process.

I turn on the radio transmitter, and fix the clip into the waistband of my jeans, adjusting the volume, and then I face the climb.

"Alice? Testing. Testing." Lars's voice crackles in my headphones. "Can you hear me, Alice?"

I press the answer button. "Yes, yes. What is it?"

"OK, listen . . . erm . . . yeah, you should take that red blanket and position it better. And the picnic basket, turn it, please. A little to the right."

I do as he says. "OK. And now?"

"Good. Yes. OK. Sit down. I'm coming. Eh . . . and keep the headphones on!"

I shrug and do as he says, sitting down cross-legged on the fake grass. As I wait for him, I nibble on my mortadella sandwich and start flipping through the agenda and the parts of the script that we still need to shoot.

Suddenly, I hear a thud and the studio has gone completely dark. I jump and raise my head, calling into the headphones: "Lars?"

No one answers. I start to get up, but without a reference point, I stagger. I realize this is not such a good idea, because I'm on top of a fake hill, nearly seven feet off the ground.

After a second, the moon and then the stars appear on the blue screen. Why do I get the impression that someone is playing around with the lights?

"Lanfranco! Hey . . ." I call again. "Come on, boys, you're going to break the computer."

I hear something croak into the headphones, but I don't understand. It seems like voices, but they are very far away.

"Set . . ." I hear, and silence. And then, "Go."

It seems like Lars's voice, but it's as if he is talking to someone else.

And now the stars start falling.

Of course, seeing it from here is a real spectacle. If I didn't know that this was only a projection for a film, I would think I were actually in the mountains, under an Oscar-winning sky.

In the background, there is music. Hearing the first notes, I tense. The song playing is "Reality" from *The Party*, which, though you wouldn't imagine it to look at him, is actually Lars's favorite movie. I give in and smile. This is a classic prank that members of the crew play on each other. The only strange thing is that usually we do it when we are a bit more relaxed at work, not when we are behind with shooting. I'm surprised by Lars, I thought he would be more professional.

"Come on, guys . . . Good one, very good . . . I get it. Thank you very much. But come on, we're behind." I return to sitting cross-legged on the plastic lawn. I'm not a killjoy who doesn't know how to laugh at herself, but I don't really know what to do anymore. And unfortunately, "Reality" makes me think of something else . . . Of *someone* else, who by now is buried in the bottom of a drawer of memories.

I turn on the flashlight on my phone to start reading the script, or at least pretending to do so.

"Victor Hugo said that 'the soul is full of shooting stars.'" Instead of music, there is a voice in the headphones.

"And perhaps, in attempting to be poetic, he wasn't really so far from the truth."

This is not the scratchy voice of Lars, but a voice that I don't recognize. My heart starts to pound in my throat.

"You weren't entirely wrong in thinking that we were children of the stars, in a sense, you know?" he says again, and I bite my lip, because deep down, very deep down, I do recognize that tone and it cuts like a knife.

"All the atoms that make up our bodies were created billions of years ago. The iron in our blood, the oxygen that fuels our lungs, the calcium that feeds our bones."

As I listen to him, the stars in the sky in front of me keep shining, falling, pulsing, and seem as alive as a human body.

"Alice..."

Only then do I realize that the voice is no longer in the headphones but just behind me. When I turn around, I see a dark silhouette, just as I had envisioned for the film scene that we are shooting, the film scene that I wrote.

I squint to try and see better, because I tell myself that it is impossible, entirely impossible. And crazy. And wrong. The simple fact of him being here is something that cannot happen. Because...

I hate myself as I feel a tear roll down my chin in the darkness, and I say, "Davide..."

I tell myself, once again, that it can't be true, simply because things never happen the way you imagine, like a scene in a movie. But here he is, coming up the hill (OK, the fake hill). He slides the headphones down around his neck and throws his jacket over his shoulder.

"Hi," he says, with that warm voice that I have struggled to forget; that voice that is still a caress, in spite of everything he did and how much he hurt me.

"Hello," I reply and my voice snaps, sharp as a whip.

Davide sits down beside me, as if we had a date to watch the stars.

"You look good," he says, studying me while that scumbag Lars, perhaps in cahoots with the director of photography, puts on soft lighting so that Davide and I can look into each other's eyes.

"Um, thanks."

He raises his hand, but is unable to touch my hair because I push the errant strand behind my ear myself.

"Why the short hair?"

"It's more practical," I explain. "You know, when you have no time to keep drying and styling your hair . . ." I make a vague gesture. "Girl stuff."

"Alice stuff," he replies, smiling.

I divert my gaze, because his eyes are too intense. "Hmm, maybe."

"But you are still beautiful. Actually, even more than before. You are . . . sophisticated."

A loud laugh escapes my lips, because, in these Roman months of working and reconstructing myself, I seem to have done everything but become sophisticated. But then I shut up because he takes my hand.

"Davide, this is my life . . . I work here. Why did you come? Why did you show up here? Today—now—after so long?"

I see him bite his lip and look at the fake sky that covers us. "I miss you."

I shake my head. "What do you miss? The goofy, hysterical girl that was desperate to be with you."

"You were never like that. You are ironic and funny; intelligent, beautiful, sweet, caring . . ."

"And stupid . . . given that I kept on falling for it. Leave, Davide. You know that it can't work between us."

He smiles. "Because I'm a Leo with a Libra Ascendant?"

"Because you're an asshole. Zodiac signs have nothing to do with it." Davide takes the blow, closing his eyes and nodding. "Sorry. I dreamed of having this conversation with you months ago and saying that. I almost know the lines by heart. Now, I realize that it doesn't really make sense anymore."

"Because it's not what you really think?"

"Because it doesn't hurt anymore. And I've learned a lot, like not needing love or a man to be happy. And I've been much happier in these seven months than I ever was when I was someone's girlfriend."

"Mmm, I know . . ."

I look at him. "What do you mean you know?"

"I knew about your job. I knew that you had come to Rome, and I knew that you had left Daniele. No." He stops me, raising his hand. "If you are going to accuse me of having followed you, or worse, of having interfered in your life, I didn't. At least, not until now. But I was happy for you, for your success, for the fact that you spread your wings and finally wanted something for yourself. Just for you."

"And now, just for me, I'm asking you to leave." I stand up because everything is becoming too painful, and I don't want to feel like this. Not here, not now, not after all the effort I've made. "It's too late. Maybe if you had come months ago, when you and Barbara broke up . . ."

"Alice, I left Barbara before Paris."

I take a step back because I need to distance myself from what he just said.

"I wanted to be with you. I loved you . . ." he says, looking into my eyes. "I already loved you then, I had done for a while, but I had an unbearable fear of what would happen if I told you, after a lifetime of trying to be enough by myself, for fear of being abandoned."

He tries to come closer, but I stop him. "No . . ." I whisper.

"I still love you now. And I know perfectly well how you feel."

"Go away."

"Alice . . ."

"You know perfectly well how I feel. Yes. Because you made me feel that way. You wanted it. You haven't come to see me for months, even though you knew that I was here . . . alone . . . even though you knew . . ." Why the hell am I crying? Alice, knock it off. Alice, wake up! You're not the same girl from months ago. You are a strong Alice, sure of yourself, a woman who knows her stuff, and who people respect.

"Go away, please. Leave me alone." I sit back down and I put my head in my hands and let the silence and darkness wash over me. I don't know how much time goes by, but it seems an eternity. Then a voice comes from the speaker in the warehouse: "Alice!"

"Why did you do this to me, Lars?" I ask him, drying my eyes and trying not to let my voice shake too much.

"Because you deserve it, honey. You deserve a chance to be happy."

I shake my head. "This is only a chance of suffering, and you know it. You know it all too well. You've been married and divorced three times . . ."

"Sure. And if a fourth woman should come along, I would do it again. Alice, you can't be happy without taking risks. You can't climb to the summit without knowing that there is always the possibility of falling." When I don't say anything, he continues, "My dear, that man that you just allowed to leave told me that he completely changed his life so that he could come back to you. That he changed his job to have a real house, to start building something, when in the past he was always afraid of becoming attached, of making something definitive and stable. And if a man does all this, if he takes seven months to do it without ever hesitating . . . Honey, it means that you can make as many wishes as you like on falling stars to help you win the lottery, but if you don't check the numbers, you'll never realize that you have the winning ticket in your hand." He turns on all the lights again, and as if by magic, my starry sky disappears, and I am surrounded by the four walls of the set, the cables, the rails for the trolley, and the stairs for the lighting arrangement. I am surrounded by my life. And I am alone.

Davide was here, looking for me. And he told me that he loved me.

My knees shake when I try to get up.

He told me that he loved me, and I sent him away.

I, who have kept loving him for a year, in spite of the distance, in spite of our astrological charts, in spite of the pain, and in spite of trying to forget him by running away from my old life.

I want to climb down faster, but this hill seems to have become a mountain. I want to run toward the door, but fear paralyzes me. I am afraid I won't find him again. And I am afraid to find him again.

"Davide!" I call, but I am out of breath and he doesn't hear me. He keeps walking toward the boulevard that leads toward the reconstruction of ancient Rome. "Davide!"

All at once, I hear barking. Davide stops and opens his arms because Flash is heading toward him at a gallop. But then the dog passes him, aiming directly for me with his wagging tail, and a second later, slams me to the ground with his powerful paws and the poorly calibrated strength of a Great Dane overcome with affection.

"Flash! Alice!"

Davide runs toward me, the *sophisticated* woman who is elegantly sprawled on the gravel with sixty pounds of dog on her stomach. And while Flash continues to yelp, Davide lifts me off the ground and hugs me tightly.

"I'm sorry, Alice. Forgive me . . . I shouldn't have listened to Lanfranco. I should have just come to you."

"Lars has a soft spot for romantic stories, especially when he gets to direct them. And . . ." I look into his eyes. "Perhaps, this time, he even managed to write a happy ending."

Davide smiles and then, as he hesitates, I am the one to kiss him. And I'm still afraid. I'm afraid of making the wrong decision. I'm afraid that Davide and I could break up. I'm afraid that we could be together for the rest of our lives. And I'm afraid of suffering. I'm afraid of the unknown, because not only is tomorrow unfathomable, but even what will happen in the next hour is shrouded in mystery.

This is what it means to live without astrology: walking out onto the stage of life without a prompter, without anyone depriving you of the beauty of discovering what you're really made of; understanding your own mechanisms without anyone telling you that it is down to your Ascendant, a wrong Conjunction, or a misplaced planet.

I kiss Davide and hold him tightly. Suddenly, I'm no longer afraid of my fears, because I know that this time the stars will only be watching.

An Astrological Guide
to Chapter Titles

Prologue: The Heavens Can Wait
Heaven Can Wait, directed by Warren Beatty and Buck Henry, USA, 1978

1. Swept Away (by a Libra)
Swept Away, directed by Lina Wertmüller, Italy, 1974

2. I'm Starting from Aries
I'm Starting from Three, directed by Massimo Troisi, Italy, 1981

3. Dog Day Libra
Dog Day Afternoon, directed by Sidney Lumet, USA, 1975

4. A Gemini for All Seasons
A Man for All Seasons, directed by Fred Zinnemann, UK, 1966

5. Libra on the Verge of a Nervous Breakdown
Women on the Verge of a Nervous Breakdown, directed by Pedro Almodóvar, Spain, 1988

6. The Libra, the Aries, His Wife & Her Lover
The Cook, the Thief, His Wife & Her Lover, directed by Peter Greenaway, UK/France, 1989

321

7. Aries of Darkness
Heart of Darkness, directed by Nicolas Roeg, USA, 1993

8. Libra Wednesday
Big Wednesday, directed by John Milius, USA, 1978

9. Working Libra
Working Girl, directed by Mike Nichols, USA, 1988

10. The Curse of the Jade Scorpio
The Curse of the Jade Scorpion, directed by Woody Allen, USA, 2001

11. Into the Wild Sagittarius
Into the Wild, directed by Sean Penn, USA, 2007

12. Libra Girls Are Easy
Earth Girls Are Easy, directed by Julien Temple, USA, 1988

13. Libra on a Hot Tin Roof
Cat on a Hot Tin Roof, directed by Richard Brooks, USA, 1958

14. A Very Little Sagittarius
A Very Little Man, directed by Mario Monicelli, Italy, 1977

15. Guess If the Sagittarius Is Coming to Dinner
Guess Who's Coming to Dinner, directed by Stanley Kramer, USA, 1967

16. Just a Question of Horoscope
Just a Question of Love, directed by Christian Faure, France, 2000

17. No Country for Old Libras
No Country for Old Men, directed by Ethan and Joel Coen, USA, 2007

18. Some Like It Taurus
Some Like It Hot, directed by Billy Wilder, USA, 1959

19. Libra in Pink
Pretty in Pink, directed by Howard Deutch, USA, 1986

20. Love in the Time of Aquarius
Love in the Time of Cholera, directed by Mike Newell, USA, 2007

21. Bread, Love, and Astrology
Bread, Love and Dreams, directed by Luigi Comencini, Italy, 1953

22. The Gemini Connection
The Chinese Connection, directed by Lo Wei, Hong Kong, 1972

23. A Story of Streets, Libras, and Crime
Camorra (A Story of Streets, Women and Crime), directed by Lina Wertmüller, Italy, 1985

24. Torture Me, But Kill Me with Leo
Torture Me But Kill Me with Kisses, directed by Dino Risi, Italy, 1968

25. Don't Bother to Knock for the Libra
Don't Bother to Knock, directed by Roy Ward Baker, USA, 1952

26. Full Metal Gemini
Full Metal Jacket, directed by Stanley Kubrick, UK, 1987

27. Libra Fever
Horse Fever, directed by Steno, Italy, 1976

28. Lions for Geminis
Lions for Lambs, directed by Robert Redford, USA, 2007

29. Catch Leo If You Can
Catch Me If You Can, directed by Steven Spielberg, USA, 2002

30. Crouching Leo, Hidden Gemini
Crouching Tiger, Hidden Dragon, directed by Ang Lee, UK, 2000

31. Leoless
Breathless, directed by Jean-Luc Godard, France, 1960

32. The Day the Pisces Came Out
The Day the Fish Came Out, directed by Mihalis Kakogiannis, Greece/UK/USA, 1967

33. A Leo Named Desire
A Streetcar Named Desire, directed by Elia Kazan, USA, 1951

34. No Sex Please, We're Libras
No Sex Please, We're British, directed by Cliff Owen, UK, 1973

35. You Will Meet a Tall, Dark Leo
You Will Meet a Tall Dark Stranger, directed by Woody Allen, USA, 2010

36. The Leo on the Bridge
The Lovers on the Bridge, directed by Leos Carax, France, 1991

37. A Night Full of Rain and Horoscopes
A Night Full of Rain, directed by Lina Wertmüller, Italy, 1978

38. Sex, Lies, and Leo
Sex, Lies, and Videotape, directed by Steven Soderbergh, USA, 1989

39. It's a Mad, Mad, Mad, Mad Gemini
It's a Mad, Mad, Mad, Mad World, directed by Stanley Kramer, USA, 1963

40. What Ever Happened to Baby Libra?
What Ever Happened to Baby Jane?, directed by Robert Aldrich, USA, 1962

41. Lost in Astrology
Lost in Translation, directed by Sofia Coppola, USA, 2003

42. The Unbearable Lightness of Virgo
The Unbearable Lightness of Being, directed by Philip Kaufman, USA, 1988

43. Aquarius of a Summer Night
Smiles of a Summer Night, directed by Ingmar Bergman, Sweden, 1955

Epilogue: The Libra Who Went Up a Hill But Came Down a Mountain
The Englishman Who Went Up a Hill But Came Down a Mountain, directed by Christopher Monger, UK, 1995

Acknowledgments

To make this journey, we've crossed the Four Elements, climbed Trines, dissected Astrological Charts, observed Constellations, rattled through Decades and come to blows with the planets ... But if Alice and I have come as far as writing this page, we owe it to a series of people without whom she may never have had a voice and I may never have completed her adventures.

So I must say thank you very much to: my agent Laura Ceccacci, my dear friends Patrizia Rizzo and Cristina Caboni; Cristina Prasso and the whole team of GeMs: Giorgia di Tolle, Barbara Trianni, Giacomo Lanaro, Marco Tarò, Cristina Foschini, Giuseppe Somenzi, Paolo Caruso, Benedetta Stucchi, Elena Pavanetto, Caterina Sonato, Viviana Vuscovich, Graziella Cerutti, Mauro Tosca, Oriana Di Noi and Laura Passarella and Simone Morandi, who had the patience to read and correct my astrological blunders. Thanks to my parents, Gisella Guidi and Roberto Zucca, and to all my family, to my sister Carlotta and her husband Fabrizio, and to my dear nephew Matteo and niece Martina. And also Jean Paul Bosco, Claudio Canossi, Jean Claude Rosseau, Corina Trotea, Valeria Sciandra, Amanda Meneghelli, Deborah Albanese, Laura Ghirigato and Serena Marranini, Valerio Grazioli, Roberto Pesavento, Pietro Cazzaniga, Marialuisa Righi, Alessandra Roccato, Raul Montanari,

Francesco Muzzopappa, Paolo Clarà, Rosa Dello Iacono, Elena Cattaneo, Carmen Vella, Marta Santomauro.

And I owe a very special thanks to my dearest cats, my sweet Musetta and Drusilla, who are now the most brilliant stars, and to Byron and Modì, who are the best company ever.

Friends, may the stars be with you. Thank you for everything.